M000190636

Copyright © 2014 by Asia Harris

Copyright © 2021 by Asia Harris

For more information log onto www.AsiaTheWriter.com

Cover Design: Brie Marielle

Library of Congress Control Number: 2021918534

ISBN: 978-0-578-90050-6 (Paperback)

ISBN: 978-0-578-90236-4 (eBook)

Dedicated to my pride and joy my grandmother, Edna B. Thorps, thank you for loving me wholeheartedly and teaching me how to be a lady.

In loving memory of David "Drilla" Hutchinson, Pierre Roberts, Shahied "Biscuit" Asad

&

Bernard "Benny" Jones

Booga-loo loves you

WE DID IT! WE FINALLY MADE IT!

"Though Life is dim, I keep shinning,"

Asia The Writer

ACKNOWLEDGEMENT

First and foremost, all praises are due to my creator. Lord, I thank you for favor, grace, and mercy. Thank you for showering your blessings upon me throughout this project and saving a sinner like me.

I am extremely grateful to my number one fan, Mommy, thank you for believing in me even when I didn't believe in myself. Thank you for your prayers and sacrifices that you made to prepare me for my future. To my bug, Muck, thank you for loving me unconditionally and teaching me how to love unselfishly. I cannot express enough thanks to my cousin Shojonae, thank you for keeping my secrets safe and being a positive inspiration in my life. Thank you so very much Aunti Snub for all that you do, New York shopping spree is on me girl. A special thanks to my cousin Randy who has been so very supportive in all my endeavors. To my godbrother Troy, thank you for always believing in my dreams. To my cousin Joy thank you for your sound advice and always being on point for me at the drop of a dime. To LBD, thank you for those 16 cakes, you know I got you Unc. To my big bro, my favorite graphic designer, Weezy, thank you for always uplifting me in my craft. To my cousin Shani Mac, thank you for always having my back. To my daddy, thank you for singing to me as a child. To Dana, B-Lo, Nip the Trip, and the rest of my family thank you for showing interest in my vision.

I cannot express enough gratitude to Dr Greenfield and Dr. Harris, who are both life fathers to me, thank you for steering me in the right direction and inspiring me to be great. To my brothers, Nick, and Darnell, thank you for seeing my potential when others counted me out. To my homegirl Kay thank you for being my ear to listen and always offering a helping hand. To my extended family, Kim, James, Pig, Boobie, Red, June, Shaunna, Bird, Keke, CJ, Rhonda, and Maal, thank you for helping me find my voice.

Finally, to, Dr. Christine List and Dr. Kelly Ellis of Chicago State University, thank you for mentoring & inspiring me. To all my readers and fans, you all are the real MVP's. I could not have done this without any one of you. I love you all.

"Writing is the geometry of the soul," Plato

LIFE'S ROLLERCOASTER

ASIA HARRIS

A NOVEL

ONE

Blood, Sweat & Tears

The trees are dancing as the wind shifts gears. Patrolling the Englewood streets, of the Chi, while I inhale the smoke which causes me to cough, uncontrollably. Home sweet home, thinking to myself. Kids are out playing even while the streetlights are beaming. Boys are shooting hoops and girls are moving their feet to the beat of the double-dutch jump rope, which strikes the cement. Abandoned buildings are in plain sight. More liquor stores are present than churches. Addicts are surrounding the area. Young thugs are shooting dice in the alleyways.

Sirens are screaming loudly. Police cars are dashing down the one-way streets, while kids continue to play. Barbeque vapors are in the sky. Cruising to a familiar melody, as I am interrupted by a loud thump that strikes my rear windshield, almost causing it to crack, then another. I hit the blunt and passed it to cuz. I swerve a bit almost losing control, but I gripped the steering wheel tightly. I hear what sounds like a rock striking my windshield, yet again.

"What the fuck is that blood?" Boom! "Nigga I don't fucking know." His eyes grow wide as saucers. "Duck B, Duck. Shit!" I grabbed my gun from my secret compartment quickly. I climbed out of my truck; Fully loaded, Chance follows suit. I toss the lit blunt full of hydro, to the ground and I cock back my 9-millimeter. The city at this time is painted red even in between the cracks. Removing the safety, I shift my index finger from resting on the trigger of my, "heat," referring to the gun that I never leave home without. Bullets are flying rapidly.

My heart is beating so fast that it might rip through my blazing chest. My nose is burning from the smelling of flesh. I wipe my free hand on my designer jeans to reduce the moisture accumulating on my palms. Aiming, and shooting like the range. Shot's pouring. I'm sure I would lose my hearing because of the erupting sounds as they echo through the foggy sky. We were attempting to get as far away from the truck as we possibly can. As we maneuver, we're careful not to step in any of the shattered glass. I'm just trying to stay out the way, while playing a game of, "Duck, Duck, Goose," with my life. Skipping through this smoggy atmosphere is becoming, unbearable.

Brains splattering like paint balls. On-lookers are crying hysterically. Others are shaking like they have Parkinson's disease, scarily fleeing the scene. My heart is thumping. "You good fam? Say something man! Bro, is you straight?" I quickly glance in his direction then back at my surroundings. Aiming, cautiously as I scope my target. The way I see it, it's either them or me and my time is not up yet, so I'm busting. Ketchup colored puddles are universal. "Cuz, get up man, and hit one of these fools." Bullets are thundering rigorously. Even with his flesh wound, he regains his composure, groggily.

He returns the fire, with his semi-automatic weapon. "They hit me cuz, so it just got real!" Cuz voice is a bit weak, but still firm. I could still here the venom escaping his lips. "I'm gone wet these clowns like super soakers." Staggeringly, cuz starts letting off rounds. A menacing smile crept, onto his cold face. It's almost as if he is getting off, on the gun fight. We were raised to shake something, push buttons, and get active. Pride is on the line. In this game we call life, anything goes. There are no rules.

These streets can be disrespectful though. The last man standing wins. A 357 Magnum tiptoed to my ears. I can't make out the shooter clearly, but it is something real familiar about that cat. I ducked, behind the parked cars, praying the alarm doesn't sound. "Shit I'm hit, fuck!" Bodies are falling like Jenga pieces. Anxious and nervous, my mind is racing. One thing I learned a long time ago, life isn't promised but death is. The truth is no matter how gutter, hood, street, or gangster you claim to be, no one wants to be carried out by six or tried by twelve. I know I'm not God and I'm not trying to be, but if you come for me, I'll hurt your soul.

If I'm strapped and trust me, I'm always strapped, I'll put an end to your lease on earth. Everybody has an expiration date, that only God knows. When your time is up, poof, just like that you're gone. If you take your life for granted your freedom will be revoked one or two ways; either by a white sheet, or some uncomfortable silver metal bracelets, choking your wrist. That's just life. You determine your own destiny. Me, I'm just trying to stay humble, stack my bread, and disappear. Trust me, they don't want no smoke with me!

Quiet Storm

I'm so irritated. This entire day has been a bit strange. Unknown callers keep playing on my phone. I really don't have time for this childish shit. I answer my phone only to hear someone breathing heavily, then I get a dial tone. Then to top it all off I received a strangely wrapped, gift box earlier today. Normally when I see a gift, I'm ecstatic but not this time, something seems off. My stomachs queasy and my head is spinning. All, sorts of unanswered questions are flooding through my puzzled brain. I place my ear to the box, checking for ticking sounds. I shake my head as I laugh at my own suspicions. Thinking to myself I watch too much TV.

I sat the box down onto the nightstand near the lamp. I grabbed my cell phone and glanced at the screen and noticed my battery was low. I called up my man and he sent me straight to the voicemail. I resorted my attention back to the gift. The packaging was kind of strange, black wrapping paper, with a green bow, that camouflages as a hint of décor. My eyes are red from crying. Nauseated, I've been running back and forth to the bathroom, all day. I threw my cell on the charger and grabbed the house phone off the base and I called him again.

"You have reached--847---sorry that mailbox is full." Tears started flowing heavily. I slowly, wiped away tear after tear. I tried to lay down, but I couldn't seem to get comfortable. I tossed and turned, for what seemed like an eternity. I'm crying out to God, and to no one in general, as I pray for answers. I couldn't fall asleep, so I sat back up and started rocking back and forth, in the middle of our bed. I went from staring into space, to focusing my attention back on the gift, repeatedly. Just when I began to get deep in thought, the house phone rang.

"Hello," I answered as I cleared my throat. The caller then spoke into the receiver, "May I speak to Miss Montgomery, Misses Isis Montgomery, please." Hesitantly, I answered, "This is... this is she," I stuttered. "Mam this is Detective John Wilson and............." The person on the other end of the receiver was trying to get my attention but I was in shock, and I couldn't respond. "Hello, hello." My body became numb. The sound of his voice is evident, but it was muted to my ears. At first, I could hear him clearly, in almost a gentle whisper but then the sound faded away. Pretty soon, I could no longer hear anything over my hysterical cries. The phone slipped from my hands and crashed to the floor.

Shoot em up Bang...Bang

The streets resembled the Fortnite video game, more bodies dropping than the county morgue. "Fuck you, you not on shit; you think you a boss?" Pop, pop, pop, pop, BANG! "That's your fucking problem; you think you're better than every fucking body." My vision that was once blurry became clear now. I was shocked by the image standing before me. "Bitch I knew you wasn't shit but an eater, you money hungry bitch. Pops always said, fuck the hoe, can't save a hoe, so pass that hoe." I laughed; my adrenaline was pumping. "Check mate, you clown," she shouts, like she was saying something clever.

"Yo, tired ass game is now ...." The stream of tears slid down her face right before the erupting explosion targeted her chest. Blood gushed from her mouth, like a leaky faucet as she falls to the ground. While I'm aiming at my opps (oppositions) a sharp pain rips open my flesh. I peeped cuz, ducking behind some branchy trees. The grip to my gun loosens and slips from my hand. An unmasked assailant kicks my gun from arms reach and hovers over me. Boom! The rain starts to pour. Last thing that I remember seeing was the street sign that read, May.

Before the blackout, I remember hearing sirens. As I started to fade away, I reflected over my life. All I could think about is, I have too much to live for. "Sir, sir," said the Asian brunette. "Stay with me sir, sir please stay with me! Clear! He's not responding, clear! Sir, please stay with us." The heart monitor started beeping continuously. "Last time. Clear." I felt myself slowly, drifting away, fading into a place of darkness, slipping into the clouds. Flashbacks entered my mind from my early childhood. I started to think about all the lost souls that I've encountered, my family, my life, and my basketball dreams. I envisioned my girl and her elegance.

I felt an aching pain in my broken heart. I thought about the lives I've crossed, the lies I've told, the laws I've broken, and the crimes I've committed in sin. A single tear rolls down my cold face. All I can think about is, is this really the end? "Clear!" The beeping sound became even louder. "We're losing him...clear. Sir, you look like a fighter, and you have probably been fighting battles all your life, don't give up. Charge it again...clear!" Those were the last words I remembered before the blackout as I faded into a deep, deep, slumber.

TWO

Love at 1ˢᵗ Sight

Mike and I have been dealing, for a while now. We became a thing back in, high school. I remember it like it was yesterday. I wasn't even a woman yet. My baby is five years older than I am, but you couldn't tell from his boyish looks. The boy is a looker. From day one we started rocking heavy, I mean you know the vibes. I am nothing like the other girls my age. At my school everyone, is sleeping, around with everyone, like one big orgy or something, but not me. I'm a young woman with morals, goals, standards, and dreams. We've been inseparable since the start, and nothing will break our bond. We're locked in for life.

Me & My Shorty

It was around the time of President Obama's inauguration that me and Isis started fooling around. Normally I just smash and dash. Now, Isis, man, Shorty, she's one of a kind on, my son. Her light brown skin lets off a slight glow. She has hazel brown, exotic eyes, you can get lost in. Her, dimples are as deep as an ocean which compliments, her smile. She has a Marilyn Monroe mole above her lip, on her left side of her face, that I find wildly attractive. These other hoes I'm used to hitting, had more work done than Kim. Not my little bitch, Shorty authentic. Isis is something poetic. Her taste is of nectar, so soft and sweet.

Her hair is sandy brown, shoulder length and naturally curly. Her smile brightens up any room that she steps foot in. Her teeth are pearly white and straight. She has a petite frame with curves like a sculpture. Her cup size is 36, waist is flat, and her hips are just right to. Shorty is no slider either. Her face doesn't even have any blemishes or acne. They be trying to shoot they shot but she not going. My Shorty has values, that other girls her age lack. As for me, on the other hand, I'm a college level sophomore. Some say I'm something like a basketball star. I'm 6 ft 3 inches tall, slim, but well built, with muscles like I did a stretch (jail time).

I'm dark brown, with brown eyes or so I've been told. I have a tattoo sleeve, on each one of my arms. One of my tats read, "Death B4 Dishonor," with some graphic art details. Another one of them read, "Trust

None." I also have a tat that says, "Boss Up," with some money bags and dollar signs. The letters carved, "Nething," on my forearm, because out here anything goes. Tatted on my neck is my favorite one of them all, "Loyalty." On my chest I have some prayer hands with the Bible scripture, *Psalm 23,* entirety. Underneath it reads, "Lord Forgive Me." I wear my hair chopped short, I don't do dreads or braids. Those styles make you an easy target in these streets and where I'm from target's get murdered by rivals and the one times (police).

Game Time

The big day came, and the seats are filled. It's barely any elbow room. I wore my hair pulled back in a ponytail underneath my white baseball cap. My medium size gold hoops laced my ears. My fitted jeans hugged my frame perfectly, along with my identical shirt that read the word, "LOVE," in pink cursive letters. My feet rested in my white, leather, strappy sandals which compliments my French, manicured toes identical to my nails. On my shoulder laid my purse which coordinates with my outfit. Mommy always keeps me looking fresh.

Now, I might not be spoiled with designer, but I am spoiled with love. We get our hair, and nails done twice a month. We get up early on Saturday mornings, eat breakfast and get dolled up at the "X-Clusive Touch." We always get our hair done by the same stylist, Khai. She could make an ugly chick look good. Some of her styles has even been featured in black hair magazines to. She has even curled up Oprah, braided up Snoop, and cut up Barack. Celebrities flew her out for main events. The shop is like a reality TV show, where you hear all the latest gossip.

Normally after we get our hair done, we head over to our favorite nail salon. Only on special occasions does, Mommy allow my girls to tag along, which doesn't happen any too often. Last time they came with us they ended up fighting over some boy. Kia and Tia are the names of my best friends. Kia is the cutest one, out of the two, but T is no monster either. The day of the game was crazy. The twins wore matching miniskirts. Barely covering their breast, were their identical halter tops. The buttons were unfastened, down to their cleavage.

The backs of their shirt's had their names in airbrushed letters. They wore name plated, oval shaped earrings to. I love them to death, but they have no class and no ambition. I wouldn't be surprised if they chose porn, like Laurence's daughter or worked at the ranch with Hef. They have always been hardhead and Mommy always says, a hard head makes a...well you know the rest. Now, don't get it twisted, I love eye candy, but that's just where it ends with me.

My girls are different though. They want to go first base and get a taste of the candy. Quiet as kept, I already heard about them throwing themselves on my secret crush. I never did confront them on it. I mean who can blame them. His eyes are dark and mysterious. It rumored that he was well packaged, like a horse. Word around town is the boy is a bit of a lady's man. I'm not gone front my move, when I hear his name, my antennas go up and I tune in like a radio station. I hear there are scouts checking for him to.

The boy puts you in the mind of the actor Idris, with his sex appeal. He gives off an aura that screams power. Other than his tattoo's, they could have easily passed for twins. Snapping back to reality, staring in the direction of the man of the hour, makes me want to believe in love. I don't know much about it though. All I know is the love that my parents share. Other than that, the only love that I know is through R&B songs.

They Get It from They Mama

Although my friends lost their virginities, a long time ago, I was in no rush. That's one thing that once it's gone, it can never be replaced. At the age of eight, the twins became sexually active. They started off playing spin the bottle and truth or dare, the "X-rated," version. By the time we turned ten, they yearned for penetration. They weren't concerned with the rumors that were surfacing. They kept their legs spread like jam. There, mother, wasn't the best role model either. Their parents have been separated for some time now.

Their father is the stricter one out of the two. Work, and family, is all that he lives for. It all came to a drastic end, one dreadful evening. It was one, Valentine's Day that he would never forget. He walked in the door of his home and saw his wife blowing the whistle of some John. He immediately charged in their direction. Pushing him to the side, he grabbed his wife by her throat. He shook her violently as he shouted, "I cannot believe you, you trifling bitch! How could you? What is wrong with you Shelenda?" Unable to respond, she remained silent. At that very moment the mystery man muscled up enough courage, ignoring Marc's display of despair.

He cleared his throat, preparing himself to speak, "My man, you need to take that up with this hoe later, I paid for this service. I gave the hoe $100. No disrespect to you, but I'm not leaving until I shoot this load. You understand right, my man?" Right then, Marc dropped Shelenda to the floor and charged towards him. Then he pounded him in his face, throwing blow after blow. Finally, able to catch her breath Shelenda, started shouting, "Stop, please you're going to kill him!" Marc ignored her as he continued punching the guy until he heard the girls screams, "Daddy no! Please stop, you're scaring me." By now the man was out, cold. Angrily Marc shouted, "Shelenda get the fuck out!" "Where am I…I mean we supposed to go? I don't have any money, what am I supposed to do Marc?" Marc stood there with a dazed look in his eyes, "I don't care where you go. Just get out of my house and take your boyfriend with you."

Bolo was finally coming too, a bit shaken. He lifted his head slowly. "Motherfucker," he shouted. He grabbed hold, to the table, pulled himself up and stood to his feet. He adjusted his clothes storming out the door, in embarrassment. He shouted, "You haven't seen the last of me, bitch you gone pay, both of you. You and your old man!" Marc turned and walked in his direction. Bolo tripped and fell down the stairs while in pursuit of his car. Marc slammed the door behind him. That was the first time that Marc had ever raised his hand to a woman.

It made him flashback on his early childhood. He grew up watching his father abuse his mother day and night. The last time that he remembered, blood was everywhere resembling a slaughterhouse. That was the day that Marc was forced to become a man. He ran into his parent's bedroom, he grabbed his father's pistol, and reappeared in the doorway of the kitchen, "Stop!" His father waved his hand. In a drunken sober he slurred, "Gone head on boy, this doesn't concern you none." Nervously, Marc yelled again, "Stop, Pa please!" His father stopped briefly, "Gone head on now, before you get some to!"

He looked down at Marc and noticed the gun in his hand. "Boy now tell me what in the hell you plan to do with that besides piss me off?" Marc cried, "Stop, please, I'm begging you Pop." "Or what? What you gone do about it boy?" Silence. "Yeah, son just as I thought, you're not a man you're a punk. I'm the man of this kingdom. I'm the…" Marc placed both of his hands on the gun and aimed in his father's direction. He closed his eyes and squeezed the trigger, until silence filled the air. When Marc opened his eyes, his father was on the floor atop his mother. Shakingly, Marc rushed towards their bodies and placed the gun on the counter before he leaned down.

He pushed his father to the side and shook his mother violently, but she didn't budge. That day changed his life forever. Snapping back to reality, to the sound of his children screams, he looked at Shelenda with disgust. She stood there, looking pathetic. "Kids quiet down now hush!" She turned her attention back towards Marc. "Marc baby, you're never home. You're never here for me. You made me do this. You did this to us, not me. All you do is work, work, work! What about me and my needs?" He stood there as he listened to her every word.

"Kids you shouldn't be down here, go to your rooms, now!" They jumped at the sound of their mother's voice. "Aw so now you want to order the kids to go to their room. You should've sent them to their rooms before committing adultery." The girl's stood up to leave. "No kids, have a seat you don't have to go anywhere." They sat back down. "But Marc." "Don't but Marc me, you are the example of what I hope my girls will never become." They cried, in almost a unison as they screamed, "Ma, and Daddy no! Please stop fighting.

Daddy don't do this. Daddy why are you doing this? You don't love us anymore?"

Those words cut him deep. "Tia, Kia, I will always love you, that will never change." He redirected his attention back at his wife. "What, did I ever do to deserve, such disrespect?" Stunned by his question so instead of responding, she walked away, to gather some of her belongings, hoping that he would stop her. "Shelenda," Marc yelled. "I knew he wouldn't let me go, sucker ass," she mumbled. "Yes, Marc honey." Silence. "You can keep the car because of the kids, but you will be responsible for paying your car note. You need to leave, now!"

She ran upstairs to the bathroom and grabbed the money that she had stashed away. Then she got dressed and rushed back into the living room. She grabbed her car keys off the table and walked towards the door. She stopped dead in her tracks and walked towards the couch to the girls. She hugged and kissed them both. "Mommy loves you. Stop crying. I want you girls to obey your father." She wiped away their tears and walked back to the door.

Marc grabbed her by the arm and with a disappointing tone he asked her, "Was it worth it?" She paused. "A girl has needs, so I did what had to be done." Once she was on the other side of the door, he slammed the door in her face. She stood there in shock hoping that he would change his mind and open the door, but he didn't. I could tell they resented their dad, because of the breakup to. They hated his rules. They, moved in with their, Mom, as soon as they could.

His Cheerleader

The game is now in the 3rd quarter, we are up by five. Mike is dunking all over the court. I'm screaming and jumping like I'm his biggest fan. Sweat is glistening down his sexy, muscular body. As he glances in my direction, my heart skips a beat. I even felt moist down low, where Mommy, always told me as a little girl, to let her know if anyone touches. On the court, there are at least 2 or 3 guys that the twins have already slept with, well those are just the ones that I know about. I looked at the guys then back at them. I shook my head in repugnance. Although we grew up together, opposites we are, but those are my dogs for sure.

I flashed back to when we all first met. We had been in the same class from kindergarten to second grade and we never even uttered a word to one another. I was a book worm even back then, so the other kids teased me. It wasn't until this one day, that I was forced to defend myself, which made us grow closer. We were in the second grade, I believe. The smelly, oversized class clown, Tominiqua Black, kept hounding me. As soon as the teacher walked out, she threw a jumbo-sized crayon at me. The first time she did it she missed but the second time she hit me in the back of my fresh hair do and the class laughed.

I ignored her at first. The next thing I know, she hit me upside my head with a dry eraser, causing me to cough from the chalk dust. Now, everybody in the class laughed except for the Kia and Tia. Surprisingly they came to my rescue. After about five minutes of being in shock, I jumped up from my desk, I turned around, and balled up my fist, preparing for a scuffle. Before anyone could say anything else, I stormed over to her desk and I punched her something good, sending her flying into my other classmate's desk. I hit her over and over for good measure. She remained in a fetal position while I used her body as a punching bag.

She was so frightened, that she lost control of her bladder. From that day forward, all the kids started teasing her and stealing her lunch money, up until she transferred. I got off on a warning and I never saw her again. Me and my girls have been hanging tight ever since and the rest is history. The buzzer sounds for half time, snapping me out of my deep thoughts.

After half time, the opposing team somehow manages to catch up with Mike's team. We were yelling, "Defense!" Sting who is on the opposing team, has just stolen the ball from Scooter. They were up by one. With five seconds left in the game Mike gets filed. Scooter makes his free throw, which was the break that we all needed. Two seconds remaining on the clock, Mike takes a chance on the most impossible shot ever and he scores. Three points were made as the timer goes off. BUZZ! The crowd went wild. The game ended, sixty-two to sixty-five.

I'm smiling from ear to ear while the cameras are flashing. Reporters are on Mike's heels to. Call me crazy but I could've sworn, as he walked out, I saw him wink his eye at me. Excitedly, I expressed my glee, with my friends. "Oh my God, did y'all just see that?" Kia responded first, "No. What happened Ice?" "Mike just winked at me." They looked at me with the yeah right face. "Hello…did y'all just hear me?"

By now I'm cheesing hard. "Girl please knock it off, for real. Ice you be tweaking. He probably just got something in his eye." They laughed. Then Kia had the nerve to say, "Girl his fine ass, don't want no virgin, the fuck. What he needs is an experienced woman that knows how to work the pole." They high fived each other and laughed. If looks could kill, the way I stared at them. Instead of responding, I just rolled my eyes.

We Won

After the game the team decided to celebrate their victory at the bowling alley. Coach Jamison had prearranged everything. On our way out the door of the gymnasium, Kia and Tia were in the corner talking to some random guys. I waited for them by the water fountain, patiently. I didn't say anything because I didn't want to come off as a hater. 30 more minutes goes by and I'm starting to get anxious because I was ready to go. I sprinted over to the stairway, grabbed the rail, and sat down on the stairs. While I was waiting on my girls, the man of my dreams, was in plain sight.

As he approached me, I could smell his sweet scent, entering my nasal passages. My stomach was in knots, so I'm praying I don't let one go. "What's up, Ma? You ready?" He extends his hand and I suddenly feel weak. His dialect is smooth yet nonchalant. I couldn't help but to smile, as my cheeks turned a hint of red and my chest heaved up. I played it off the best that I could. I continued twirling one of my spirals in between my fingers trying to gather enough courage to respond.

"Ready for who? Ready for what?" He laughed sarcastically, "Ready for a Boss!" His laughter was replaced by a sly smirk. Trying to act all cool I responded quick, "I was born ready." Silence. "I like your style, Ma, what's your name?" He looks into my eyes as I shied away. "My name is Isis." "Oh, Isis huh? I like that name Ma, that's different. What side of town you from?" I paused. "I'm from the South side. What about you?" "State to lake, Shorty," he said as he flashed his million-dollar smile. The twins were still, being grouped, hemmed up by the lockers. I was in no rush to leave.

THREE

Ghost

Ghost was a hustler. He's been an outstanding member since he was 10. Chicks flocked to him. Trapping is all that he knows. His, mom, provided him with the best life that she could. A father figure subtracted from his life a long time ago. As a kid, he looked up to the older hustlers that were known in the hood as trap stars or local dope boys. In the neighborhood where he grew up, bums were on every street corner. He had promised his, Mom, that he would never drown in the waves, of the streets.

As he walked down the street, to school he passed dope fiends, bucket boys and dealers, it was like that in the jets (projects). He stayed in and out of fights. It had gotten so bad that his mom, lost her job attending one to many parent teacher conferences. Rumors surfaced that he had gotten caught having a three-way with the principal and his teacher, but no one knows that to be true. By the age of thirteen he had saved up enough of his money to buy his first whip (car). He purchased his car from one of the old heads named Cat Daddy.

Cat Daddy was a real OG, a street legend. He was a green eyed, old cat and as yellow as the sun. He wore loud colored, suits with matching Gators. He was medium built, and he stayed clean. His circle was limited. Cash, who could've easily passed for DMX's twin, voice included, was his right-hand. He was the muscles of the operation. You name it, they sold it, from clothes to hoes. They were real game changers to. They owned ice cream trucks that they trapped out of in the summer months and food trucks that they hustled out of in the winter.

Cat Daddy saw something in Ghost, and he sold him his first car for a little or nothing. He respected Ghost's hustle and he took him under his wings. He taught him a lot about the game. His only stipulation was that he finished school. He knew firsthand that street knowledge, mixed with an education is a lethal combination. That would be one of the many attributes that would separate him from the rest of the hustlers around his way.

Isis The Diva

If there is one word that could describe me, I think that it would have to be, diva. I'm not thick but I have a few curves. I'm not the finest but I am cute. I've heard boys refer to me as sexy to. I'm not the slutty type either. My friends always say that everybody has a price, but I don't know about that because I can't be bought. I would never sell my princess parts for material or financial gain. My Mama always taught me that a woman should always remain a lady. In my eyes being paid for any sexual acts is a form of prostitution. Now, don't get me wrong, I don't knock anybody's, hustle but it is what it is.

Money

Money was ten years older than Ghost and five years younger than Cat Daddy. He had been watching Ghost flip cars and get money, for years. He liked his demeanor and the way that he conducted his business. He knew that he would be an additive to the team. Money taught Ghost some of what he knew about the game. "The game's cold, but it got to be played," one of the old cats by the name of Johnny Carter Jones use to say. Now that brother was notorious. He was affiliated, he was like the Godfather of the streets. Money was more of the flashy type. He wore jewels, like he owned a jewelry store. He's like a mixture between street and Hollywood.

Money had a hard time trusting people based on his upbringing. He tested Ghost's loyalty on numerous occasions. The last test was when Money and his crew was forced to make an example out of this older cat. The guy had been scheming. The situation escalated and it got bloody. The media ate that story up. The Chicago police department offered, a $50,000 reward for information regarding the murder.

Ghost kept his mouth shut. In the hood for that type of money, some of the guys a give up they own, mother. That was around the time that Money started calling Ghost his son. After the murder, the detectives saw Ghost as a potential target, young, black and had a few dollars. They tried to coerce a confession out of him. They couldn't break him though, he was hardbody.

Based on the lack of evidence they pinned a petty case on him. They prosecuted him and sentencing him to a 5-year stretch. The only reason they were able to make a case against him was because he left his DNA near the crime scene.

That was the first time that he had ever seen a body, but it wasn't his last. While incarcerated, Ghost books stayed stacked. While he was down, his ride was stolen, and his mentor, Cat Daddy was murdered. Rumors surfaced that they found his body in one of his rides, with his throat slit from ear to ear. Hearing about his death while he was incarcerated hurt him to his core. Money's complexion was an Almond shade.

He has deep, dark eyes and a permanent scar above his left eye. He has tattoos all over, like a mural: Skulls with blunts and guns with, "Live as if you will die tomorrow," in italics on his chest. Half Angel half devil on his right arm, and tombstones that contains the names of his loved ones. He even has rolls of hundreds, seeping through the front of his hand in 3D. He has a 5 o'clock shadow and he wears his beard full to. He has a deep voice, with a chilled stare. His hair is low cut, but it stays freshly tapered.

He pushes all types of rides (cars) all of which is customized. He was raised by his drug addicted, mother up until she died. He never knew who his father was. By the age of twelve he had dropped out of school, and he started hustling. He started with an eight ball, and he kept flipping until he was pushing weight. He envied the other kids that had normal lives. Kids teased him because of his misfortunes so he stayed in fights. Often, he would walk in on his mother having sexual intercourse with random men, which bothered him. One of her suitors was the first body. She didn't realize it then, but she was molding him to become a heartless demon.

It's A Boy

She was two months pregnant, when she finally mustered up enough courage to come clean about her pregnancy. Irma started calling her all sorts of degrading names as soon as she heard the news. "You and that bastard child of yours, can get the fuck up out my house, with your fast ass. You are a disgrace to this family, and I hope the baby dies," her mother spat callously. Disowned by her family she was kicked out on the streets. With nowhere else to turn, so she slept in shelters and abandoned buildings. She dropped out of school right before her 8th grade graduation, which caused an onset to depression.

The friends that she once had, were forbidden to have any form of contact with her. She had to dig in garbage cans to feed her growling stomach. With limited options, she was forced to sell her pregnant pussy. She used drugs as an added boost of courage. She started off by popping pills. The pills blocked away the torture and the mental anguish. The drugs mixed with alcohol relaxed her mind. It was the pills that sparked her urge in experimenting with other drugs. The day her son was born it was a cold and rainy.

She had just finished taking it roughly, up the ass. She needed money to get her next fix and to pay for a one-night stay at a nearby motel. She wobbled her pudgy belly to the front desk, of the rat infested, bed bug consumed, motel. She ran her fingers through her holey pockets, grabbed the money she had made and handed the balled-up bills to the front desk clerk. Then she grabbed the key and rushed to her room. Upon entry she snatched the curtain string and wrapped it around her arm and inserted the drug intravenously.

She began to nod until she was interrupted by the excruciating pains that filled her stomach. The pain was so severe that it caused her to nearly fall to the floor in agony. She grabbed a hold of her left side then she felt something wet between her legs. She opened her mouth to scream but nothing would escape. She noticed a damp spot on her pants which was full of blood near her crouch area. Although she tried, she just couldn't seem to force herself out the chair. The mixture of the drugs, the alcohol, and the pain overpowered her.

Finally, she gathered up enough strength to stand. While slouched over, she dragged her legs across the floor as she attempted to leave the room. Tears were cascading down her face. Every step that she made caused her more pain. She walked, down the street, until she fainted, landing in a puddle of water. By the time she regained consciousness, she was in an unfamiliar setting. She scanned the room for some familiarity.

Everything was a blur. The pain that she was now experiencing was different than before. She fumbled around but nothing seemed recognizable. She attempted to retrace her steps in her mind, which caused her to have a headache. She moved her hands to her side as she felt the cold steal of the bed rail. That was when she realized that she must've been in a hospital room.

As, her eyes adjusted to the light she was able to see clearer. She rubbed her hand on her stomach and noticed her belly was no longer full. For only a slight moment, she felt relieved. Moments later a nurse entered. "Mam, how do you feel? (No reply) It's okay Miss if you're a bit overwhelmed and you aren't up for conversation, I do understand. I just wanted to inform you that your surgery was a success. You delivered a beautiful, baby boy. He was 2 pounds and 10 ounces?"

Tamekia looked at the nurse with a blank stare. "With all the blood loss you are lucky to be alive. Would you like to see your son now?" Silence. "No! I don't want to see the little bastard that helped to destroy my life. I mean look at me and look at what he did to me. I don't wish to see him, not now, and not ever!" Shortly after, the caseworker walked in. Tamekia rolled her eyes and smacked her lips. The caseworker got straight down to business, "How old are you?"

"Seventeen, why?" The caseworker continued on, "Have you considered adoption as an alternative? Is there any family member that we can call? Do you wish to contact the father of the child?" The nurse interrupted, "Her grandmother was in the waiting area earlier, but she left." Tamekia became hopeful that her mother had come to save her, but she never showed face. Six days had gone by when Tamekia decided to go and see her son. She slid her feet, across the floor, one by one. She felt a draft entering, from the opening of her gown so she held it shut. She walked into the nursery, unattended.

As she entered, tears slid down her face. She stood there in silence, staring at her son. She glanced away, daydreaming, looking through the window as the sun crept through the blinds and jumped when she felt a hand touch her shoulder. When she turned around, Ms. Jackson was standing there smiling. Tamekia sobbed uncontrollably. Growing up, Ms. Jackson and her grandmother were good friends. Tamekia extended her arms, and they embraced in a hug.

Once separated, Tamekia refocused her attention back on her son. Ms. Jackson lied to the hospital staff to

27

prevent the young girl from foster care, but not before Tamekia agreed to move in her building and to check into a rehab clinic. As soon as she was released, she was back to her old tricks. When her son was released Tamekia was, so high that she forgot to pick him up. Ms. Jackson went to get him for the hospital. She took a special interest in the boy, she took him to his doctor's appointments, and made sure that he took his seizing medication.

Tamekia

Her once perky, breast, were dried up like prunes and her body had deteriorated. She gave up on life a long time ago. Every night from the age of six to twelve, she was being molested by her father. The assault tugged away at her soul to the point where she started slicing her own wrist. When her, mother, got word of the abuse she contacted the authorities, and he was sentenced to 25 to life. Irma Mae went into a state of depression and refused to testify on her daughter's behalf.

She ignored the sounds that she heard escaping her daughter's room, at night. As time has it, Wade had been a sexual predator since a boy. His sister was his first victim. He still didn't know if he had fathered his sister's child. As the story surfaced, multiple women started to come forward accusing him of rape. Immediately following trial Tamekia was thrown out on the street.

She cursed the day her son was born and left him in soiled waste for days. She was forced to shoot up in between her toes because most of her veins had collapsed. At the age of 6 Tamekia introduced him to a life of stealing. By the age of seven, he was stealing from the neighborhood food markets. The only thing that Tamekia had ever given her son was the nickname, Money and she scolded it in his head that he was born to be her money maker. Ms. Rosa Jackson, or Ms. J as she was known, looked after him and gave him an allowance in exchange for the chores he completed around her house.

After completing his chores, they talked for hours. One day as, they were talking, Ms. Jackson reached out to hug him and he squealed, from the twinges, inflicted by his mother. Afraid of being placed in foster care, he never told anyone about the constant abuse he faced. He had been on a first name basis with his mother since he learned to talk. One tragic day, when he walked into his apartment, he immediately became shook. He was heartbroken when he found his mother sprawled across the floor, motionless. He rushed to her side. He grabbed cup, filled it with water, and poured it on her face.

He slapped her, a few times but she was unresponsive. Tears began to weld, in his eyes but he couldn't bring himself to cry. He kissed her on the cheek and whispered in her ear, "I love you." For the first time, in a long time, she wanted to live. She tried fighting, away, her demon's but she just couldn't shake them off. At that very moment she wanted to tell him that she loved him, but her time had come. He, ran next door to get Ms. J. She could tell by his facial expression that something was wrong. She sprung forward rushing across the hall. As she entered the apartment her stomach turned. She clutched at her heart, at the sight of Tamekia's lifeless body and dialed 911. She grabbed him by the hand and stayed with him until the response team arrived. Shortly after Damontae, moved across the hall with Ms. J.

Heartless

Money stayed in altercations, especially with the older boys at his school. The last fight that he had was brutal. It had been 5 years since the death of his, mom. One of his classmates cracked a joke about his mother and he put him in the hospital. After getting suspended for the umpteenth time he dreaded going home. He hated disappointing Ms. J. He peeked his head inside of J's room. He walked over to her bedside and pain shot right through his body. He nudged her, but she didn't move. His heart dropped. Tears started flowing freely. He grabbed the phone and dialed 911, then he wiped away his tears. He kissed her on the forehead, grabbed the money he had saved, and left.

That was the day the beast in him was unleashed and he disappeared into the cold streets. He started jugging (hustling) as he became drafted in this game of life. With nobody else to depend on but himself, he started drug trade-operation. He got his GED, and he took some college courses to keep his promise that he made to Ms. J. He even worked a few side jobs for the city. Word traveled fast, how some new kid, had taken over the city. Older cats started getting upset because he was cutting into their pockets, but real bosses respected his grind. Tired of getting a set with the cards he was dealt, he refused to let anyone get close to him again.

FOUR

Caged in Shackles: Ghost

While incarcerated I managed to get my GED. I studied Business and entrepreneurship courses as well. After working out I was back to my books. My celli (cellmate) was my homie Fly. Me and Fly chopped it up a bit and he told me all about is relationship with his girl. "The only one in my corner is my girl, La-La and she a rider, like no other. I love my crazy ass bitch." Although I couldn't relate, I listened intensely. "That's what's up, homie. That's what's up. So how y'all meet fam?" "I met the hoe at a bank when I was cracking cards. I cuffed her from some clown she was dealing with that use to beat on her, and I made him disappear. My chick goes harder than a lot of these snake ass niggas, dirty. When my homie turned states on me, she was ready to catch a body." "Man, Fly, I hear you, big dog but I ain't never putting that type of trust in no bitch, straight up."

The Release: Ghost

Money was sitting outside the joint (jail), flipping through the CD changer. He rapped all the lyrics to the song, "Made Men," while waiting on the release. He was sitting so high in his truck that it looked like he was sitting in a booster seat. The jet black, Range was fully loaded. The guts of the ride had black leather, with silver trimming bucket–seats, with grey suede interior and butterfly doors. The 24-inch, chrome "Menzari, Z11 Viaggio," rims also complimented the ride to. The steering wheel contained the letters, "G-H-O-S-T," and the speakers were designed by Bose.

Walking out a free man gave me a new prospective on life. It was no more soy meet or jailhouse burritos for me and that was a blessing. As the wind hit my chin, I couldn't help but to smile. I walked in the direction of the only foreign ride sitting out front of the housing unit. Getting closer to the ride, Money jumped out to embrace me. He, smiled big, showcasing his new grill, he gave me a pound, along with a brotherly hug. I took a step back and pointed my hand to the sky, as a gesture to thank God.

It's a big deal making it out, unharmed, no paperwork, and alive. Before I jumped in the truck, I stooped down and kissed the ground, because it's nothing like freedom. Pop's smiled, looked my way and threw the keys in my direction almost hitting me in the head. "This you, son. Welcome home." I smiled. "Love, OG." Money hopped in on the driver side and he pulled off. I sat back trying to recollect my thoughts as I got reacquainted to the streets.

"You made it out that jam, on my dead homie, it's up my boy. Yo, sorry I never got around to visiting you, but you know how this go." "Yep, it's smooth." He flamed up a wood (blunt) and started filling me on business matters. As soon as I hit the blunt, I started coughing like an amateur. "Slow down, fam, you a born-again virgin. It's been a minute." I laughed.

Loyalty

After 4 hours of cruising, we made it downtown. We ran into Neiman's and spent a few bucks. I ain't gone front my move, Pop's got me right from my shoes to the jewels. He copped me a Rollie (Rolex) with, "Loyalty," engraved on the back. I hugged him, real manly like. "Thanks Pops." "Naw, son, on some real shit, thanks for staying down. Always remember man, loyalty is a priority not a casualty, facts." He flashed a smile, but it slowly diminished when he looked at his caller ID.

I became intrigued, by the street life, as a young boy, shortly after my old man split. I saw my, moms, struggling so I did what I had to, and I haven't stopped applying pressure yet. I never did get around to meeting my, dad's, folks either. He left us high and dry, no calls, no money, no post cards, no visits, nothing. He went cold turkey and left us behind like a bad habit he was trying to kick. I stayed up many nights, listening to my mom's cries. To help around the house, I managed to land myself a part time gig at a gas station. It didn't pay very much though. I was only 8 then, I was just a boy myself, learning to be a man.

After I stacked enough bread, I invested in the streets. I flipped like a tumbler, I doubled up, and I never looked back. Some hustlers hustled all day and all night and then jagged they bread on some pussy. Not me though, once I get the right play, I'm gone. My Mom did the best she could as a single parent raising two kids. My little sister is only two years younger than me, but I spoil her like she's, my daughter. I promised myself a long time ago, that those two women in my life, would never want for any good thing and I'm standing on that. By the age of twelve, I wasn't holding to the point where I could move us out of the hood yet but, I was straight to the point where my mother was able to quit one of her jobs. My OG didn't ask me any questions about where the money was coming from, so I never gave her any explanations, I just made it happen.

FIVE

The Celebration: Isis

"Strike Out," bowling alley, is where the celebration all started. There were balloons, banners, and crowds of people everywhere. We were all here for the same purpose, to celebrate the team's victory. Announcements were being made, constantly, over the intercom welcoming the team's success. There were scouts present to, who were talking to the coach about his star athletes. My besties were up to their same old tricks. I peeped them, letting some random dudes feel all over there assets yet again. Mike and I were sitting around making small talk, so I was good for the moment.

"So, um Mike, what do you do for a living? Do you work?" "I'm an entrepreneur, punching a clock is slave men work." "Aw okay. I guess." I was unimpressed by his response, so I changed the subject. "So, um what's your major?" "Damn, Shorty, am I on trial or something?" I rolled my eyes and sucked my teeth, irritated by his comment. "Never mind Mike, I was just…that's okay."

I turned my head in the opposite direction and I crossed my arms. Then he redirected my attention back on him. "Shorty, it's smooth. I'm just playing around, no need to get your panties in a bunch." I laughed as I punched him playfully in his shoulder. "My major is Business, Shorty. Business and Accountant are my two fields of interest." I shook my head in agreement. As I looked into his eyes, it felt like I could see his soul.

"So, um Mike where's your little girlfriend at? She not gone run up on me, right?" "Wow, little girlfriend huh? Naw, I don't have those type of problems. The only person you safer with is Jesus. All I'm missing is you." I blushed. I really didn't know how to respond to that, but I knew I had to think of something fast. "Well, if you play your cards right, I might be able to be your first lady. I might be your Michelle."

We both laughed. I saw his coach pointing in our direction, so I nudged him. We stood up simultaneously and headed in his direction. He introduced me to him and a couple of his teammates. Once I was up close, I could tell that his coach was a nice-looking older guy. He was medium built, with a baldhead and a salt and pepper beard. Afterward their brief talk, we walked back to our table.

Looking around the room, everyone seemed to be having a good time. Hours had passed since I last laid eyes on my girls. While Mike was talking to one of his guys, I became a bit antsy, so I decided to interrupt them. I tapped him on his shoulder, and he could tell from my facial expressions that something was to be wrong. "Yo you good Ma?" "No not really. I don't know where my friends are. I'm looking around but I don't see them anywhere."

"Don't panic, Ma. I'm sure they straight. Did you call their phones?" Embarrassed I replied, "I don't have a one Mike." He reached down in his pocket and handed me his cell. I snuck and saved my number in his phone. Then I dialed them up a few times and got the voicemail. I looked up at him, with a look of uncertainty. "Don't worry Ma, I'm sure they'll turn up. Maybe they're in the pool room." "Uh okay," I said before I turned and walked back to my seat. As I started walking away, I could feel his eyes glued on me, so I walked a little sexier. I sashayed across the room, and I tripped over a loose cord that was hanging from the wall.

I was so embarrassed that I didn't even bother turning back around. Instead, I sat down at the nearest seat to me. Mike walked over to where I was sitting.

"Why don't you go check and see if your friends are in the game room? They are probably just cooling out with some of the homies." "Okay Mike thanks you're probably right, I will. I'll be right back." He nodded in agreeance, and I walked off. I looked around but I still didn't see them anywhere. My stomach started bubbling so I walked to the bathroom, and I immediately drew suspicion.

Surprisingly the lady's bathroom, line was full of men and the men bathroom line was empty. Baffled, I ran back and got Mike. Without saying a word, he grabbed my hand and we walked to the front of the line. I was startled, once we walked in. As soon as we entered the bathroom, the waterworks started. Seeing my girls gagged, naked, incoherent, and restrained, broke my heart. I rushed to their sides. Come to find out, the guys had been taking turns forcing themselves on them. I tried to push them off, but they were too strong. Mike saw my reaction and pushed the men away, forcefully.

Then Mike started going back and forth with one of the guys. "The party is over, nothing left to see. Everybody, get out, now!" "What the fuck man? These hoes for the streets?" I don't remember exactly what happened next but all I know is dude must've grabbed Mike and Mike sent him ass flying across the room. He looked at me and yelled, "Get them out of here." "I'm trying Mike, I'm trying!" "Mike man, what the fuck," I heard another one of the guys say.

Then Mike got all up in his face and screaming, "This not cool man, this is fucking rape." After the commotion settled down, the others left. I untied and ungagged the twins. I adjusted their clothes and dragged them to the door leaving Mike in the bathroom arguing. I left the bowling alley shortly after. I found a nearby bench, and we sat down. I checked the girls for their phones, but they were gone. I saw a payphone, so I dialed 9-11. I gave them our location and then I sat back down on the bench. I almost gagged when I found my hand accidently on somebody's else already chewed gum. Twenty minutes in passing, and the police and the ambulance arrived. I gave them my statement and hopped in the ambulance with my girls.

Miracles Hospital

We arrived at, Miracle's hospital, and headed straight to the ER. I asked one of the officers to borrow their phone and he agreed. I called their mother first, but I didn't get an answer. I did make a mental note to self, that her number was programmed in his phone under unknown. I called her a couple more times and got the same response. The tall, slender, officer started questioning me as soon as I ended the call. I erased the call from his call log and handed him back his phone. While answering questions like I was being interrogated they're fathers number came to mind, so I asked to use his phone once again and he agreed.

Placing the phone to my ear while it rang, I was a nervous wreck. I didn't know what to say. On the third try, I finally got an answer. I pretty much kept it short and sweet. I told him the girls had been in an accident and I gave him the address to the hospital. Not even twenty minutes had gone by, and Mr. McNeil came flying in. We hugged briefly and he thanked me for the call. It had been years since we last saw each other. I filled him in the best that I could.

Afterwards he excused himself to talk with the doctor. I overheard the officers, walkie-talkies, sounding, "I'm requesting backup, at 5555 S. Woodward

Lane Road Drive. Proceed with caution, the subject is said to be armed and dangerous." Then the channel 7 news interrupted, one of Maury's episodes, with a breaking news coverage story: "We interrupt this regular scheduled program, for a special bulletin. This is Nancy Savolski reporting to you live... We are at the scene of the crime where a woman who looked to be in her mid-forties, has been brutally murdered...They have just identified the victim as, Shelenda McNeil...No known subjects have been apprehended. If anyone has any information, please contact Detective Jonathon Wilson at the 8th precinct at 312-555-5555, now back to your regular schedule program."

It was at that very moment that I could no longer contain my tears. I looked up and saw Mr. McNeil heading in my direction. The next thing I know those same two officers were approaching him vastly. Suddenly I heard him yelling out in agony, "Oh my God, no! Please God No!" I couldn't do anything except shake my head. "Mr. McNeil, I'm sorry for your loss. I know this is hard, but I have to ask you some questions...Sir can you think of anyone that would want to hurt your wife?" "No, I cannot imagine who would have done this to her."

The shorter one of the two proceeded, after scribbling something down onto his notepad, "Sir, if you can think of any information concerning this case, please give me a call." Then he reached inside his jacket pocket shoving what looked to be a business card in Mr. McNeil's face. Before leaving out the exit door, one of the two officers said to Mr. McNeil, "Good day sir. We will be in touch."

Shortly after that the doctor, approached him. "Hello, Mr. McNeil I am Doctor Hubbard. I am pleased to announce that the girls have regained their consciousness. They were deeply inebriated." Silence. "I don't understand, my kids don't partake in any drugs or any illegal activities." "Needless, to say sir their blood levels showed a high dosage of alcohol in conjunction with methylenedioxy-methamphetamine commonly known as ecstasy. Luckily, they arrived when they did. Each of their stomachs have been pumped."

"Do whatever that needs to be done Doc. Thank you." "Sir, your daughters are asking for their mother. Will, she be accompanying you?" Something inside of me, told me to check on my friends so I willed myself, until I gained enough strength to stand to my feet. As I stood up my knees became wobbly, and they felt like some noodles. I walked in the direction of the girl's room. I grabbed hold of Kia's door, and I was stopped abruptly. "Isis I know you're concerned but I think it's best that I go in first." "Sure, sir."

I walked back to my seat and sat down. He went in Kia's room first. "How are you feeling baby girl?" "Daddy, I'm okay. I'm just sore. Are you mad at me?" Silence. "I'm sorry, I let you down. I'm so... sorry." "Sugar, it's okay you girls did nothing wrong. We are going to get through this, together, as a family. Let's just focus on you getting well." "Okay daddy, where is Mommy?" Silence. "Baby I need to talk to you about something." Silence. "Daddy what is it? What's wrong?" Silence. "Daddy, you're scaring me, please tell me what's going on. Where is Mommy? I want to see Mommy can you get her on the phone for me? Daddy, what's wrong?"

He paused. "Baby your mom, She---lenda, oh my God baby, she's gone... Baby she's really gone." By now, Kia is crying and shaking hysterically. "What do you mean she's gone, gone where?" Then Kia started trying to remove her IVs from her arms. "Daddy, what do you mean? What are you saying?" Her voice became increasingly loud. "Daddy, I don't understand. I need to go home, take me home, NOW!" "Honey, your mom... your mom...she's...she's dead." Silence.

"What? Stop saying that, no she isn't." Before he could respond, Dr. Hubbard, accompanied by a nurse came in the room. Kia screamed to the top of her lungs, "Daddy please. Daddy I need Mom. Daddy what are you saying? Let me out of here!" The nurse rushed to her side to calm her down, but she was irate, so she grabbed her. "Let go of me." "Baby, please calm down." "I can't calm down until you tell me what's going on with Ma. Stop, I need to get out of here. Are you stupid? Let go of me!"

"Baby please calm down, do it for me." "No, Daddy make them stop. Take me to see Ma. What are you doing? Stop it, please, Daddy, help me. Tell this stupid woman to let me go." "Sir please calm her down or we will have to sedate her," said the Nurse. "I'm sorry mam, Kia please baby, it's going to be okay." Kia failed to comply, so they restrained her and injected her with a mild sedation which knocked her out immediately. Drained he walked to Tia's room. Everything went pretty much the same way, with one exception, she bit the doctor and scratched the Nurse. The last thing Tia said before being sedated was, "This is all Isis fault, I hate her, and I never want to see her again!"

After exiting her room, Mr. McNeil walked towards me. I stood up, out of respect. "Thank you so much Isis, for saving my girls." "No need in thanking me, those girls are the only real friends that I have, no, scratch that sir, those girls are my sisters. When can I go and see them?" He paused. "Isis, it saddens me to have to say this to you, of all people, but (shaking his head) I can't let you go in there yet. The girls are kind of angry and well..." "Well, what?" "They blame you for tonight's mishaps." "Wait what? They blame me?" Silence. "I'm sure they're just overwhelmed with all that has transpired. I wouldn't take it personally if I were you. Just give them a couple days to cool off. You understand, right?"

I nodded my head, but deep down I was crushed. "They're resting now but I will update you on their recovery process." I stood there, barely able to respond. "I just don't understand, what I did wrong?" "Nothing, my dear child. Isis you did nothing wrong. Isis, honey you know you are like a daughter to me. Take this $20 so you can catch a cab ride home. I would drive you myself, but I don't want to leave the girls, especially now. I know your parents must be worried sick about you." That's when it dawned on me, that I hadn't even called them yet.

"Thank you again dear. I'll call you a cab. Don't worry about the girls they're just hurting right now." "Yeah, I guess," I said dryly. "Now if you'll excuse me, I have to go and check on the girls." Before he was out of eyesight he hollered over his shoulder, "Isis the cab will arrive in 20 minutes." I nodded my head. When the cab pulled up, I was already outside. I jumped in his ride so fast he barely had a chance to park. I slammed the door kind of hard. Then I fastened my seatbelt. I could tell by his accent, that he was an islander. He put you in the mind of Ox. "Don't break my door off the hinges mon. Where to mon?" Silence.

I had so much on my mind that I didn't even hear him when he was talking to me. When I snapped back to reality, he sounded agitated. "Hello...Miss, excuse me. Where to mon? Hello." Then I blurted out my address. I remained silent the entire ride home. Before I knew it, we were pulling up in my driveway. I shoved the twenty-dollar bill in his face and told him to keep the change. "Oh, wow mon, .75 cent I won't spend it all at once, mon." I was already in a mood, so I didn't even bother responding. Then I slammed the door even harder than before. While the driver was speeding off, I couldn't make out what he was saying but I know he was probably saying something smart. It had been such a stressful day. I'm just happy that I made it home safely.

When It Rains It Pours: Marc

The twins were still out cold, so I found myself pacing the floor. About 15 minutes goes by before I was approached by the officers again, but this time I was asked to identify my wife's body. I was petrified. What hurts me the most, is, we haven't spoken since our separation. "Sir, would you like us to escort you to view the body?" "No offense but this is something that I have to do on my own." "I know this is a hard time for you and your family sir. We will bring forth justice." "Yeah, thanks." "Sir are you okay?" "Officer, I honestly don't know, hopefully I will be with time."

I turned away from them and I started my stroll down the hall. Despite my better judgement they followed closely behind. Walking through the doors, a chill went down my spine. I stood in silence and through my tears, I confirmed my own suspicion. I kissed her one last time. Then I signed the paperwork that was needed for her autopsy. I leaned down and whispered in her ear, as if she could hear me, "I love you." Who knows, they say the dead can still hear you while their soul is transitioning.

Then I turned to the door and walked out of the room without saying a word. I walked into Kia's room, and I sat down in the chair closest to her bedside. The nurse waved her hand, signaling for me to step out into the hall so I walked out the room and headed towards the nurse's station. "Hello, sir I am Nurse Kristy, and you are?" I extended my hand. "I'm Marc... Marc McNeil. I am the father of those two beautiful girls in there." "Very nice to meet you sir. I just wanted to let you know that your girl's vitals are stable. I think it would do us all, some justice if you went home and tried to get some rest. I will personally, keep an eye on those girls for you." "Well, um, I guess you're right."

I handed her one of my business cards. "I'll go home only on one condition." "Sure, sir what's that?" "You have to call me the minute that they wake up and if they are any changes. Those are my girls, and they are all that I have left." Her smile was warm which gave me the reassurance that I needed. "Sure, sir I have all of your contact information right here. I will see to it that your information is added to their whiteboards, and I will also make a notation on both of their charts to." "Thank you, Nurse Kristy."

Home Sweet Home: Isis

I eased my key in the door trying not to make too much noise. When I got home the entire family was woke, including my cat, Smokey. I could tell by my mom's puffy eyes she had been crying. "Isis Montgomery, where in the world have you been? Do you have any idea what time it is? This is absurd, young lady, totally unacceptable. It is 2 o'clock in the morning, and it is, way, past your curfew," said Mommy. Daddy didn't waste any time jumping in either, "You could have at least called to let us know that you were okay breathing. This is so unlike you and very irresponsible of you."

Mama chimed back in to make matters even worse, "A young man by the name of Mike has been calling you, nonstop every hour on the hour. He says that it's urgent that you get in touch with him. Where have you been Isis? Answer me, answer me right now! Silence. I called both the twin's parents but neither one of them answered. I know they must be worried sick about them girls. What is your problem young lady?" Feeling overwhelmed, I cried. "Sorry I didn't call but, Ma, Daddy please… it has been a rough day. Honestly, I don't even know where to begin."

"Oh my God Isis, honey what is it? Did somebody touch you?" "No, Mommy no one (sniff, sniff) touched me." Daddy sighed before he spoke, "Well, honey that's a relief. I would kill the man that forced themself on my, Sunshine." "I'm…I'm okay, but the twins and Mrs. McNeil." I paused, as I felt like the wind was being shifted from out of my body. My voice started to tremble. "Oh God Mommy." I rushed over to where she was standing and wrapped my arms around her tight. "The twins…they were… they were… raped and drugged."

"Oh my God, Isis. That is terrible news, honey." "Yes Mommy…and Mrs. McNeil, is—is, is…" I paused. "Mrs. McNeil…is dead. I have been at the hospital all night. I am so sorry for not calling but (sniff, sniff) I wasn't thinking clearly. You have to forgive me," I blurted out. My mom looked at me with the look of pain in her eyes. "Wait a minute honey, what did you just say, Isis?" I continued. "I don't have a phone to call you guys otherwise I would have. The twins are in the hospital and Mrs. McNeil was murdered."

"Lord have mercy. I hate to have to say this, but I just thank God that my child is home safe. I can't even imagine what their father must be going through right now. That poor man…That poor, poor man. The McNeil's are definitely in my prayers." "Thanks Mommy." "I know you're tired Sunshine, so run on upstairs, get out of those dirty linens, and try to get yourself some rest." "Thanks Daddy." I kissed them both before disappearing upstairs. As soon as I got to the top landing, I headed straight to the bathroom and pulled off l my clothes. I turned on the hot water and applied some apple scented bubbles to my bath. Then I heard Smokey clawing his nails at the door, so I let him in locking the door behind him. I sunk my body into the bottom of the tub, and I overheard, Ma talking to me from downstairs, but her words were muffled. I didn't even bother responding. I closed my eyes, while the bubbles danced all over my aching body.

Marc

I was walking in the parking garage, while trying to locate my keys. I sounded the alarm to my Cadillac, yanked on the door handle, hopped inside of my truck and I pulled off. Heading west bound, I rubbed my face with the palm of my hand. I powered on the radio trying to find something soothing. 20 minutes later and I was parking inside my garage. Once I shut down the engine I cried like, never before. After I released some of my pain, I unlocked my door and walked inside my empty house. The first picture that I saw upon entry, on the mantle was of the twins, which warmed my heart. I went to the bathroom and shaved my beard, before showering.

I brushed my teeth and washed my face. Then I headed to my room. I sprayed on my deodorant, threw on my boxers, and hopped into bed. 6 hours later, I hopped up and got dressed. While I was slipping on my shoes my phone rang. "This is McNeil." "Good morning

Mr. McNeil. This is Nurse Kristy Johnston calling from Miracle's hospital." I paused. "Yes, go ahead." "I'm calling to inform you that the girls are awake, and they are asking for you. So, I..." Before she finished her sentence, I intervened, "Thank you for calling. Please let them know that I am on my way." I disconnected the call, rushed to my car, and headed to the hospital.

Nurse Kristy Johnston

It has been 2 years since my publicized divorce. I've come a long way, and it hasn't been easy either. With the help of counseling, and plenty of prayer, I can finally say that I am starting to feel like my old self again. My ex-husband was a former pro-football player who was referred to as, "Jake the great." In the beginning our future seemed promising. It wasn't until his injury onset that he was sent to a state of despair. It had gotten so bad that I contemplated committing suicide. It wasn't until I ran across an Old Testament, pamphlet that an older woman had given to me awhile back that I was able to start to heal.

I felt like that was a sign from God. The following Sunday, I rejoined church and I never looked back. The physical abuse started when Jake lost his contract. He never left any visible bruises on my person. He threatened to kill me and himself if I left him, so no matter how bad he hurt me I stayed. The lavish gifts and the watered down apologizes, started getting old. Too embarrassed to tell any of our family and friends so I was forced to face that pain alone. I have always been a good woman to him. I cooked, cleaned, and I helped him to raise my six-year-old illegitimate son.

To this day, I treat him like my own. Jake being the only man that I have ever been with, holds a special place in my heart. The only reason that I have any form of contact with him, is because of our son, Derrick. I tried getting custody of him, but he lawyered up on me, just so he could stay in control. He fought me to the point where I could never conceive a child of my own. Derrick's biological mother Kiosha sold him like he was a toy. Jake met her at one of his football retreats, out of town. A couple months after Derrick was born, I started receiving estranged phone calls and emails, from unknown senders. The media was all over it to. Despite the rumors Jake denied the allegations.

In search of the truth, I hired a private investigator. I thought about contacting the show, "Cheaters," but I decided against it. When that was unsuccessful, I snuck and did a DNA test and that is when my entire world came tumbling down, and my biggest fear became a reality. After I did the leg work, Kiosha started extorting Jake. She threatened to expose him claiming that she had compromising videos of him. He paid her $50,000 dollars for her silence, custody of our son, and for her disappearance. As far as I know she has kept her end of the bargain. After our messy divorce, I built a steel wall to protect my heart. Although he scarred me, I yearned for the type of love that you only read about, in those sappy romance novels.

Rise & Shine: Isis

The next morning, I woke up to the screaming voice of my mother. I immediately became irritated, until I heard her say that Mike was on the phone for me. I was so geeked, I almost fell out the bed. "What time is it Ma?" "A quarter to ten." "Oh okay, Ma thanks." I jumped out of the bed and rushed to the bathroom. I glanced in the mirror at my appearance. I took one of my hands and held it in front of my mouth as I blew out hot air into my hand. Then I screamed downstairs, "Hey, Ma tell him hold on, please." I brushed my teeth and freshened up a bit. I even applied some lip gloss before heading downstairs, to get the phone. I grabbed the phone from off the table and I headed back up to my room.

"Hello. Are you okay?" He laughed. "What's up, Ma? Yeah, I'm straight. I should be asking you that, as long as it took you to answer the phone. I thought you didn't want to talk to a nigga." "Nah, it's nothing like that, Mike." "I was calling you Ma, because I needed to holler at you." "I'm all ears, what's up?" Silence. "Hello, Mike you there?" "Yeah, Ma I'm here but we gone chop it up later. Your buddies, cool though?" "Yeah, they are okay." "That's what's up Ma. Can you get out today?" "Uh yeah Mike, I'm not a baby. Of course, I can get out." "Okay then cool." Before hanging up we agreed to meet up at the library. I was so thirsty that I ran back downstairs trying to pick Ma and Daddy's brain.

"Y'all not going to work today?" "No not today, Ice, your father has a doctor's appointment." "Aw ok." "I called your school and told them you will be out for the rest of the week." I shook my head. "Okay Mommy cool, well, can I get some money?" "For what Sunshine?" "Well Daddy, I need some money in my pocket so I can go and meet up with Ash today. We have to finish up our history paper." Ma looked at me like she didn't believe a word I was saying. "A paper huh?" I looked at her and smiled. "I don't know about this Isis." "Honey let the girl go and work on her schoolwork. You know how she is about those grades." "Thanks Daddy." I looked at Ma and started pouting.

"Please Mommy, please." She rolled her eyes. "Okay now, Isis don't miss your curfew." "I won't Ma, I'll be home early today, I promise." Daddy reached in his pocket and handed me two twenty-dollar bills. I hugged them both before I ran back upstairs. After, prepping for two hours, I was ready to go. I glanced over in the mirror briefly, making sure everything was intact. Then I gave myself an approving wink and I headed out of the door.

SIX

Blissful Magic

It was nice day outside, so I decided to take the bus. The noisy, graffiti tagged, bus, got me to my destination in record timing. I pulled the lever once I reached my destination. I hopped off the bus and sat down on the closest bench. Feeling nervous my leg started shaking. I was humming one of my favorite tunes when Mike appeared, and we locked eyes. As soon as I saw him my heart started to pound. He was looking good to, he had on some distressed Purple brand, jeans with the matching shirt. His feet were laced with some blue and red colored Js to. I couldn't help but to notice, the bulge that was protruding through his zipper.

"What's good Ma?" "Oh, Nothing, much." "What's on the agenda for today?" I stopped myself because I wanted to blurt out you, but instead I remained calm. "I'm just chilling that's all." "Aw okay, That's what's up, Ma. I'm just asking because I got us a little room downtown, so we can chill, you cool with that?" "Yeah, uh… that's cool I guess." I stood to my feet and followed his lead. We walked over to an onyx colored, Jaguar. He held my door open, I got in, and we left. While in traffic, he glanced at me and smiled. "You look good, Ma." Unable to contain my excitement, I blushed. "What this old thing? Aw, thanks."

"Answer me this Ma, you ready to let a real nigga, snatch you?" "If you think you can handle me." He must've noticed my nervousness, so he grabbed me by the hand, and started rubbing it in a circular motion. He took his eyes off the road momentarily, he glanced over at me and smiled. Then he redirected his attention back on the road. "Isis I knew when I laid my eyes on you, that you were for keeps, Ma." I listened closely while I stared out the window watching the birds fly in the sky.

"That's messed up what happened to your friends the other night." "Yeah, it's sad." "You know I would never let anything happen to you right?" "I hope not Mike." While we were deep, in conversation, we arrived too the hotel and parked near the valet booth. I didn't know what I was going to tell my parents, but I'm not missing my beat, period. I'm not gone lie I might be grounded for a year after this stunt I'm about to pull. Mike hopped out of the car and handing his keys to the valet attendant. He walked over to the passenger side and opened my door. Then he extended his hand, I grabbed hold of it, and I stepped out.

Casually we entered the hotel lobby. The inside looked amazing. The crystal chandelier hung perfectly in the middle of the ceiling, and the crème colored, seating and the two-toned, circular rugs were exquisite to. The distinct shaped, crystal center pieces complimented each of the cocktail tables. I continued scanning the room, while Mike checked us in. After the woman at the front desk handed him our key cards, we were off. I followed him as he led us over to the glass elevator. On the ride up, we rode in silence. He got off the elevator first, but I wasn't too far behind. He slipped the key inside the door and instantly a lavender scent invaded my nasal passages. Flowers were everywhere. We were stationed on the 19th floor, in the penthouse suite. Our room had a balcony overlooking the entire city. The jacuzzi was full of red and white rose pedals, adjacent to the bathroom. The kitchen was small but very dainty. There were 2 champagne bottles atop the mini bar that was next to the fridge. The bed was oval shaped.

An assortment of rose peddles were evenly distributed. "What's wrong Ma? What, you don't like the room? If you don't like it, we can always go someplace else. Sky's the limit, Ma. I got you." I smiled. "As long as you play your part, Shorty, you gone be good." This was all sounding too good to be true, so I started rambling like I did whenever I get nervous, "Yea I hear you Mike, but how do I know you're not just running game on me? I mean, a guy will say anything, to get in a woman's pants. They be placing bets on me like a trifactor."

He looked at me and frowned. "Awe that's what you think this is, you think I'm trying to get some ass. Shorty, no disrespect, but I can have any girl I want, facts!" "Well, Mike, I need to know, what the deal is? I mean we just met, and you already got us a room." A bit emotional I started to cry. I cried tears of sadness because of the twin's situation and tears of joy because I've never seen anything more romantic in my life. He took one of his hands and pushed my bang to the side.

He wiped away my tears, and lifted my chin, slowly. Then he looked into my eyes. "Don't cry Ma, I got you." I blushed, it was the tone, for me. "Ma, we don't have to do anything. No pressure. I just thought you was feeling a nigga but it's smooth." "That's not, it," I sobbed.

"What is it then, Ma?" "The room is gorgeous and I, I... I love it. I'm just.... scared that's all. I just don't want to get hurt." He rubs my hand, gently, while placing soft kisses on it. Then he looks up at me with his mesmerizing eyes. "Games are for kids, Ma. With all due respect, pussy ain't shit to a boss. I was just trying to show you something different, Shorty, that's all." That was just the confirmation that I needed. I don't really remember what was said next, all I remembered was our lips interlocking. He kissed me passionately and with my eyes closed I tongued him back. His touch made my body tingle, but in a good way.

I had never experienced this feeling of ecstasy before. He lifted me carefully from my seat and he cradled me in his arms. He laid me down on my back, gently while the flowers tickled my uncovered flesh. I kicked off my shoes. He got on top of me and started caressing me, kissing my neck fervently. The mixture of his soft touches and warm kisses, makes, me get wet in places, that I have never experienced before. While we were wrestling with our tongues, I stopped. "Wait Mike...I'm a..." I stuttered, so uneasily.

"Mike, I don't know how to tell you this but.... I'm a..." He jerks back. "Just spill it, Ma. You're a what, Shorty just say it." I paused. I took a deep breath and I blurted out real fast, "I'm a virgin." He looked at me and burst into laughter. "Oh, shit, is that all? It's all good, Ma. That's what's up. That's nothing to be ashamed of. Don't know man want another man's leftovers." We shared a laugh and I laughed so hard that

I snorted. I covered my mouth from embarrassment and we both laughed again. "I thought that you would be disappointed because I wasn't experienced like the girls that you're used to." He looked at me strangely.

"The girls that I'm used to Ma. What is that supposed to mean? There you go worrying about the wrong shit." I frowned. "The wrong shit, how, Mike? I'm just protecting my heart." "It's all good we can just chill, no pressure." By now, I was irritated and turned on by his collected demeanor, all at the same time. Then he started caressing me. "Just say the word, Ma and I'll stop. Do you want me to stop?" I paused. "No, Mike don't stop." I purred. "You sure Ma?" "Yes, I'm sure I'm just scared so be gentle with me." My voice must've been enticing to him because I could have sworn, I felt his private, jumping, through my clothes. He removed my shirt effortlessly.

He unhooked my bra, in one swoop exposing my grape sized nipples and medium sized breast. He took one of my nipples into his mouth and flicked his tongue all over it, fast, then, slow, until my nipples were as hard as an erection. I laid there reserved, panting, and biting down on my bottom lip, as he explores my body. He nibbles away, from my chest, down to my navel, until I felt moist. He smiles, slyly with a mouth full of my breast. He stops for a moment and looks me in the eyes. "Don't worry baby, I got you, but if you're not ready, we can cool it." "No, please don't stop." I cried out in ecstasy. "I want this, I mean I want you, and I need to feel you inside of me." He slid down my pants exposing my lace covered boy shorts. Then he pushes my panties to the side and massages my clit.

With two of his fingers, he moves them in and out of my vagina and his kisses increases. He kisses me on the nape of my neck while I removed his belt and his jeans mechanically. He kisses my navel, while looking into my eyes. Soft moans escaped my lips. I couldn't believe those type of sounds, were coming from me. Just when I thought that I couldn't feel any better, he slid my panties all the way down, exposing my trim, and puts his face in my place and says his grace. He tickles my pearl causing my legs to shake, uncontrollably. I squeezed the pillow for dear life, struggling, to catch my breath while he tastes me. He removed himself, from his Polo shorts, and stood strong at full attention. His member was shaped like a python with a slight curve.

I almost exploded when he started rubbing his tool up against my clitoris. I tensed up when he slowly pushed his erection inside of me. At first, his key ejecting from my jewel box. His kisses made me relax a bit more. He got into rhythm. It was like an indescribable, pain. Loving every moment of it, I slowly started getting into the flow of things. Then I started throwing it back at him, bucking my hips to the rhythm of his beat. As our tempo, connected we became one. I matched his every thrust.

He talked dirty to me and surprisingly, I liked it. "Yea baby throw that pussy back at me. Yeah, just like that." The more he talked, the more I started to feel myself. I bit down on the pillow to keep from screaming. I grabbed a hold of his head and kissed him slowly. Then I shoved my tongue down his throat, demanding him to go deeper inside of me. "Oh, Shit," he shouted in ecstasy. An hour into our heated passion and we started to cum. As I came my body shook violently. Then he laid on top of me barely able to catch his breath. "This, my, pussy now. You better not ever give my shit away. Do you hear me Ice."

I smiled. "Okay Zaddy. I won't give your goodies away, I got you." I stayed the night like I didn't have a trouble in the world. The rest of the night pretty much went the same way. He fed me strawberries and we sipped champagne, while he held me in his arms. I couldn't hide my excitement, even if I tried. He made me feel warm inside. For the first time I felt safe, I felt whole. He is my, Mr. Bliss.

The Party Over

Walking in the door of my home, I had an unfamiliar, womanly glow about myself. Mike took me shopping before dropping me off, so I had on a cute little fit and I had a couple bags in my hand to. After jiggling my keys around for about 5 minutes or so, nervously, I finally got in. My heart nearly beats up out of my chest when I walked in and saw Mommy and Daddy, sitting in the dark. I jumped at the sight of them. I have never been in any trouble, so I didn't know what to expect. "Where have you been young lady and what is in all of those bags, library books, I hope?" I didn't even get a chance to respond before my father started going off at me.

"Isis what is your problem? You couldn't pick up the phone?" "Where have you been? We have been worried sick about you. Isis what has gotten into you lately?" I really wasn't in the mood to be chastised, so in an aggravated, tone, I went there with them. "I was out with a friend. If I had a cell phone, I would've been able to call you guys. Furthermore, had I told you that I wasn't coming home last night you guys would have gone through the roof just like you're doing right now. Sorry I scared you guys, but I'm getting older now and I..." Then in midsentence, ma reached over and smacked me so hard that I felt fire on both sides of my cheeks.

I grabbed my cheek and rubbed it. "If you're going to be living under this roof, there are rules that you must follow young lady. No daughter of minds will be galloping around town like some sort of tramp." Without saying a word, I stormed passed them and I went upstairs to my room. When I got inside, I slammed and locked the door. I flashed back to last night's bliss. I heard my mother yelling at me from downstairs, "Isis Desire Montgomery, we're not done with you yet. This sort of behavior will not be tolerated. Get down here now!" Instead of responding I grabbed my headphones, I plopped down in my bed, and turned my music up to the max to tune her out. I laid in my bed and cried myself to sleep. It was the next day and my parents were still angry. Mama yelled after me.

"Isis Desire Montgomery, get down here this instance." I sprinted downstairs. "She gets on my last nerves," I mumbled underneath my breath. I got to the bottom of the stairs, and she had the audacity to tell me, I was grounded. She looked at me and rolled her eyes, then she turned back around to finish washing the dishes. "Well Isis, let me make this perfectly clear, for your little grown ass, if it wasn't for Mrs. McNeil's funeral you would not be stepping foot in any hair salon. Do you understand me, Isis?" "Yes mam."

R.I.P. Tee's: Isis

I still couldn't get over the fact that I hadn't talked to my girls. This is the longest we have ever gone without speaking. My feelings hurt, and I feel like everybody's against me. First them, then my parents and now Mike. I remained quiet the entire ride to the funeral home. I heard Mama say to Daddy that I needed to fix my attitude before she fixes it for me. Instead of my father he increased the volume on his radio. When we arrived, I hopped out instantly. As I walked in, all I heard was sobs and babies crying. We had just made it in time for the end of the wake. I saw a few people wearing R.I.P. t-shirts to. After viewing Mrs. McNeil's body, I hugged everyone on the first row, including the twins. "Sorry for your loss, your family is in my prayers." One of them spoke dryly, "Thanks." Even when we hugged, it felt estranged. After the preacher spoke about life, death, and choices a plumped woman, approached the podium. Her dress was elegantly worn. She grabbed the microphone and she cut up while singing, "Eyes on the sparrow."

There wasn't a dry eye in sight. She tore that song up, like she wrote it. It was almost like being in church where Whitney sang lead, before meeting Bobby. I could hear Kia and Tia crying the hardest. I saw some familiar faces in the crowd, some of which I hadn't seen in years. I heard Mr. McNeil, shouting, "Why? Why? Why my family? Oh Lord why didn't you just take me instead?" In desperate need of some fresh air, I excused myself. I walked towards the bathroom to rinse my face and apply a fresh coat of gloss on my lips. As I sashayed through the hallway, my heart nearly skipped a beat when I saw Mike's fine ass.

I tried walking in the opposite direction, but he quickly caught up with me, looking casket sharp. He was draped in a navy Armani suit. His tie, belt and shoes were made by Louie. He grabbed me by the arm. "What are you doing here Mike?" I stood there, with my lips poked out. "I knew my baby needed me. I told you, you mine, Shorty, you think this a game?" I looked away. He grabbed my chin and turned me back to face him. When we locked eyes, he kissed me so softly. After we embraced, he shoved a cellphone in my face. "Huh, Ma this you." I hesitated at first but then I grabbed the phone. "Don't be mad at me I just got back in town, Shorty." "Yeah, whatever Mike." "Don't be like that Ma, I cut my trip short so I could be here for you." He tried to hug me, but I yanked away. Before I knew it, I saw my mother and father walking my way.

Undetected, I slipped the phone in my pocket. Feeling, awkward, I didn't know what to say. Mike turns around to face them and he extends his hand to my dad while he flashes his captivating smile. Daddy frowns. "Isis." "Yes Daddy." "Let's, go...now! I don't want any daughter of mines wasting her life with some nickel and dime thug." "With all due respect sir, thug I am not. I am a man, an intelligent man, at that, might I add. I have never been a thug, nor ever will I be. I am a boss, I own my empire, and by the way if you're ever looking for employment, please don't hesitate to call."

Mike handed him one of his business cards. My mouth hit the floor. Ma didn't utter a word. I felt the need to speak on his behalf, so I did just that. "Daddy, please don't do this. This is my boyfriend, please don't make me choose." "Aw so now you have a boyfriend huh, Isis? Let me make this perfectly clear to you. While you are living underneath my roof, you don't have a choice. I make the decisions for you," said Daddy and he stormed off. "Nice to meet you, young man," said Mommy before running to catch up with my father. Discomfited Mike breaks the silence. "Your boyfriend huh. I'm your boyfriend now, Ma?"

He smiled then he slapped me on the ass. Without saying a word, I walked away, leaving him standing there. I finally spotted the car, so I put the phone on silent mode and shoved it inside my purse. When I got in the car, I slammed the door. When we were pulling out the lot, I saw Mike hollering at some of his boys. He must've felt my presence because as soon as we came near, he turned around and made a signal gesturing for me to give him a call. Although I was mad, I smiled. Then I leaned my head back and enjoyed the long ride home.

Prisoner in My Home: Isis

The ride home was so intense, I didn't think we would ever make it home. As soon as we stepped foot in the door, my parents started tripping again. "I don't know what your problem is Isis, but I can tell you this, you will not be seeing that boy again while living under this roof young lady. If you don't like our rules, then there is the door." By, now Mommy is an emotional wreck. I remained silent. "Isis, honey your father is right. We love you dearly. We just want the best for you [in between sobs] don't mess up your life baby, please. That boy is nothing but trouble. I can feel it in my bones Isis." I didn't bother responding. After they finished scolding me, I ran upstairs, and closed my door. I stripped down to my underwear. Then I laid in the bed while I let my pillow absorb my tears. I needed something to cheer me up, so I contemplated on calling Mike.

I grabbed my cell and I glanced down at the screen noticing I had 3 missed calls. A smile appeared on my face when I saw his name flashing on the screen. I got up, locked the door, plopped back in the bed, and I returned his called. "Hey you." "Hey." "What's wrong Ma?" I hesitated. "Nothing." "Something's up, I can tell, talk to me, Ma." I paused. "Well, um.... Mike it's like this...my parents gave me an ultimatum." Silence. "And...that is?" "Well, Mike, they told me that as long as I was living underneath their roof, I could no longer see you. I'm sorry. I really don't know what to do Mike." "Wait, what are you saying Ice?"

I paused, "Mike, I like you, I really do, but I can't risk getting kicked out on the streets. I mean where am I going to go?" Silence. "First off Ma, I know those are your parents and all no disrespect but how they gone give you an ultimatum like that? Ma, what's your address?" I told him... "Hold on a minute Ma, let me take this call. Say less. I'm gone hit you when I'm in the front." Silence. "When you're in front, wait a minute... hello... Mike.... hello..." Silence. I hid my phone inside my purse. Then I got up and jumped in the shower. I ran back to my room and got dressed. Thirty or forty minutes later, I heard a horn blowing like crazy. I looked out of my window and just as promised, there he was. I grabbed my purse and my overnight bag. I picked up my pace and headed for the door. While I was heading out, I overheard Ma talking to my dad. "Aren't you going to do something? Are you going to just sit back and let her l ruin her life?"

My pride wouldn't allow me to back down, so I continued walking to the door. Daddy looked at my mother and then backs at me. I'm doing everything in my power not to cry. Before I got out the door good, I heard my father saying, "If you walk out of that door, Isis Desire Montgomery, so help me God, don't bother coming back." Nervously, I dropped my bag to the floor contemplating my next move, while the horn continued to sound. "Isis don't do this baby please," said Mommy. "Go ahead and ruin your life, I'm done," Daddy stated coldly. Before twisting the knob, I turned around to face them. "I love you both, I just have to live my life." I turned back around, grabbed the door and I headed out. As I got on the other side of the door, I could hear my mother calling after me, but I kept walking.

I hopped in his ride, I stared out the window and we drove off. "You good Shorty?" I shook my head no.

"What am I going to do Mike? I don't have any clothes or any money. My parents hate me and I'm homeless." He grabbed me by the hand, and he rubbed. "Don't trip, Ma. I got you. We can go grab you a few items after school tomorrow." I shook my head to say yes. I was hurting, badly. "Of course, you say everything is going to be okay, Mike, you have a place to live, and clothes on your back. I don't have anything anymore. There is no telling how long this will last, then what am I supposed to do?" He laughed but I didn't find anything funny. "Ma be smooth. You straight, trust me. This can last long as you allow it to. Just play your cards right." I snatched my hand away, but he jerked it back. "I guess but what if your family doesn't like me, then what? What am I supposed to do then Mike?"

I had so many questions flooding through my brain. "You good Ma, my people, gone love you, just be cool. Cheer up Shorty, your parents will come around." I managed to crack a weak smile. "Okay." "Ma, you have to take risk in life. So, take a chance with me and stop being so uptight. Get your panties out a bunch." I laughed from his comment. The rest of the ride, we let the music do the talking. We stopped in a couple of stores before heading to his house. I grabbed myself a fit, some under garments and some toiletries. "That's all you want Ma?" "Oh, uh…yeah. I just needed something to wear to school tomorrow." He reached in his pocket and paid the bill without hesitation. Then we left.

SEVEN

The New Place: Isis

When we arrived to his him, I was stoked. The place was password protected and the landscaping was beautiful. As soon as we got inside, he gave me a grand tour. The living room was humungous. The entertainment system contained an 85-inch plasma television screen with some Bose speakers. The fireplace was adjacent to the entertainment system. There were marble floors seen throughout. The black leather and suede couches were a classy additive. The Lennox crystal sculptures were also delicately distributed, on each of the end tables. To the left of the living room was the dining area the dinner table placed at least 8.

Following that was the stainless steel filled kitchen. The cabinet doors were made of glass and the counter tops were of marble. The circular shaped, glass, kitchen table was very elegant. Throughout the house amongst the walls were paintings by well-known artist. There was a spiral staircase leading to the upper level. The multi-unit 5 bedrooms, 6-bathroom home with vaulted ceilings was spacious. "Close your mouth Ice, before a fly enters your trap." I punched him playfully in the shoulder. "Your house is astonishing." He smiled. "Thanks, Ma. I purchased this house so that I could move my family out of the jets (projects). That's how I got started in the real estate business."

I admired his humbleness. He grabbed my hand and guided me from room to room, minus the two bedrooms with their doors closed. His basement resembled a modernized recreation room. Along the walls were the all-time favorites, he had every full-sized arcade game from Ms. Pac man to Street fighter. The 88-inch flat screen complimented the look. His built-in projector was perfect for any family gathering. The entertainment system was identical to the one upstairs. The candy apple, leather couches, was nice to. The sunken love seats were indistinguishable to the couch. Centered in the middle of the floor was a pool table. His leather bar was stocked like a liquor store. The basement was closed off, like a separate entity of the house and it was also password generated. I also noticed there was a nice size jacuzzi in the bathroom to.

He grabbed me momentarily and held me in his arms. He whispered in my ear, "I told you, you were going to be mines, Shorty." I smiled until my cheeks turned a shade of red. As we shared a kiss, he palmed my ass. For a moment, just for a moment, my pain disappeared. Once we broke free, we walked back, upstairs. Once we were on the other side of the door, he keyed in the lock code. Then we walked back into the living room and headed up the stairs to the master room. I swear his room was as big as a one-bedroom apartment. His black suede sectional sofa matched his love seat. The glass swivel cocktail table, meshed well with the rest of his ensemble. His flat screen, television was a nice size to.

He had the seven deadly sins, picture hanging over his, black leather headboard. His surround sounds put you in the mind of a movie theater. His ceiling mirror was kind of dope. Gucci signature bedding was draped across his king size bed. His dresser looked like a cologne counter. The jacuzzi in his bathroom, was the size of a small swimming pool. His triangle shape rug showcased different shades of blue. He also had a blue, "Fleur-De-Lis," pedestal sink which looked like it had wings. "Ice, I need to holler at you about something." "So...what's up, Mike? Just tell me." He grabbed me by my chin, and he stared in my eyes. "Ever since the first day that I saw you, I wanted you to be in my life. I told myself that day you would be mines." "Boy is that all? For a minute you scared me." "I told you I got you Ma.

You'll see." He looked at me with a sly grin and I smiled. Then leaned forward and kissed me.

Mourning: Tia

Immediately following the burial was the repast. My sister and I seem to be taking it the hardest, well other than Dad of course. We have been through hell and back in the last couple weeks. Isis, our supposed to be best friend is a no show, which comes to me as no surprise. Rumors surfaced how she put on quite a show at the funeral to. She has always been a conniving little bitch, that everyone thinks is so perfect. It's always an Isis show. Everyone always caters to her and I'm sick of it.

Kia is spaced out. Dad is in so much pain that he didn't even say his goodbyes after the eulogy. Nurse what's her name, Karen or Kristy came to the funeral with her son Derrick. She claims that she came for moral support, but I'm not buying it. She better fallback, before I make her life a living hell because she cannot fill the footsteps of my mother. They say I'm a splitting image of Mommy, looks, and attitude included. I take that as a compliment. No matter what anybody says, she's, my hero. I just hope that she knows just how much I love her.

EIGHT

I Could Get Use to This: Isis

So much had transpired I didn't even get a chance to stop by the repast. Mike and I talked for hours. I'm not gone lie his voice makes my soul shiver. We talked about my aspirations, and I told him that I planned on going to Harvard to study law. I could tell he was impressed. "Mike what do you want from me?" With a smile he answered, "Everything Ma. Your loyalty and your heart." "Oh, that's easy." "Yeah, alright, Ma we gone see. That loyalty shit is hard to standby. Everybody not built for it. I need you to be die hard for me, stay on top of them grades, fuck me when I need to bust a nut, and come too few of my games, that's it." "I guess I can handle that." "You guess?"

After School Surprise

After school, the next day my boo was outside waiting, just like he promised. I must admit it feels good, having somebody checking for me. There, he was sitting in his dark colored, Range truck, sitting up high, like a supersized Tonka truck. Walking in his direction, my smile disappeared when I peeped, some random chicks, lined up by his truck. Now I know with every star comes fans, but they look like some attention seekers. I sashayed from the school door to the truck, while my hair bounced off my shoulders. I mustered up a fake smile increasing the depth in my dimples. I walked in between their circle, and I bumped one of the girls on purpose, daring one of them to try me.

Then I opened the door to the truck on the passenger side, I hopped in, and I shut it tight. I kissed Mike on the lips, real seductive like, just to give them a show. Afterwards, I checked the mirror to see if my lip-gloss was still intact. It seemed to be fading so I applied some more. I rubbed my lips together and then I ran my tongue along my lips, making them look even juicier. As "You're temporary just like the rest of them so don't get too comfortable boo-boo, he just out on loan." I didn't even bother entertaining those hoes. Next thing they heard were the tires screeching.

Living Lavish

"How was school, Ma?" "It was cool." He could tell I was salty. Then out of nowhere he burst into laughter. "What's funny?" "You, Ma, you." Unsure of what to say, I turned my head and faced the window. He grabbed my hand and massaged it. "Play your part, Ma, and everything will be smooth. Shorty, I'm not checking for none of them hoes. No disrespect Ma, but you my bitch, now, you paid foe." I looked at him crazy. Now, don't judge me, judge your mama, but I was offended and turned on, at the same time. "Man, Ma, I don't want you to get wrapped up in your feelings worrying about them ran through ass hoes. Those hoes got more miles on them, than a used car. "Yeah, I hear you, Mike."

"Ice you say you hear me, Ma, but I need you to feel me. Don't be worrying about the wrong shit. The game is cold, but it got to be played. A hoe a get you whacked (killed). I need somebody that's gone be down, can you handle that?" "Yea, I can handle it." He laughed. "Well, you don't sound too reassuring, let me know something, so I can turn around and holler at one of them hoes." We laughed. Then I punched him in his shoulder playfully. "Mike, stop playing with me."

Why Me?

As soon as we entered the paid parking facility, out of the blue I started rambling. "Why me Mike? You can have any woman that you want, so why did you choose me?" He parked his car closest to the door and shut down the engine, placing his ticket on the dash before answering. "Why not you, Shorty? Ice it's real simple Ma, I been wanting you on my team. It was a minute ago when we met. It was something about your demeanor, that drew me to you." "When was this, Mike? I don't remember that."

"You and your home girls were at the corner store. Ya'll were in line waiting to checkout and you were short changed. I walked over to you and handed you a fifty-dollar bill and told you to keep the change, but you said no. If I looked hard enough, I could see the dollar signs, in the eyes of your friends. After you paid for your stuff, you handed me my change. When y'all left out, I overheard your girls, clowning you for not keeping the money but you stood your ground. Shorty no cap, after that, I went into that store for a week straight trying to bump heads with you, but I never saw you again, until that day, at the game." "How did you know that it was me?" "Ma, the eyes never lie. When I saw you on the bleachers, I knew I recognized your face from somewhere, on my son." "Wait, what, you have a son?" He laughed. "Naw, Shorty it's just a figure of speech. I heard from one of the old heads a long time ago, that what comes twice comes nice and I wasn't gone let you slip away from me again."

I sat in my seat, intrigued. I started to drift away revisiting that day. "Wow, Mike, that was a long time ago, but I remember that day, vaguely." He smiled. "Come on Ma, we can chop it up later. Let's go run through some cash. If we keep sitting here the stores gone be closed." "You right about that one, let's go." He shut down the engine and we hopped out.

Retail Therapy

It felt like we had bags from every store in the mall. He got me this pretty ass D&G bag with the matching sneaks and grabbed me a pair of heels to. I told him I couldn't walk in them though. He spent so much money on me that I felt guilty, so I talked him into grabbing himself something to. "Thanks, Mike." He nodded at me, "It's smooth Ma." We went into the Louie store, and I could've sworn that I saw those same shoes he bought me, on Mary at a red carpeted event. He must've noticed my awkwardness, "Nothing but the best for my lady." I blushed. We stayed in the mall until closing time.

"You hungry Ma?" "Yes, actually I am." "Okay, cool. What you got a taste for?" "Filet mignon and lobster." He smiled. "I like your style, Ma. Let's go eat." He carried most of our bags, to the car. He pushed the remote starter to his ride, threw the bags in the trunk and we pulled off. We talked with no discretion. The more we talked the more that I felt our chemistry. "Thank you, Mike. Thank you for everything." "Stay down, and you gone be straight, Shorty. I got you, Ma."

He drove us, to some Brazilian steak house, but there was a long wait. I overheard the greeter telling the family ahead of us that the wait time was an hour and forty-five-minute. Mike whispered something in the greeter's ear, and we were seated, immediately. Now that was impressive. The food was immaculate. I ate until I was completely stuffed. While I was taking my last fork full, I noticed Mike staring at me, so I stopped eating and I looked up at him in embarrassment. "I don't play about food, Mike," I managed to say with my hand covering my mouth. He laughed. "I see, Ma. I see." He signaled over our waitress, but by the time she made it to our table she was on the phone. He placed his hand over the speaker. "Check please." He paid the tab, added a tip, and then we left.

NINE

Some Things Never Change

Me and Mike been together, 9 months now. I still hadn't heard anything from my parents or the twins. It was my mother's birthday, so I swallowed my pride, and I gave her a call. Nervously, I dialed her up. "Hello." I almost cried when I heard her voice. "Mama is that you? It's… it's…me." "Me…me, who? Hello…If you don't tell me who you are, I will hang up." "Mama, please don't hang up It's me, Isis." "I don't know anyone by that name, you must have the wrong number. Please don't call here again," she said and disconnected the call.

I'm not gone even lie, she that my feelings with that one. I heard the door close downstairs, so I wiped away my tears and ran down. Ma and sis was coming in with groceries, so I grabbed some of the bags, and helped them to put them away. Since, I moved in everybody has made me feel so welcomed. Mike's mom, his sister, and I go to the same salon that I use to go to with my mother. To avoid running into her, I made sure that we didn't go on the same days. Mike's little sister is the sister that I never had. She talks to me about everything, from school to boys and I never tell her secrets either.

"Is Mike home baby?" "No, Ma he left about an hour ago to run some errands. He said he'll be home for dinner though." "Okay, baby. Thank you." In exchange for their amiable hospitality, I kept the house clean, and I cooked most of our meals. I also made sure that my sis, stayed in her studies. My baby keeps me fly, with money in my pockets, and he knows how to lay the pipe better than a plumber, so I don't mind helping around the house.

School Chronicles

Even though me and my BFFs are still not on speaking terms, I've been meaning to reach out to them. I spotted them sitting at a table near the door in the lunchroom and decided to head over. I cleared my throat before speaking. "Hey y'all, what's good?" Kia looked up from her phone. "Nothing much." "Aw uh, hey Ice," said Tia dryly. "How you two been?" "We good Ice, we good but what's with the 21 questions? What you the law or something?" At that very moment I had to catch myself before I slapped her little simple ass, but I played it cool, and I laughed it off.

Kia looked at me with pleading eyes. "We…" Before she could complete her sentence, she covered her mouth with her hand and rushed over to the trashcan and she hurled. I looked at her then back at Tia. "Yea girl, we are straight. I got us, so go ahead on, on your high horse, we don't need your kind over here." I know they both hurting but I will not be disrespected. I grinned, trying my best to refrain from spitting on her ignorant ass. Refusing to stoop to her level, I reiterated her statement, "My kind, now what is that supposed to mean, huh?"

She ignored me, grabbed some of those hard ass napkins off the table, and walked over to her sister and handed her the napkins. I got up and walked away, down the hall to my class. After last period I picked up my pace and exited the building. I already knew my man would be outside waiting for me. As soon as I saw him, I powered walked to his truck and I hopped in. "Hey baby." T "What's good, Ma?" "Nothing much." He paused. "After the game I'm riding home with some of the guys. I got some business I need to handle, so you can just take the truck. I'll meet you back at the house later." I was kind of salty, but I didn't even trip. I don't want our relationship to be based on false presumptions and adaptive rules. I wanted us to make up our own rules. "Ok baby that's cool. I have a paper due soon, so I'm going to go straight home, after y'all win, and get a fresh start on it. Plus, I have finals coming up to."

"So, what you want for your birthday, Ma?" I paused. "Uh I don't know yet, baby. I just want to be with you." He nodded, "Good answer." We headed home, got dressed in a hurry and we left back out. Pulling up to the game, we jumped out the truck and he tossed me the keys. Lately, it seems like Mike was so wrapped up in his real estate business that his passion for joining the league is fading. I hit the alarm button twice. We entered, the gymnasium, I wished him good luck and we went our separate ways. Then I headed over to the bleachers and found myself a seat.

Game Changer

While I was watching the game, I noticed two chicks starring me down and mugging but I didn't cause a scene. The twins were sitting a couple rows down. I screamed as my man scored points on the court. We won the game, and the crowd was going crazy. After the game Mike, walked with me back to the truck. He kissed me before opening my door. As soon as I hopped in, I adjusted my mirror and noticed those same hoes from earlier walking in our direction. I immediately got in defense mode. I swooped, my hair in a ponytail and I jumped out of the truck real beastie like, unnoticeably. I walked over to my man with the sounds blazing.

"So, Daddy, when are you coming home? What color you want to see me in tonight, Papi?" I asked him as I bit down on my bottom lip. They looked at me with hate in their eyes and I loved it. The ringleader seemed pressed. "Sweetie, he's with us tonight boo, Zaddy's not coming home, so don't wait up. We triple the trouble unless you want to join us." I looked at her with a mean mug out of this world. With my eyebrow raised I said, "There is nothing funny about me except for these jokes that I crack. Trust and believe me boo, I'm all the woman that my man needs period." Mike turned around from talking to his guys with his face all twisted up.

"This bitch thinks she's all that, with her little prissy ass. I'll take dude from her stuck-up ass." I didn't say a word but right then something in me just snapped and I stuck her, right in her mouth because she talked to much. Then I punched her in her nose. I knew that I was outnumbered, it was four of them, but I wasn't backing down. Once I hit her once, I didn't let up. Her friend jumped in, and I slung her to the ground to. Before I knew it, I was on top of her throwing blows. One of them grabbed my hair, but I kept punching away.

Then the other chick tried to run up on me and I cleared her to. Out of nowhere the twins appeared and started jawing them. While we were tussling, a guy tried to jump in. Mike wasn't haven't it though. "Stay out her business, don't play with her." Then he fell back. Onlookers were uploading the fight to social media. Not much longer after we heard sirens. I gave them hoes a kick to their stomach and one to the face. Mike grabbed me by my waist. He loosened, his grip and I jumped out of his arms. I ran and got the twins and we hopped in the truck. We pulled off with, Nip blasting through the speakers. Kia broke the silence, "Now, what the fuck was all that Ice?" I looked back at them, "What? Man, they came for me. They were asking for trouble."

T laughed, "Ice you already know, we don't play about you. I know we had our differences but you still our girl and we rock with you the long way, no cap." "Thanks girl, but I had they ass. Ya'll could've just watched the show." "Yeah, we seen you putting in that footwork, but we got your back, you're our dog fa sure. Check you out, Little Miss Prissy, done got herself a hood nigga, now you about that life," said T. "First of all, I am not prissy, why does everybody keep saying that to me? I'm just confident, and my baby is not hood, he's a businessman, so boom." We laughed. "Now Ice, you know you been spoiled and uppity your entire life so cut it out," said Kia. "Excuse me, Mam. I have never been uppity. I just carry myself like a lady boo-boo and some mistake my confidence for arrogance so boom, leave a message."

Rider

Mike started snickering, so I had to ask, "What's funny?" "Baby, I'm not gone lie, seeing you get busy out there, got my dick hard," he said with a sly grin. I smiled. Then he shouted back at my homegirls, "Where to? Me and the wifey got some unfinished business to attend. My boys still trailing us, I got to let them know something." "Your guy's, shit, you should've let one of them take us home," said T. Mike ignored her comment. "Where, to?" Then one of them finally spoke up and shouted out their address. "Gotcha, I know exactly where that is." Mike called up one of his boys. I couldn't hear what the caller on the other end was saying, but based on his response, I could tell they were talking about me. All I know is whatever he was saying had Mike cheesing extra hard.

When we pulled in front of the twin's crib one of them blurted out their number and told me to give them a call and I agreed. They got out the truck, and we didn't pull off until we made sure they were in safely. "Damn Ma, you never seem to amaze me." Bashfully, I smiled. Then he called up another one his homeboys and told them he would meet up with them tomorrow and they stopped trailing us. We pulled in the garage, and I started getting mannish. I reached down and stuck my hand inside of his joggers. Then I glided my hand up and down his controller skillfully and I continued to stroke him just like I did his ego.

I leaned forward and placed my mouth down on his rock hard. I positioned him in my mouth while I licked his erection and played with his balls. I leaned down further, tickling his balls with the tip of my tongue. I flicked my tongue on his head just like he likes it, and he grabbed a hand full of my hair. He forced feeds me until he felt my tonsils. I came up for air, I spit on my hand, then I spit on his member. I continued make slurping sounds while I took care of his tool.

I squeezed tightly, but not too tight. I sucked him slow and then fast, fast, and then slow, repeatedly. I gagged when I felt him hit the back of my throat, but I kept going like a pro. "Right there, Ma, don't stop. Shit eat that dick, bay. I love seeing your pretty face eating this dick." Hearing him talking dirty to me always gets my pumped. I kept slurping and bobbing my head on his erect, long, thick, pipe. Then I stuck two of my fingers in my panties and I started massaging my clitoris. "Baby I like that nasty shit." He looked down at me, while I was going to work on him. I held my head up and looked in his eyes while I let the saliva drip from my lips to my chin. His facial expression changed I could tell he was turned on.

I kept one hand on his erection and the other in my panty's. He got jealous of my fingers, and he pulled my hand from out of my pants and replaced my hand with his. In eyesight of him I sucked my juices off my fingers. Then I put my mouth back on him. I continued licking and slurping until I heard a familiar sound, "Oh shit! Right their baby, oh shit." "You like that baby?" "Yes, baby… right there! Oh shit." I rode his fingers, while I sucked him up, like a vacuum. Barely able to catch his breath, he said, "You bet, not ever give my pussy away, you hear me? Yes, shit baby yes!"

At that very moment, I couldn't take it anymore, so I hopped on top of him, and I rode him like a horse back rider. He lifted my shirt exposing my nipples and he teased my breast with his tongue. I rode him until he almost went limp. We shared a kiss while I gyrated my hips. I swayed my body, rolling and bucking my hips up and down, in a melodic motion. I was trying to feel every inch of him. I bit down on his bottom lip. Then I whispered in his ear, "No baby not yet." I slid off him right before he climaxed.

Then I took him back inside my mouth. This time my mouth stayed on his pole until his volcano erupted. I drank his lava, sucking him dry as the Sahara. After my performance, I licked his head, slowly, as I teased his shaft with my tongue. I got up and slid back over in the passenger seat. Then I adjusted my clothes. I wiped the corners of my mouth and hopped out the car. Walking to the door, I stopped when I heard him say, "Isis, You…you my bitch fa life." I smiled. "I know baby. I love you too." Then walked out the door and headed in the house. As soon as I got in our room, I ran into the bathroom and ran myself a bath.

TEN

Gossip

As soon as Kia had visuals on me, she flagged me down. Hesitant at first, I walked over to their table. "Hey girlies," I said as I sat down. "Hey Ice, I mean Miss Tyson," joked Kia. It feels good to be sitting with the girls, again. "You really handled yourself out there yesterday, Ice," stated Tia. "Yeah Ice, we have never seen that side of you before." We laughed while Tia did an instant replay making hand gestures. "Let me ask y'all this. How did y'all know that was me out there?" "Well Ice we heard the commotion, and we had already peeped them staring you down at the game, so we just put two and two together." "Aw okay cool."

"Ice I know we've had our share of differences and we been acting funny with you, but you're still our bestie," said Tia and Kia agreed. "It's all good." The bell rang before we could discuss anything further. "Call us later Ice," said Kia. I nodded, "Okay. I will." We walked out of the lunchroom making small talk. "So, y'all ready for prom yet?" They didn't answer my question, so I left it alone. "So, Ice, what's up with one of Mike's boys? Put us on girl." I didn't want to come off seeing like a hater, so I let them down easy, "Girl my baby keeps me put up. I don't be around his friends like that. Besides that, most of them are already taken."

I could tell they were salty by what I said. "Good talking to you girls, I'll catch you later." I rushed outside knowing that my man would be on point, waiting for me but he wasn't. I tried reaching him on his cell, but

I got his voicemail. Irritated I called myself a cab, hoping and praying the driver didn't take all day.

Irritated: Isis

When I got home, Mike wasn't home, so I cursed him out in a text message, which I hardly ever do. Then his ignorant ass had the nerve to come in the house at like 5 in the morning smelling like a distillery. He gave me some lame excuse, but I wasn't buying it. I didn't even trip because that very lie, cost him a new bag. No relationship is perfect and yeah, he has pulled a couple all-nighters on me, but I could never stay mad at my man. Wait now, don't get it twisted, I'm not condoning infidelity, but I don't go snooping around looking for trouble either.

My parents been on my mind heavy, so I swallowed my pride and I dialed them up. I hated the way that we left things. I called a few times, but I didn't get an answer. I started getting worried, so I called once again, still no answer. Before I could get my shoes on good, the phone rang, and it was my dad. "Hello." "Hello, Sunshine is that you? How are you? I see you finally decided to call your old man. For a minute I thought you had forgotten about us over here." Hearing him call me by my childhood nickname, mended broken heart. "Hey Daddy, I've called you guys a few times, but Mommy always hangs up in my face. How did you know it was me?"

Tears formed in my eyes, but I fought back the urge to cry. "Isis a father knows, plus this isn't the stone-age darling, we still have caller ID. Your name pops right up when you call." I laughed at his sarcasm. "Daddy, you still got jokes huh?" We shared a laugh.

"Sunshine, you know we love you very much, that's something that will never change. Your Mom is just stubborn and I'm guessing that's where you get it from, too. It really did hurt her when you left, (paused) correction, it hurt us both." I listened to him with reason. "You guys kicked me out. I thought you two didn't love me anymore. Daddy, you told me that I could never come back home."

He paused. "No, Sunshine, you made a choice. I know that I can't make you stay a little girl forever, but you can't blame a father for trying. You are still my little girl." I smiled. "Well Daddy, I miss you both and for what it's worth, I will always be your little girl, no matter how old I get." "That's good to know baby. That makes an old man happy." "So, Daddy, I was calling to invite you guys to my graduation and my prom send off. You don't have to answer just yet, but can you just consider it, for me?" "Isis Desire Montgomery, what is there to think about? We wouldn't miss your big day for anything in the world. I've been calling your school, checking up on you. Glad, to see that, that young man hasn't distracted you from your studies. I'm proud of you honey."

"Thank you, Daddy. Nothing can stop a woman with visions." "That's what I love to hear, Sunshine. I understand that you must live your own life, it just took me a minute to realize it. One day when you have children of your own, you'll understand why we are so hard on you." I listened carefully as he spoke words of wisdom. Daddy and I talked for about an hour. "Let me ask you this, Sunshine, is that fella of yours, treating you right?" "Yes, he is Daddy, he's the best. He treats me like a princess." "Okay, now that's good to hear, because I don't want to have to load up my shot gun." We both laughed at his comment. Then we ended the call by saying, "I love you" but not before he made me promise to meet them for lunch. He told me to hold the tickets until then. I felt relieved, after we spoke.

Stressing: Tia

Kia had been experiencing stomach pains and vaginal bleeding for the last past week now. When I finally told, our dad, he rushed her to the hospital. I was bugging up because if something were to happen to her, I would be as good as dead. They ran all sorts of test on her. I was so nervous that I bit my nails down to the meat. When the doctor, returned he told us she was pregnant, which was a shocker to me. "She's what? Doc this has to be some sort of mistake she can't be." Daddy silenced me. "Hold on Tia. Wait a minute, let the Doctor finish. I'm sorry about that interruption, please continue." Dr. Obolsky cleared his throat before speaking, "Of course sir, well first we will need your consent, because an emergency surgery has to be scheduled immediately to stop the subchorionic hematoma. An ultrasound will also be conducted prior to, to locate the bleed." "Of course Doc, I understand. I give my consent please show me where to sign?"

Anxious

Mike caught me prancing around, bare, and started rubbing his hands down my spine. Every time he does that to me, I get the giggles, like a childish little schoolgirl. I tried to break free from his grip, but he wouldn't let up. I couldn't resist him, so I had to get me a quickie in. After my 15 minutes of pleasure, I hurriedly fixed my hair, clothes, and makeup so that I could meet up with my parents for lunch. I had my hair pulled back in a pony with my AX signature hat resting on my head. My jumpsuit matched my hat and my designer bag, matched my shoes.

Walking in the restaurant, a slight nervousness overpowered my excitement. When I reached the hostesses booth, Daddy waived me over. Chewing on a piece of gum, I nearly bit down on my lip when I saw them. As soon as I reached the table, Ma started crying. Daddy stood up to hug me as he whispered in my ear, "So much for tough love huh, Sunshine." I smiled. He kissed me on the cheek and gave me a once over. "Looking good kid looking good." "Thanks Daddy." "You know how mushy your mother gets, Sunshine." I laughed as I shook my head because we all knew that to be true. "Hi Mommy," I said, sounding like I was about 3 years old. She stood to her feet, and we hugged, no words were needed. After about five minutes or so we finally sat down. Then Ma broke the awkward silence.

"So where is this Marcus fella at?" "Ma, his name is Mike. He is actually doing some last minute, prom shopping." "Oh, okay Isis, I was just curious that's all but as long as you're happy that's all that matters sweetheart." I smiled, "I really am, Mommy, he makes so happy. He really treats me like a lady. So, are you guys coming to my graduation?" "Now of course Sunshine, we wouldn't miss it for nothing in the world." "Great Daddy, here are your tickets," I said as I slid their tickets across the table to him. Lunch went great.

As we talked, it felt like old times. Standing to my feet, I placed the money on table to pay the tab, and I left the waitress a $50 tip. Daddy argued me down, demanding to pay the bill but I insisted. "I got this Daddy. You can get it the next time. Mike sends his love. He says lunch is on him." Daddy looked at me, with his eyebrow raised and surprisingly he smiled,

"Okay Sunshine, if you insist." "We love you so much Ice." "I know you do Ma, me too. I'm sorry for everything. I never meant to hurt you guys." We hugged and said our goodbyes. Before I was out of eyesight, Ma, called after me. I stopped and turned to face her. "I'm sorry Isis." I smiled. I blew her a kiss, then I grabbed my keys from my purse, and I left out.

ELEVEN

A Night to Remember

Prom night was finally here. I had literally been in the shop getting pampered all day. I decided on going with a soft, spiraled, updo. I rushed in the house as I was pressed for time as usual. I wanted to be dressed before our guest arrived, so I moved quickly. Mike made sure everything was perfect to, from the champagne to the decorations. The black and red balloon garlands that were shaped like a champagne bottle, were tasteful. Hopping out of the shower, I dried off and I got dressed. I sprayed on some, Dior and applied some body glitter from my shoulders to my bosom area. My cream-colored Versace dress, with the red trimming, fit me like a glove.

In the front of my dress was a V shape, from my neck, down to my navel. The top portion of the back of my dress, was cut out, in crisscrossed slashes almost to my buttocks. My dress slightly flared at the bottom. Mike's suit contained identical colors to my gown. My 6-inch Red Bottom, pumps with embellished crystals matched my clutch purse. When Mike got home, he was also rushing to get dressed. His belt, shoes, and handkerchief were compliments of Ferragamo. Our guest arrived on time. Tia, Ma, and Daddy along with Mike's boy D were waiting on our grand entrance.

Mama and Shayna were our hostesses for the evening. Sis is serving our guest champagne and finger foods while the music is escaping from the speakers. As soon as I was in eyesight, cameras started flashing from every angle. We sipped out of our crystal, flute glasses, while indulging in conversation. I even caught Mommy and Daddy talking to Mike for a minute or two. I worked my way around the room. I took pictures with everyone and smiled until my face began to hurt. We were saying our goodbyes, while everybody followed us to the car.

I could feel Mike's eyes glued on my body, so I walked even sexier. Before I knew it, he started acting all mannish, grabbing me by the arm, whispering, "You look hot, Ma, keep walking like that and we might not see the prom." He winked at me, and I hit him playfully, "Boy you crazy." His smell was intoxicating. "Man, Ice. I want to rip that dress off you!" I blushed. "I knew you couldn't take a real diva." I could feel his manhood rising as he walked close to me. He opened the door to our, cream colored, Phantom rental, with the back cut out. Our family was still snapping flicks of us.

We waved goodbye and we sped off. Pulling up to the prom the onlookers were starstruck wondering who we were. I'm not gone lie there were some nice-looking rides there to. I'm seeing Yukon trucks, sitting high, all white with the silver glitter with a mean grill. In passing I see a few new model Lexus's, Jeeps, Cadillacs, and Beamer's that are nice too. The only other ride that can even halfway compete with us is the fluorescent colored, Tesla coupe, now that was nasty. I checked the mirror making sure my makeup was intact before we hopped out. We took a couple pictures, and I mingled a bit. I didn't see my girls, so I made a mental note to call and check on them later. I did run into Ash at the punch bowl, which made me smile.

When we were in proximity, I introduced him to Mike before he walked over to holler at one of his friends. Ash and I stood there for a minute shooting the breeze. We exchanged phone numbers, then I left him standing where I saw him. After about an hour in a half of taking pictures, and socializing the excitement, had worn off. I started to get bored, so we ended the night early. We drove through the city, sipping champagne and talking about some of the hideous outfits we saw at prom. Shockingly my baby, had booked us a suite downtown. Our room was breathtaking.

The bed was in the shape of a gigantic heart full of white and pink rose pedals. There was also a sex swing hanging in the closet. We finished off our bottles of champagne before we started fondling each other. We made love in every possible position until I fell asleep in his arms. The next morning, we ordered some room service, we ate, scheduled a late check out, and we headed home. Pulling up to the house I felt so drained. Mike had some errands to run so he showered first. We still had the rental for another week. I overheard him talking on the phone about some out-of-town trip that he was supposed to be going on. I stayed in my own lane; I didn't even mouth a word about it. I wasn't tripping long as he made it back before my birthday. He kissed, me on my forehead and left out the door.

TWELVE

Trap Talk: Ghost

Pops and I been busy tying up loose ends in these streets. Lately our operation has been expanding drastically. We out here in the trenches, pushing, so much weight that our plug can hardly keep up. We're vested in this, spending hundreds of thousands a week. We run a 24-hour trap house, in this multimillion-dollar drug trade. Our workers already know what the fuck going on, so they know not to play with us. The few workers that tried us, were bodied. This lifestyle of mines is complicated, and it's not for the weak at heart.

Me and Pops were planning on heading to Miami to meet up with the Columbians. Fucking with the Cartel can be costly. That's one mob I never plan on being at odds with. To do business with these guys, they require your whole resume. They want to know where your mother lives and where your kids go to school. If you cross them, they'll wipe out whole family, including the dog. The Friday before we headed out, I collected all our money from the streets. I double checked to make sure I had my passport, picked up Pop's, and we jetted. I slept the entire plane ride.

Boss Moves: Ghost

We counted a couple mill so we could take it to the plug. The plane ride was smooth. I didn't feel any turbulence at all. The meeting went quicker than anticipated. Meeting Pablo and EL Jefe is the first thing we did when we touched down. By their looks, you would never be able to tell that they were the ones holding the weight. They both had that preppy look. They frowned upon weed like it was beneath them, so we didn't even flame up none of that strong. Pablo insisted that we had a drink, I declined at first, but by the facial expression on El Jefe, I could tell that he wasn't used to being rejected. I didn't want to come off as being disrespectful so, I ordered up a shot of that 42, while they drank on their whisky. Pablo was the older one of the two, brothers. They inherited their family business that had been passed down from generations.

I can tell from our conversation that, El Jefe, was the brains of the operation. Pablo seemed to be the humble more assertive one. His presence screamed enforcer. I did my research and found out that their family had been dealing dope since the early 60's. In their family, by the age of 10, boys are considered men. If they didn't join their family organization, they would be cut off, for good. They are trained in smuggling, murdering, money laundering, and weaponry.

Pablo assured us that upon arrival back home, our shipment would be waiting. He claims our inventory will be shipped in some oversized teddy bears. I gave them half of the money up front and told them that the other half would be wired upon receipt. After everything was finalized, we stood to our feet and shook hands. "We'll be in touch," said Pablo. I nodded my head in acknowledgement. Then we left. In desperate need of a shower, as soon as I got to my room, I jumped in. I threw on my Versace shirt and jeans along with my Balmain belt and kicks. My diamond, bezel, Cartier watch completed my fit. No homo but Pop's got fresh to, he was sporting a money green Burberry shirt, some Off-White jeans and some money green, steppers that were bloody at the bottom.

We headed out and went to some club called, "F.U." Pulling up, the first thing that caught my eye was the giant middle finger, with the diamond ring and bracelet spinning on top of the building. Word on the street, this was the place to be, so we had to slide. We arrived in a black Audi truck same year as the current. We handed the keys to the valet attendant, and we gave him a couple hundred to keep our ride parked near the entrance. The line was wrapped around the corner. Passing, the onlookers we headed straight to the front. Walking up we saw the bouncers at the door, guarding the entrance way and telling people that they had reached their capacity.

I pulled buddy to the side, threw him a few hundreds and he stepped aside without even searching us. As soon as we got in, we ordered a bottle of Avion 44, for $1250 and a bottle of champagne before heading to the V.I.P. We tipped the bottle server girl something hefty to. The club was humongous, all 3 levels was wall to wall. I walked through the crowd, squinting trying to adjust my eyes to the fluorescent, flashing lights. I scanned the place for safety precautions because you can never be too sure. The bar was directly underneath the light. The crowd was mixed, and the attire was upscale. Meek and Ross were on stage performing, "Ima Boss." Everybody in the club was going crazy.

Keyshia was hosting the event, so I know Gucci wasn't too far. Women were dancing in cages doing all types of tricks. These women were beautiful, all ethnicities to. Me and Pops was just cooling, blowing on some Za (weed). The atmosphere was nice, the waitresses and bottle girls were topless, looking bad. Looking ahead, I saw these thick ass hoes, heading our way. The one in the red was looking real fuckable. Her buddy with the green on was cool to, so I nudged Money. She didn't waste any time going in, "Excuse me, is anyone sitting here?" Money reply was quick, "That depends." She stared him down before she continued, "That depends on…."

He smiled. "That depends on, who wants to know?" Then, Shorty in the red spoke up with a fucked-up ass attitude, "Yo, my home girl and I were wondering if we could sit with y'all, what up?" I couldn't resist so I had to jump in, "Hold up Shorty turn around really quick. I'm trying to see something." She smacked her lips, but she did what she was told. She spun around confidently. "Look can we sit the fuck down or what? Don't nobody got time to be spinning and twirling and shit? This not no free peep show, the fuck!"

Money interrupted, "Bitch who the fuck you think you talking to?" Then he stood up getting ready to slap the hoe. I laughed before I diffused the situation. "Pop's it's smooth bro, fall back one time." Then her buddy spoke up, "Excuse my friend, we were just wondering if we could accompany you two gentlemen, it's my birthday and uh my feet are killing me." She extended her hand to Money. "My name is Candi, and this is my girl Kiki." Money reached for her hand, and he kissed it. "It ain't shit, y'all two sexy ladies can have a seat with me and my man's." They grabbed a chair and sat. Not really caring, I asked, "So what brings y'all out tonight." "Well, it's my girl Candi's birthday and I'm trying to show her a good time," said Kiki.

"Aw okay that's what's up," I stated dryly. I could tell Money was feeling oh girl. "Aw yeah…Happy Birthday, what's your poison?" "Aw…Thank you Money, I'm not a heavy drinker so I'll have to say, a *Sex on your beach*." She laughed. "I mean a *Sex on the beach*, my bad." Then the jazzy one spoke up, "The fuck wrong with you Kiki it's your whole birthday. Is you cool? Champagne us please, the fuck."

I laughed at her little simple ass. Money ordered them up a bottle of Rose' and two Long Islands. I didn't have nothing for them though. Oh girl, Kiki reached over trying to grab my bottle from out the ice bucket, but I grabbed her by the wrist, stopping her. She snatched her hand back quick and rolled her eyes. I never cared though. I laughed. Then I poured myself another drink. I could've sworn I saw oh girl throw what looked like a vitamin in their bottle to. They started taking pictures, so I moved out the way. Under the table oh girl, Kiki started grabbing my dick and I let her to.

I felt my phone vibrating, so I reached down and grabbed the phone from my pocket. I sent the caller to voicemail. I stood to my feet needing to take a leak, so I gave Pop's the word, and I dipped. The bathroom was empty, so I was in and out like a robbery. On my way back to our table, I felt something hard on the smalls of my back, so I hesitated. Then I heard a male's voice say from behind, "Little nigga, you know what it is." I reached for my gun, before realizing I had left it in my jacket pocket that was back at our table.

I balled up my fist because I wasn't going down without a fight. I spun around nervously. As soon as I turned to face my assailant, I was caught off guard. I couldn't do anything except laugh. "Bro I almost cleared your ass, straight up." "With what fam?" I held up my fist. "These two right here!" We both started laughing. "Damn, your Chi town swag, got you lacking huh blood?" "Never that, my boy, I keep it on me." "Yeah okay, I hear you big dog." "Cuz you already know how I'm coming. A motherfucka' would have to body me, on Shorty." He gave me some dap and he laughed. "Same oh, Ghost, I see. What's been up cuz? What brings you to my neck of the woods, bro?"

"Shit, you already know, what it is, business." "I'm, already knowing blood say less. Who you up here with? Where y'all posted?" "Cuz we in the V.I.P., ain't no paper shortage." "Aw yeah. Are they treating you good in here?" "Yep, everything straight." "Cuz man, this you?" "Hell yeah, something slight. I had to switch it up, before I got bagged. You know ain't no cheat codes in these streets." I nodded. "I should've known this was yo spot. The name of the club has your name written all over it. You a fool with it." We laughed as we walked to the back of the club to his office.

His décor was on point to. I could see myself owning something like this. His desk was all white, with Italian leather and his chair had the number seven with gold crowns on its peak. The number seven was customized on the arms of all his chairs to. He had a surveillance monitor, on the left side of his desk, overlooking the entire club. His office also housed a tiny kitchen area adjacent to his personal bar, with cherry wood cabinetry. Cuz, was only 28 and he was caked up. "Cuz, this shit saucy as hell, on bro."

"Thanks blood, it started getting crazy around the way for your boy. I messed around and got shot." "Word." "Yeah, they tried to take me out my glow." "Damn Seven, that's crazy blood. What went down?" "Man, cuz Diamond, man, that bitch a rider. I was in it heavy, feel me, with no way out. When I got shot, I was lit, rolling off the E (Ecstasy). These clowns must've backdoored me, followed me from one of the guy's parties. I was so faded that when they upped pipe (gun) I tried to wrestle oh boy to the ground. I guess my bitch heard the commotion because she started 'yakking' (shooting). Later I found out that I had been set me up by girl's niece. My bitch shot her niece and got grazed while she was pregnant to. She dropped two of them clowns to the ground and the other one ran off." "Damn cuz she a real one."

"Yeah Ghost, man. I figured it was only a matter of time before the ABC boys (feds) grabbed me and my girl got snatched up by a legit nigga, so I had to make some changes." While he was talking, he walked over to the bar and poured us both a shot of 42 and he slid one of the glasses to me. We raised our glasses, threw the drinks back and slammed them on the table. We chopped it up for about another 30. My phone kept going off, but I ignored the call. We exchanged numbers and I gave cuz some dap. Before I left out, cuz hollered, "Yo, Ghost man tell my aunt and my little cousin I said what's up, it's been a minute." "Got you blood."

I nodded my head and I left. When I got back to the table, I peeped Money and oh girl, seemed to be getting a little cozy. I sat down, grabbed my stick (gun), and slid it back on my waist, unnoticeable. 20 minutes later a chilled bottle of Cristal was sent to our table with a sparkler attached. I smiled. I reached in my pocket and peeled off a few $100 dollar bills to tip, but she held up her hands to stop me. "This one's on the house." Pops looked up at me strangely.

I didn't say a word though. Out of respect, I held up the champagne bottle and I nodded my head in the direction of one of the camera heads, gesturing a thanks because I already know he was watching. "What happened man, did you get lost or something? Shit I almost had to T-up in this bitch." "Naw, man it's smooth, I ran into some of the old heads." I grabbed a fresh glass from off the table because I didn't trust a soul. Then I poured up. Oh, girl Kiki downed her drink and headed over to the dance floor. Pops and oh girl were deep in conversation.

While I was sipping my drink and enjoying the vibes, my eyes fell on Kiki. She was grinding on some random cat. She took one of her hands and placed it on the back of homies head, while sucking on one of her fingers. Dude reached underneath her dress, but she stopped him. She used both of her hands to glide them up and down her entire body, as she danced to the beat of the music. I smiled, intrigued by her moves.

She continued twerking and grinding on dude, until he tried lifting her dress, again. This time she slapped him simultaneously he slapped her back. Then he grabbed her by the neck and started choking her before slinging her to the floor. Pops looked up noticing the commotion and he stood up, to assist. I stopped him because that wasn't our beef. Her friend ran over to her defense and jumped on his back, but he slung her ass on the floor to. Security swooped in and kicked him out of the club. When they came back to the table, she looked mad. Shortly after that, the DJ announced, last call.

We finished up our bottles and we headed out. Pop's hopped in the car with oh girl and the other bitch, Kiki hopped in with me. As soon as I got in traffic, she wasted no time putting her mouth on my pipe. When she came up for air, I asked, "Where to?" She smiled, "Well baby, I live about 30 minutes away. Want me to give you, my address?" "Naw, you got a few options," I said as I moved her hand off my member while I adjusted myself. She sighed, "Okay what options is that?" "You can grab a cab to the crib, or you can go to the hotel with me." "Okay, well, I choose option B for $200 Daddy." I laughed. "Yeah, alright cool."

The Suite: Ghost

When we got to the suite, I made her wait out in the hall, so I could make sure my belongings were put away. I hit Pop's on the line to make sure he was good. Shortly after, I let her in. "You seem real tense I can tell you single baby." "Actually, I gotta bitch." "Man fuck that bitch, that's your problem, not mines." "Aye yo watch your mouth, Shorty." "Well, I can't tell you gotta a bitch, the way that bulge, pointing at me. She must not be taking care of you right, but I'm gone take real good care of you baby." Already seeing how this was gone pan out, so I went with flow of things.

"Yeah, you right, let me get them lips." She walked over to me, dropping her clothes to the floor. The closer she came, the louder she reeked of alcohol. She leaned forward trying to kiss me, but I turned my head and she almost hit the floor. She reached down, grabbing a hold to my dick and she started stroking me, while talking dirty. "I know what Daddy want's and I know what Daddy needs." Then she dropped to her knees and sucked me so skillfully that she seemed toothless. I exploded in her mouth within minutes. After I emptied my clip, I pulled out and adjusted up my Ethika boxers.

I gave her an approving high five then I rolled over and entertained her with my snoring. When I woke up the next day, she was sitting on the edge of the bed with her lips poked, out. Since the liquor had worn off, she wasn't looking as good as she did the night before. Pops was feeling her friend, so I remained cordial. While we were in town we clubbed it, in the hottest spots and dined in some of the upscale restaurants to. Candi ended up staying with, Pops the entire trip. Oh girl, Kiki gave me her number, but I didn't plan on calling her. She sucked me up one last time before I had to leave to catch my flight. I did however throw her some cab fare though.

At the Crib: Ghost

I made it in the crib around 10. I tip toed my way up the stairs careful not to wake anyone. As soon as I walked in our room I headed straight for the bathroom and hopped in the shower. My girl wasn't in the room so that blew me. I grabbed my phone out my pocket and dialed her up, but she wasn't answering either. I could feel my blood boiling, instantly. I called her a few more times but I kept getting the voicemail. I looked up and noticed a flashing green light on the nightstand. So, wherever she was, she had messed around and left her phone in the crib. Steaming, I started thinking the worst.

My brain started flooding with questions. What, this bitch out here doing dicks? Is she outside turning her hoe up? The more I thought about it, the angrier I became. All I know is that I needed a drink and fast. I headed downstairs to the basement. I stopped upon entry as I became caught off guard. "Shit!" Seeing the wife, sprawled across the pool table in her, fishnet yellow onesie, immediately got my dick hard. I stood there for a minute admiring her beauty. As I was walking in her direction, I heard her say in a phone sex kind of tone, "We miss you, Zaddy, me and Ms. Kitty. Come taste her." I watched carefully as she started to touch herself.

She dipped one of her fingers in her mouth, then she used that same finger and placed it in her wetness. As soon as I was close enough, I started kissing her lips, while massaging her thighs. I stopped kissing her briefly and I walked over to the bar and poured myself a shot of Remy. I threw it back and grabbed a bottle of champagne. I undressed, until my dick was swinging against my legs. I watched her as she played in her own juices. Hearing that familiar squishing sound, was melodic to my ears. She moaned out in pleasure. I sat the bottle down and I started feeding her strawberries with one hand. Then I ripped off her lingerie with my free hand. I grabbed the cool whip, and shook it up, before spraying it all over her body. Then I popped the champagne open, poured it all over her chest and I licked it off. After that I pushed every inch of me, inside of her warmth.

THIRTEEN

Graduation Day: Isis

Four long years and the day has finally come for me to walk across that stage. After showering and spraying on my Prada perfume, I walked over towards the bed. I nearly cried when I laid my eyes on the prettiest crème D&G jumpsuit, that I have ever seen. The jumpsuit had spaghetti straps with a swoop in the front. On the side of the fit was a bag that reads, "Big Brown Bag," so I know it must've come from one of my favorite stores. I opened the bag, and feasted my eyes on a Chanel box, enclosed with a crème crossbody, oval shaped bag, with the black double C's, a pair of six-inch pumps, and shades identical to the purse.

I smiled. There was a note attached which read, "Congratulations Ice! Put this fit on and use these keys. I got some running around to do. Call me before you leave the crib. Mike." I turned on some music to get myself in the mood. I started dancing around in my undies. I slipped into my outfit, carefully. Then I threw on my shoes and switched purses. I placed my shades, on top of my head, just for show. I applied my makeup, but I didn't add to much. I checked the mirror to make sure that everything was intact. I twirled around and I smiled at the image standing before me. Walking towards the door, I stopped almost forgetting my keys, so I turned back around, grabbed the keys off the bed, and I headed downstairs.

I was trying my best not to be late for the lineup. I sounded the alarm, locked up the house, and walked down the stairs. As soon as I reached the bottom landing, my heart nearly ripped from my chest. Full of glee, when I saw the most dazzling, black, Infiniti coupe that I had ever seen. I looked down at the keys, noticing the Infiniti logo on the Gucci key ring, that read, "Ice's coupe." Super geeked, my mascara is now running down my cheeks, from my tears. In complete shock, I hopped in my ride. The interior was nice to, as it contained red leather bucket seats. I immediately adjusted the mirrors and the sunroof to my liking.

I noticed there were some flowers on my dash, so I grabbed them, and I buried my noise in them. Then I placed them in the seat next to me. My stereo system was made by Bose. I had customized TV's built-in the back of my head rest's and a much-needed navigation system in the mid-section of my dashboard. If that wasn't enough, I saw a card sitting on my back seat, so I grabbed it. I was so nervous that my hands were shaking. I opened my card and read it carefully. Inside the card, I counted, 10 crisps, one-hundred-dollar bills. He snapped on my gifts, so I had no other choice but to call him.

When he finally answered, he was acting nonchalant. "What's good, Ma?" "Thanks baby, (sniff) thank you so much." "What are you talking about, Ma?" I can tell he was smiling through the phone, but he was still acting modest. "What's up, Ma you like that fit I got you?" "Baby, I love you so much, I absolutely love all of my gifts. You snapped on this one!" "I told you stay down, and I got you Shorty. Now let me handle this business, I'm gone hit, you back." I was so excited I drove around for minute before going to graduation. Riding through my city, with my sounds blasting, I must admit it felt good. I had my sunroof cracked, while the breeze kissed my cheeks.

After cruising around for about twenty minutes, I finally arrived, and I was late as usual. I pulled up and I parked right in front of the venue. I hopped out like I owned the place. I hit my alarm twice and proceeded to enter with the sexiest, most confident walk ever.

Prancing in, and it seemed like all eyes were on me and I loved it. The graduation seemed longer than usual, I wanted to sneak out, but I couldn't because I had to give my Valedictorian speech. After graduation, I received some nice gifts from my family, but nothing could top my gifts from my man. Immediately after we went to grab a quick bite to eat at this nice little seafood joint. We ate good and talked for hours. Mike fronted the bill to. This was our first formal, family outing combining our families. It was going great. I couldn't hide my happiness, not even if I tried.

FOURTEEN

Missing You

I'm starting to feel some type of way, my man has been neglecting me, lately. He really has me all in my feelings. Since graduation day, he has been too busy for me. Other than his games I hardly ever see him anymore. Apparently, his right-hand man is toting around some new chick. For whatever reason my man has been distant. Eavesdropping as I pretended to be asleep, I overheard him talking freely about some random ass chick that his homeboy was hanging out with, tough.

It seems like every time I walk in a room, lately, he rushes off the phone like he is hiding something. I'm starting to think that he's seeing somebody else. I don't know what's going on with him, but all I know is, I miss him, and I miss us. This is lowkey ripping me apart. My friends, including his homies main chicks are always, trying to convince me to go out, and meet new guys but I never do. Feeling a little frustrated, I decided to clear my mind and go for a ride. To relieve some stress, I ended up stopping at Saks, for some retail therapy.

Some women eat when they get depressed, as for me, I shop. Don't judge me, judge your mama. I'm not gone lie; I ended up buying his creep ass a few items to. That's my man, so when I grab myself something, I automatically get him something to. I didn't see anything that caught my eye, so I shopped small. I got myself a Fendi bag and some cute ass blue jeans. I also copped my baby some Balenciaga sneakers, with the belt to match.

In Her Feelings: Ghost

I hadn't even smashed the little bitch and she's tripping. Pop's say oh girl been sweating him to be his main thang, but I don't think it's a good idea. I told him to watch himself though. Since we got back in town, Greedy hasn't really been hanging around too tough. I made a mental note to holler at him to see where his head was at. It's all politics, if his paperwork good, I don't trip. I heard his baby mother

Sheena was pregnant again, with twins, though. I believe that's gone be their 4th or 5th pregnancy but I'm not sure. He been complaining about his ends, like he's not eating, and that's beyond me. Me and Pop's founded this empire, and all our squad of savages, got plenty to eat on their plates. Greedy just be mismanaging his funds. Bro, driving a silver Expedition, that's paid for, and he has a nice little town home, that's decked out to. The boy be getting money trust me I know because I got him on salary. The problem is he spends it faster than he makes it. Despite his best efforts, G can't get right for shit. I guess he pay for the pussy to make up for his short comings, no-homo but he's the ugliest one out of the guys. The hoes say he fucks like a jack rabbit and his shit small to. Black's, country ass, hasn't even been fucking with him and that's his right hand. I don't know what's up, but I'm gone get to the bottom of this, soon.

He Doesn't Love Me Anymore: Isis

To say that I'm crushed is an understatement. I'm just over it like for real. I been waiting and waiting on my acceptance letter, from Harvard and there is still no sign of it. My nerves are shot. I've been getting acceptance letters from everywhere else Stanford, Spellman, and even Hopkins. My number one choice is Harvard and I've worked my ass off to secure my future. I woke up kind of cranky today and I should be happy, after all, it is my 18th birthday. This is really a big deal. I called up my mother, since I was bored.

Do you know she had the nerve to act like she was busy, on my holiday? The nerve of her. That blew me. I would've called the twins, but they gone be broke as usual and I'm not sponsoring nobody on my day. Mommy and I agreed to grab dinner later so that was cool. I dressed simple, yet classy. I strutted in my candy apple, fitted, lacey Halston, mini dress that makes my ass look plumped and my girls sit up extra high. My feet rested in my YSL, pumps, indistinguishable to my clutch. My diamond stud, solitaire, earrings, sparkles so elegantly. I was spraying on my smell goods when my boy Ash called. "Hey Ice, what are your plans for today?" I was too embarrassed to tell him the truth, so I lied, "Mike and I are going to dinner, nothing major."

We talked for about another 30 minutes or so, until Ma interrupted the call. She told me she was downstairs, so I rushed him off the phone. Daddy dropped her off at the gate and she had volunteered to drive so I let her push the ride. She must've known I would need a designating driver because I plan on having myself two, maybe three, or even five drinks. Yeah, I said what I said. I hurried downstairs in my flats, with my heels in hand. I did a quick inspection one last time in the mirror before heading out. I sounded the alarm and locked up. I hopped in my ride and drove to the gate. I leaned out the window and punched in the security code. As soon as the gate expanded, Ma, was standing there with the about damn time look on her face. I slid over to the passenger side and signaled for her to get in.

She adjusted the seats and mirrors, and we pulled off. I'm not in the mood for any I told you so antics, so I kept my business to myself, and I stared out the window. I turned to face my mom. "So, Ma, where is Daddy at?" She glanced at me briefly and then refocused her eyes back on the road. "He's out golfing with his friends." "Oh." "What's wrong baby? You're mighty quiet for it to be your birthday." I smiled briefly before the tears surfaced. "Everything Mommy everything. I haven't received my acceptance letter yet and Mike done forgot my birthday."

"I told you not to worry about that acceptance letter, you can always start off at a community college. Now, what do you mean he forgot your birthday? A real man would never forget his woman's birthday. Maybe it's time for you to come back home and live with us." She responded the way I knew she would, making me regret opening my big mouth. I cut my eyes something hard at her. "No, I'm good Ma."

When she spoke, her words cut deep. "Your father has never forgotten my birthday Isis, you know why?" "No, why Ma." "Because I would kill him," Ma said as she forced a smile out of me. "See, Isis you should've never left home that young to start with. You were just a kid yourself." I sat in my seat, and I listened. "Just leave him he doesn't deserve you anyway baby, trust me baby. A mother knows." "Ma, I know you're just trying to help but I'm not the same little girl that I was when I left home. I'm a woman now. Thank you, but I have to figure things out on my own."

We pulled into the parking lot near the valet booth to some new restaurant that she wanted to try. The line to the spot, next door to the restaurant was longer than an amusement park ride. The lot was full of all types of foreign rides. Ma sees me deep thought, so she snapped me right back to reality. "Baby girl don't worry; everything will be as it should. Now, what's that word you kid's say today? Aw yeah, I know, let's turn up, it's your birthday!" I laughed so hard until there were tears in my eyes. "Ma, have you been watching reality TV again?" We both fell into laughter. The valet driver approached us. Before hopping out, I switched from my flats to my heals, and I touched up my makeup.

I turned towards Ma with a smile on my face. "Thanks Mommy." "For what baby girl?" "Thanks for always being here." She smiled back. "That's what mothers are for, and before I forget to tell you, I am so proud of you baby. I love you, happy birthday Isis." Hearing those words warmed my heart. "It's all about you today, now cheer up, turn down for what!" I laughed again but this time I snorted. "Girl, you are, too much, for me, no more reality TV for you."

We laughed. Then we hugged momentarily, but not long enough to start up the water works. We stepped out of the ride, handed the keys to the valet attendant and I shoved my ticket inside my purse. I took a quick glance at Ma, and I saw just how radiant she looked. Ma notices me, noticing her, "What?" I smiled, "Nothing, Ma you just look stunning." Walking in, I powered off my cell, because I wanted to make sure I was unavailable for him just like he has been for me. He can keep that same energy, because two can play this game.

Unbelievable: Isis

Mommy and I were walking side by side when I went the other way and headed to the bathroom. I'm smiling on the outside, but I am heartbroken on the inside. I splashed some water on my face and reapplied my makeup the right way then I left back out. The place was flooded with people of all ethnicities. I can tell that everybody was in their best attire to. It's more diamonds in the building than Treasures. Somebody big, must be in the building. While I was admiring the atmosphere, I saw Shante out of my peripherals.

She walked over attempting to make small talk and I rolled my eyes, not sure why. I never really cared for her like that. Over the loud music I asked, "Hey who's party is this?" "Isis I don't know girl, but it's lit and them, boys are definitely, in the building. This shit busting. I was just riding trying to find something to get into for the night and I saw the crowd was looking decent, so I pulled in the lot." I was dry as hell with my reply, "Aw okay girl, it figures." I walked off, but not before, she grabbed me by the arm, and said, "Isis, girl we should hang out. What's your number?" Then she pulled out her cell. I stood there with my mouth all twisted up then I yanked my arm back and I left her standing there.

I sashayed through the lobby area, trying to locate Ma. "Ma, I thought that we were going to eat at this restaurant." "Girl, it's your birthday let's go have a drink first." She must've been reading my mind because I could use a drink right about now, a double should at that. "You're right Ma, it is my birthday." I walked my pretty ass, towards the red carpeted event. To my surprise the bouncers looked at me and slid to the side without even carding my underage ass. They didn't even ask me for a cover charge either.

Entering the red set of double doors, I almost fell and lost my balance with my clumsy ass. I clutched my chest as I was startled when I heard the crowd yelling in unison: Surprise! Ma grabs me and gives me a huge bear hug. "Happy birthday sweetheart. I love you." Then she hands me a gift, wrapped box. The next face I saw was my baby, Mike. There he was smiling from ear to ear, looking as good as he wanted to. I felt like a complete idiot after the way I've been behaving thinking he had forgotten my birthday.

My man walked up, styling like it was his birthday. He had on a black and gold Amiri fit with his black Ostrich Prada's. I couldn't see his belt but I'm certain it matched to. The closer he came, the more it felt like my legs would give out. His scent was enticing. I smiled and gave him the biggest hug ever. We kissed softly but not before I punched him playfully in the shoulder for putting me through all of this. He laughed, "Damn Ice, what's all that for?" "You made me think you had forgot my birthday." I looked around at the décor, and I could tell he spared no cost. Everything looked astonishing. I whispered in his ear, "Thank you baby. I love you." I saw Tia in the corner getting her flirt on. She lifted her glass when we made eye contact.

Mama, sis, Daddy, and plenty others were mingling in the crowd. Some of my guest, I hadn't seen in years. All of Mike's boys that I know showed up to. I can see the diamonds twinkle as they beam off the light. I have never had so many people that I love, under one roof, other than a funeral. Mike even flew in some of my family members in town and covered their expenses. I can feel the jealousy and the envy from some, as they watched my every move. I smiled because I know with the glamour, and the fame, comes, artificial love and hate. I was extra excited seeing my cousin Makayla. I remember wanting to be just like her when I was a kid.

In my eyes she was a premium chick. She was like a real life, black Barbie. She seemed, flawless, perfect teeth, pretty smile, and pretty skin. She stayed in designer labels that rappers talked about. All the men around the way wanted her, the nerds, the thugs, and the professionals. It rumored that she's even dated some basketball players to. My smile expanded when she walked up. "Look at my little cousin, looking, like a star, you sharp! You are the true definition of a diva. I see you, shinning, Ice." She gave me an approving smile, followed by a hug and I smiled from ear to ear.

The roles have truly reversed. Now, don't get it twisted, she's still nice looking, but she just isn't as jazzy as I remember her to be. We exchanged numbers before I excused myself. Walking through the crowd vibing to the music, my ears were pleased, when I heard, "Birthday Sex," escaping through the gigantic speakers. Mike was making his way towards me as if the song was reserved for us. I grabbed my man so close that I could feel his breath on my neck. I turned my back towards him, and I started grinding on him, like nobody's business.

We were really a whole mood. I bucked my hips seductively but not enough to expose myself. As we danced, I felt his joystick rise, and at that very moment it felt like no one else was around. I swayed my body to the beat. He grabbed me by the waist and kissed me on the nape of my neck. I spun around, looked him dead in his eyes, and I kissed him passionately. When we broke free, his voice tickled my ears as he whispered flirty notations throughout the song. I blushed. His electrifying touch had me wanting to take him down on the dancefloor. After that song came to an end, we made our way to our reserved table preparing ourselves to eat.

Mike catered all my favorite foods from steak to lobster to salmon to greens. I didn't want to spill anything on my dress, so I ate lightly, and I had Shayna make me a to-go plate. After dinner I made my way to my thrown and I sat down. Not long after, everybody started approaching me one by one, hugging me, and telling me how beautiful, I looked. Mike summoned for a champagne toast, so everybody reverted there attention back towards him. He popped, a bottle of Aces that was only reserved for the VIP's and he filled my glass to the rim. Shortly after that he told me it was time to open my gifts. After a few glasses of the bubbly, I was feeling myself. "Rose that's my nick name," I sang along with, the song. He insisted that I opened his gift first, so I did.

He handed me a long wrapped giftbox. Then he shoved a single white rose, with an envelope attached in my face. I took another sip of my drink, and I sat my glass down on the table next to me. "What is it, Mike? Come on baby, you have to give me a hint." He shrugged his shoulder not saying a word. I ripped through the paper like a kid on Christmas. Once I opened the life sized, box, that stood taller than me, I feasted my eyes on a beautiful, full length, snow white,

Chinchilla, that had my name engraved. I threw the box to the floor, yanked the coat, and tried it on.

It fit me perfectly. When I spun around, I felt something hard, in my left pocket. Curious, to know its contents, so I reached down inside my pocket, and I pulled out what looked to be a medium sized, silver trimming blue, ink pen box, with a silver bow. Inside of it, was a beautiful white gold charm bracelet, with one single charm, that had our anniversary date engraved. Speechless from all the excitement, all I could manage to say was, "Thank you baby." I felt another box on the opposite side, so I pulled it out to. The wrapping was the same, the box was just smaller. Inside the box was a heart charm engraved with, "Mikes Ice," and boy was it icy. He smiled from my teary-eyed reaction.

I could no longer hide my eagerness, so I hugged and kissed him until I felt slippery down below. Cameras flashed from every direction. I had almost forgotten about my card so as soon as it dawned on me, I grabbed it and read it aloud slowly, *"Ice, I never had a heart before I met you. You're the one I need by my side, You my bitch fa life. Happy Birthday, Love, Mike."* I smiled while the tears cascaded down my cheeks. Just when I thought that it couldn't get any better, I felt another box that had a necklace with the matching charm. I was completely outdone. From then on, I moved graciously to the beat of the tunes.

In between opening my gifts, sobbing, and sipping champagne I slid across the dance floor. I had been racking up on gifts and I don't mean the cheap ones either. I dried my face just long enough to snap a few pictures, smiling until my face started to hurt. I grabbed the microphone signaling for everybody's attention as I began to express my gratitude to my guest. "May I have everyone's attention please. I would like to say thank you God for allowing me to see another year. I would also like to thank the love of my life, Mike, baby thank you for making this birthday magical. Lastly, thank you to each one of you for helping me celebrate, my special day. I love you all. Now let's keep this party going. Cheers."

I held up my glass and I took a sip. My smile started to fade, when I noticed a couple of odd balls in the corner that seemed to be out of place. I continued mingling, while I popped another bottle of Aces, rapping along with the music. My antennas went up when I saw some unfamiliar hoes, posted up near my man. One of them were rubbing all over his head. I instantly wanted to bug up, but I played it cool and stormed towards them like a raging bull. As soon as I walked up, I grabbed Mike's arm forcefully, separating the two.

I extended my hand to the one that was all in his face and introduced myself, rudely, "Hi, I'm Isis, Mike's wife and you are?" She frowned and rolled her eyes, disrespectfully. "Hey I'm Kiki, Mike's lover." Right then it took everything in me to refrain from grabbing that hoe by her throat. Before I could reply Mike intervened, "Bitch quit lying, this my wife right here." Then he turned to face me with pleading eyes, "Baby, this bitch is, D's girl's friend. I'm not fucking this bitch." Dismissing his lies I reverted my attention back at her because I needed some clarity.

"Excuse me, sweetheart, you're his what? Bitch stop playing yourself," I said real nasty like. Then her ignorant ass had the nerve to dismiss me and look at him saying, "You wanted me here Mike baby, you didn't tell her about us?" I looked at Mike ready to slap him and her ratchet ass. "Mike I'll deal with you later," I said to Mike before I redirected my attention back on her. "I don't know who invited you sweetie, but this is a private event, invitations only. I think you should leave before this gets real, ugly for yourself."

Now I'm trying to stay calm, but man listen, she gone fuck around and get these hands if she keeps playing with me. I can tell she was, big mad to. Oh, girl that was standing by Mike's homie D was quiet as hell. I guess she knew that I meant business. She looked me up and down then told her friend she was ready to go. Then they walked towards the exit but before leaving out she shouted in a drunken slur, "You his wife, huh bitch? Where was you when he was ripping up these guts in MIA? Mike baby when you ready for a real woman you know how to find me, hit my line."

By now all my guest are staring at her and I am so embarrassed. Not long after the security guards came over and escorted them out. No longer in the partying mood, I turned to face Mike, "How could you do this to me? How could you do this to us? I really thought that you loved me." He tried to run some lame ass game on me, but I shrugged it off. "Isis, I do love you baby and only you. You are all that matters to me. Shorty lying, Ice." "Stop it with your lies Mike, like for real. Just stop." I turned around to walk away. He grabbed me by the arm and looked me in my eyes.

"Let's not do this here baby. There you go worrying about the wrong shit again. Fuck that hoe, Ice." While Meek was escaping through the airwaves, the tears began cascading down my face, uncontrollably and I hauled off and smacked him. Then I grabbed a drink off the table, and I threw it at him. He wiped his face with his shirt and although he didn't say it, I could tell he was mad to. Without responding to my mixed emotions, Mike started giving orders. I was under the influence, so I gave Ma, my valet ticket and told her I would stop by and get my car in the morning.

Mike had Shayna and Mama gather my gifts and take them home. Not really wanting to be bothered with anyone so I stormed off. Mike runs after me, but I really wasn't feeling him. Exiting the building, I threw a rock at his head, lucky for him I missed. I walked towards the front of the building trying to flag down a cab. Mike catches up to me and he grabs me by the wrist trying to explain himself. I snatched away, as the anger continued to build up, I began to punch him in his chest. He picked me up and threw me over his shoulder. I started kicking and biting him. He was out of breath, tussling with me.

"Be cool, Ice." Valet pulled up, he walked to his truck with me on his shoulder, shoved me inside, fastened my safety belt and pulled off. Staring out the window, I decided to break the silence, "Mike can you drop me off at the nearest hotel please?" He looked at me momentarily, but he never responded. Then he turned the music all the way up, which further made me angry. I contemplated on jumping out of the car, but he was going too fast for that. All I know is after the stunt that he just pulled I will never be able to look at the same.

This Shit Crazy: Mike

I don't believe that after all the money I spent, I'm stuck in the doghouse. I know my baby in her fe-fe's (feelings) and she has every right to be, but she's doing too much. Since her family kicked her ass out, I been the one playing daddy. When she hopped out the ride, she slammed my door hard as hell. I ran in behind her and grabbed her, but her stubborn ass yanked away and flew upstairs. When I got in the room, she was loading her Louie duffle with clothes.

"Ice, baby where do you think you going? It's late, you been drinking, and your mom has your car. Shorty, can we sleep this off and talk about this in the morning?" She looked up at me with hate in her eyes, "No, need in talking now, Michael. I'm leaving. I can't do this anymore. This isn't what I signed up for." Ignoring her comment, I grabbed her arm carefully and pulled her close to my chest. I placed my arms around her frame as I rocked her side to side as if we were swaying to a beat. She tried to break free, but I held on to her tight. "Michael, I need some air. It's like the walls are caving in on me and I can't breathe. I think we should just, take a break."

I paused. Then I looked at her. "A break. Ain't no fucking breaks, Ice. Shorty you paid foe. I'm not feeding you to the wolves." I stood their looking into her watery eyes. "You ain't shit, Mike. I can't trust you anymore. I thought that you loved me. (Laughing) I guess I was wrong." We went back and forth for about another hour. "I can't do this anymore. I just can't Michael." Then she grabbed her phone and started dialing some number, but I snatched the phone from her hand and put it in my pocket. We stood there for a minute without saying a word like we were in a stare down. A few minutes later I heard Ma, and sis coming in the door, downstairs. "Mike, are y'all home?"

"Yeah Ma." I guess Ice new I wasn't gone let her leave, so she dropped her bags to the floor and stormed down the hall to one of our guest rooms. "Ice, baby wait," I called after her, but she ignored me. She slammed and locked the door before I could reach up to her. I had never seen this side of her before. I went back down the hall to our room and boy was I fuming. I laid her phone on the dresser and fell asleep. That was the first night that we slept apart since we started messing around.

The next morning as soon as I got up, I headed straight for the guestroom. I twisted the knob and found the room completely empty. She had made the bed so neat that it looked as if she hadn't even slept there. All that was left was her scent that was lingering in the air. I checked the remaining parts of the house, but it was useless. I ran back to our room noticing her luggage and her phone were gone to. Angrily, I quickly showered and got dressed so I could make a move. I know, Ma and Sis gone be siding with her as usual, so I wasn't trying to stick around and hear that shit.

I drank my cup of coffee and headed out. While I was in route to her parent's house, I called her mom and she told me that Ice had already come by earlier to pick up her car. I cut the conversation short and disconnecting the call. I blamed D for this. I busted a U-turn trying to recollect my thoughts. I started hitting a few blocks, just thinking. Since I met oh girl, she been beating my line. The last time she came in town we did a three-way, and she came through with a fine ass Asian brunette. Shorty was built like a sculpture to. I did hit her with a few bucks behind that episode, Joe. Since then, the bitch been doing the most. It's all bad for your boy, I need a blunt.

In My Bag: Kiki

"I need's my cut," I said in my Lady Capone's voice. "You know I stay in my bag. I'm not gone lie Ross was right when he made that song, "Money make me cum," because I feel that shit in my bones. I'm so sick of these hating ass hoes, trying to rain on my parade. They need to fall in line before they get ran over. I look way to good, to be denied any coins, the fuck. I'm not a hater, but that hoe not even cute in the face, she just has pretty eyes. If he like a bitch with pretty eyes, I can go buy some contacts, feel me.

Bitch, gone come for me, talking about she's his wife, bitch please. All of them gifts and her ungrateful ass tripping, off little ole me. That should've been me instead of her living lavishly. I'm the one putting in all the extra work doing 3-ways and shit. I been rocking for a minute and all he done threw me was a couple racks, but clearly that's only chump change to him. After seeing all that designer shit, he got her, I got to up my game, feel me?" I did a quick spin and a squat to emphasize my point.

"Candi, hello, earth to Candi. Are you even listening to me?" Candi looked up from her phone and glanced at me, "Yeah, huh, oh yeah, I hear you Ki, like I've been hearing you now for the last 24 hours; you are getting too worked up over nothing, I told you that." "Well, they got me fucked up." "I know boo, I know." She in the way of my riches, so she has to be eliminated." "Ki, wait a minute now I hope you not about to do anything stupid. Think about your probation. Isn't it enough that you ruined the girl party, what more do you want?" "Damn Candi, you are acting, like you on her side or something. Fuck them papers and that weak ass party."

"Ki please calm down. I'm begging you to just let this go, please. It's not worth going back in. Besides that, I don't want you to mess things up with me and my little boo either." "Man, fuck dude, clown ass to. Wait, are you catching feelings for him?" "I mean Ki, he's okay and I'm not gone to lie...I like him. Why you got to be so negative and messy all the time."

"Anyway, like I was saying, that outfit she had on probably was a fake. She thinks, she's fly with her bougie ass, she bet not let me catch her out in no club either cause it's up and it's stuck." Silence. "Hello, Candi do you hear me talking to you? Damn, bitch, talking to you is like talking to the air." "Ki, you know I hear you. I'm sitting right here. I don't have a choice but to hear you." "Now, I know I wasn't formerly invited to that party, but oh girl stuck up ass didn't have to spaz the out on me like that. If she would've been nicer to me, I might've spared her, her feelings." We high fived one another and I laughed. "Candi, pass me the blunt, what you think you taking one to the face?"

"Man, Ki calm down, hoe you just passed me this shit besides I'm kind of salty too, my man is not answering my calls. I'm trying to get him to give up his keys to his crib." "Aw so now he's your man?" "Here you go again with your negativity Ki." I rolled my eyes, because clearly, she was tripping. "Girl I'm not being negative. Dude not on shit, get his money, fuck a relationship bitch. See that's where we're different, because I'm not trying to keep a nigga not trying to be kept, period." "Yeah, whatever you say, Ki."

"I can't believe we stuck in this trashy ass hotel. I need to make some moves and fast. Shit my money ain't been right, since my old man, Zap, got locked up. I'm starting to miss him, well not him but his paper. He used to hold me down something serious, no joke. Soon as he left, I ran through his cash like a marathon, sold our crib, and changed my number. I don't do collect calls or jail time with nobody. I been hearing rumors around the way, that he's out but I don't even know or care. I'm not checking for his ass no more anyway.

That chapter closed a long time ago." "Ki, I hear you girl. I know that's right." "Candi, what are you over their doing?" Silence. "Candi, bitch, what the fuck got you so quiet girl?" "Huh, uh, oh yeah, what did you just say Ki?" "Girl, what the fuck is you over there doing?" "Aw, shit my bad Ki, I'm trying to text my baby, something might be wrong with him." "Candi, is you forgetting the rules. There is no love in this. Fuck that clown anyway he's probably somewhere getting his dick wet." "Ki, I love you and all but sometimes you can be so damn extra sheesh." "Girl, I know you not falling off track, you better hit him where it hurts and that's his pockets." I guess she wasn't trying to hear me, because her face was still glued in her phone, so I started thinking of a master plan.

I already know after that little stunt that I just pulled, Mike might not be fucking with a bitch like that for a minute. It doesn't matter though because, I keep me a spare or two. Oh boy Kevin been on my heels, so I guess he's my next stain. "Candi bitch, remember when we met at that Puffy party?" "Huh, uh yea Ki." "I gave Kevin some of this snatch, in the bathroom and the dick wasn't bad either. He peeled me off $1,500 on site. He been blowing me up, I think I'm gone hit his ass up to." "Huh...oh yeah...that's what's up Ki."

FIFTEEN

The Aftermath: Mike

It's been a whole week since Ice birthday, and we still beefing. My pride is crushed, not knowing where my lady is. Deep down I really felt guilty. I hate to have hurt her the way that I did. Ma and sis still aren't speaking to me. I been calling her folks daily and they claim they haven't heard from her. They were probably lying though. I had one of my homies running all my errands, because my mind was somewhere else. I could use some fresh air, so I decided to slide on my cousin and blow one with him.

Chop it Up: Mike

I pulled up, with my sounds blasting. First person that I saw when I jumped out, was my cousin's BM (baby mama) so I spoke, "What up Keesha?" Then, Jr. runs up to me demanding some dap. He loved when I came around because I always had something for him. That's my little homie though. "What's good Little Man?" "Hey cousin, Mike, what's up? Did you bring me something cool?" I laughed, as I reached inside my pocket and handed him the first bill that touched my palm. His eyes widened. "Oh, gee, thanks cousin Mike. I'm going to buy a whole lot of toys and candy with this." He walked off, screaming, "Mommy, Daddy look what cousin Mike just gave me."

Chance stopped him dead in his tracks. "CJ what do you say?" CJ hollered back at me, "Oh, yeah thanks cousin, Mike you're the greatest." "No problem, Little Man, be good." Chance, walked up, gave me some dap, then he jumped in the truck, no words exchanged, we sped off. "Mike, what's been up, cuz?" "Man cuz, just out here trying to get it." "Oh yeah," said Chance. "I've been thinking about opening up a club, a carwash, or something. I need to do something different. I need a change of scenery." "Good shit, blood. That's the move right there." I flamed up the wood.

"So, you in or out?" Chance turned around, shook his head and hollered, "Hell yeah. Let's get it!" I laughed because I already knew he would be down.

Chance was a couple years younger than I was, but we grew up more like brothers. He was no stranger to the streets either. My Aunt Michele and Uncle Charm were replicas of the legendary duo, Mickey, and Malory. He became a major key in the streets after he branched off forming his own alliance. Cuz, is no dummy either, he also has his Associates, in Business I believe. "Chance man, as soon as I put this play together you already know what the fuck going on." "Word cuz."

Breathless: Isis

I'm still hurting from that scene that Mike's little girlfriend put on, but I blame him. I was always taught to blame the trick not the chick. How could he invite one of his floozies to my party? Is he that damn dumb? I considered going home a few times, but I talked myself out of it. I can't even call Ma and Daddy because they would only make matters even worse. I'm not gone lie, this is a nice ass hotel, but I miss my home, I miss my man. This is the longest that we've been separated. I kept on replaying the entire night over and over, in my head, like an instant replay.

Since I left home, I had been drowning myself in booze and crying myself to sleep. The next day, I woke up feeling sluggish. I haven't really been having an appetite lately but to avoid getting sick I forced myself to eat. I drug myself out of bed, charged my phone, and jumped in the shower. Afterwards, I threw on my Nike joggers. My body felt achy, and I needed to relieve some stress, so I decided to treat myself to the spa. I normally make my appointments in advance, but not today. Kofi and Ona are the best masseuse ever. As soon as I walked in, I was greeted by name.

Without hesitation they directed me to a private room. I undressed and laid flat on my stomach as I listened to the soothing music. I was trying my best to relax and clear my mind. Ona took her time with my deep tissue massage. As soon as the massage started getting good, they switched places. Kofi's strong, masculine, hands felt so good that I almost made a mistake called him Mike. After my massage, I got dressed and tipped them both something generous. On the ride back to the room, I powered the radio off, and I drove in silence. As soon as I walked in the door, I grabbed my phone off the charger and powered it back on. My message indicator started blinking immediately but I was in no rush to check it.

Restless: Mike

I been sleeping downstairs in the basement since my baby left. The bed felt cold, without her. Ma and sis alternate coming down leaving food by the door. I hadn't really been having much of an appetite lately. Coach pulled me to side the other day to talk to me about all the practices that I've missed. I had, D pretty much running the show, taking care of things. I was chilling at the crib, blowing (smoking) trying to clear my mind.

I been trying to get in touch with Ice, but she's been dodging me. I don't know who she thinks she is. I poured myself a shot and I pressed the play button on the stereo. Sitting back on the couch and all I could think about was my baby. Lately my pain has become amplified, and all my nights seem restless. The thought of another man being anywhere near her, is starting to cloud my vision. For all that I know she might be out there trying to even the score. A million what ifs are floating through my mind.

Lonely: Isis

I called my parents to let them know I was safe. After I got off the phone with them, I checked my messages, and noticed my mailbox was full. Ninety percent of the messages came from Mike's retarded ass. The last message that I heard was strange. The caller was unknown, all I could hear was someone breathing heavily and a female ending the message by calling me a bitch with a high-pitched voice. I deleted all my messages except for that one.

I started daydreaming until the phone rang, derailing me from my train of thought. Glancing down at the screen, I saw Mike's name flashing, so I hit the end button. He called me again, but I still didn't answer. Then he started calling me back-to-back, so I went ahead and picked up. Angrily I answered, "Yeah." "Yeah, what you mean yeah, Ice? Who you think you talking to bro? Where you at so I can come grab you?" Silence.

"Mike, I'm drained, you won. I don't have the energy to fight with you anymore, it is what it is. I'm going to come and grab the remainder of my things." "Ice, quit fucking playing with me." I laughed because that was the only way that I could keep from crying. "Mike, I'm not about to play with you. I mean you got a new chick, so I'm gone give you, what you want. I'm gone just fall back and let you live."

"Baby, your home is with me, you're just mad right now. Don't do this Ice. You need to come home so that we can talk." "No thanks, fam, I'm straight, I'm gone let you do you. Clearly, I'm not what you want," I said before I disconnected the call. As soon as I hung up, he started blowing my phone up like crazy. I answered again a bit more aggravated than before, "What Mike? What's up? I can't do this anymore with you. I just can't, let you keep hurting me. I'm done." He took a dep breath before responding, "I don't want to fight either Ice. I messed up, but Ma, come home, that bitch don't mean nothing to me. What do you want me to say? I'm not perfect, how can I make this right, Ice, tell me?"

I sat there in silence, listening to his pleading voice, as he spoke out in agony. "I don't know anymore, Mike. I just don't know." "Ice, can we just, start over, fresh? I didn't fuck the bitch?" I paused. "Nope Mike, wrong answer. You're a liar Mike, and I don't trust you anymore. I can't be with someone who refuses to let me in. We're over Mike," I said to him before ending the call. Then I powered my phone off completely. I wasn't in the mood to hear any more of his lies, everybody must be held accountable. Stressing like crazy so I laid down and I cried myself to sleep.

A Little Advice: Mike

After Ice hung up on me, I called up Ma. I just hoped she didn't hit me with that, "Women's lib," bullshit. I needed some sort of sound advice. She basically told me that I was 100% wrong and anything worth having is worth fighting for. I agreed, but I just didn't know where to start. That's why I love my mother she always keeps it a buck. She told me that I needed to find my way back to her heart. That night I could hardly sleep thinking about what Ma said. The next morning, I got up earlier than usual. I showered and got dressed.

I needed to hear her voice badly, so I called her up hoping that she answered. To my surprise, she did.

Silence. "Ice, you there, baby?" "Yeah, I'm here Michael. I'm here just like I always have been." "So, what you gone do Ice, you gone just give up on us? What you don't you love me nomore?" She cleared her throat before speaking, "Michael, of course, I love you but right now I just can't do this with you. You hurt me to my core and now… I just don't know anymore. You got your side hoes trying to check me like I'm the slider. A real man would never, but it's cool Mike, it's cool."

"A real man damn Ma I'm human. I'm not perfect I make mistakes. Ice you know how hard I go for you. I fuck with you the long way, Ma." "Alright then Mike." "Alright then what, Ice? You on your way home or you need me to come and grab you?" Silence. "Hello…Mike you still there?" "Yep, you on your way home or what?" "Mike…I just can't…I can't do this anymore. I'll be there to pick up a few of my things. Goodbye Michael be safe."

Home Sick: Isis

I looked around the room making sure I didn't leave anything behind. After carefully gathering my belongings, I paid my tab and checked out. For about an hour, I just road around in silence. I passed by one of my favorite diners and I decided to drop in. I grabbed a ham and cheese bagel sandwich, and some green tea. 20 minutes or so later and the waitress approached my table. Then she handed me a napkin, so I reached for it slowly. To my surprise there was a note left on the other side. I read the words carefully, "I'm sorry baby, please come home."

I scanned the room a bit confused. My heart started to skip a beat when I locked eyes with Mike.

There he was with his fine ass, standing near my car, with his puppy dog face, which always makes me give in to him. I figured he wasn't moving from that spot any time soon, so I reached in my purse to pay my tab. While handing the money to the waitress she lifted her hand informing me that my bill had already been paid. I stood to my feet, left a tip and I split.

Not really knowing what I was going to say once we were face to face, so I walked slowly in his direction. "What are you doing here Michael?" He smiled slyly, "I'm going out of town in the morning. I'm wondering if you would accompany me, Ma." I stood there for a few minutes unresponsive. "Why me, what your little girlfriend busy or something?" I smacked my lips and rolled my eyes as I stood there with my head tilted to the side with my lips all poked out.

"It's always been you, Ma, it's us Shorty, never them." He flashed his million-dollar smile that always makes me feel weak inside. Refusing to give in to easily, I played along, "Yeah, right Michael. Anyway, how did you know that I was even here? What are you stalking me now?" He stood there shaking his head, "First off Ice, I know everything that happens in my city. Shit don't move unless, I give the order. Aw and by the way I don't take hoes on trips? A hoe can't get a crumb from me. The shit I do for your spoiled ass, I wouldn't do for any other bitch, no cap. So, what up Ice?"

I'm not gone lie, when he talks to me like that, it turns me on. I don't know if it was the base in his voice or what, all I know is it does something to me every time. Part of me wanted to jump, in my car and speed off, but my heart, was telling me to forgive him because I really do love this man with everything in me. I still wasn't letting up, but I didn't want to miss my beat either. "Yea, I'll go with you Michael, but you're not getting any." He flashed a smile as I turned to walk over to my car. Then I heard him mumble, "Yeah, we a see about that." I paused. "What was that you said?"

"Shit, Ice everything's smooth." We hopped in my car and we road in silence. I drove through the gate after he entered the code. I parked my car, hit the alarm and I walked ahead of him trying to avoid conversation. Soon as we got in the door. I headed straight for our room. Call me petty, but I needed to snoop around and make sure that there, was no trace, of another woman in our home. I searched high and low like a crime scene investigator but lucky for him I didn't find anything. I walked in the bathroom in need of some relaxation and there were candles, lit, everywhere.

Red and white rose pedals were seen seeping through the bubbles of our Jacuzzi. As if on cue, I felt Mike's hands grabbing me by my waist. Feeling his warm, strong hands on my body made me feel those sparks that caused me to fall in love with him. He planted soft kisses on my neck, tickling my spot with his tongue. I closed my eyes as I tried to savor that moment, never wanting it to end. No words were needed. As he kisses me on my neck, he pulled my hair, positioning my head to the, right, side, aggressively.

I tried to resist the temptation, but I just couldn't shake it off. Feeling his manhood pulsating near my behind made my cookies throb. I tried to fight back the urge to feel him inside of me, but my lust was overpowering me. As he continued kissing me, he snuck his hand down in my pants and started massaging my moistness. I bagged my ass up against him and I grabbed a hold of his manhood as I stroked his hardness through his pants. I unbuckled his pants like a pro, and I touched him slightly. I couldn't get the grip that I wanted, so I turned around to face him, and I grabbed a handful of him. I lifted my head, and we shared a kiss.

He removed his shirt exposing his muscular chest. His designer jeans dropped to the floor. I pulled my hand out of his drawls and applied spit to moisten my palm. I moved my hand up and down his erection mechanically. He unbuttoned my blouse exposing my breast. Then he unfastened my jeans. I slid my jeans down my legs, and I kicked them off to the side. He lifted me swiftly and he pinned me to the wall. While my legs rested on his shoulders, he kissed my lips until I screamed.

I begged him to stop, but his face only went deeper. He continued plunging, his face in my juices until my leg began to shake. He devoured me so graciously that I didn't have a choice but to return the favor. Before I started, I had to ask, "So uh Mike, she hasn't been down here, today, has she?" Aggravated he frowned. "'What Ice? There you go, with these crazy ass accusations. Damn, you sure do know how to fuck up the mood?" Snottily, I replied, "I'm just saying I don't know what or who you been doing. I used to think it was mines, but I don't know anymore Michael."

"After what I just did to you, how you gone ask me some dumb ass shit like that?" While we were going back and forth, I noticed his manhood was getting limp. "Ice If that's the case I can ask you the same shit. I don't know where you been or who you've been with. Has anybody been hitting my shit? Bitch, you the one been not coming to the crib." I looked at him with my face all scrunched up, "Excuse me? You got some nerve, Michael." "Ice baby, I'm sorry, we miss you," he said as he placed my hand on his pole.

My juice box was soaked, and I had a fake attitude. So, I did what any real woman would, I took my anger out on his pole. I dropped to my knees, tickling his navel, and kissing his inner thighs with my tongue before going for the kill. I never could stay mad at him anyway. I grabbed his joystick, and I didn't waste time putting my mouth on him. I sucked him like I was super head and drank his milk like its dairy.

He pulled me up and kissed me in the mouth, then he carried me to the Jacuzzi. We made love and we played with one another for the remainder of the night without any verbal communication. After the water became cold, we got out, and went to the room. I fell asleep in his arms and although I will never tell him this, it really felt good. The next morning, I woke up to two plane tickets on our nightstand. We got in the car with Mama around 3 so she could d (drop) us off to the airport. I guess he could sense that I was distant, so he tried to spark up a conversation.

"What's wrong now, Ma?" "Nothing Mike. Just, don't hurt me." He looked me in my eyes, before he spoke, "Ma, I would never intentionally hurt you. We gone be straight Ice alright." "Mike, I know you a man and all, but don't let your dirt soil our home." "Excuse my language, Shorty, but don't no other bitch mean shit to me but you. When I say I got you Ma, trust me, I mean it." "Yeah, I hear you Michael, but I'm warning you don't play with my heart." The rest of the ride we rode in silence. I was still salty, but no relationship is perfect. Besides that, I love my man so bad.

SIXTEEN

At the Hospital: Mr. McNeil

The doctor extended his hand to me congratulating me on the birth of my grandchild. Relieved I smiled. "Mr. McNeil you'll be glad to know that there weren't any major complications to the fetus. Your daughter did great. You are welcome to visit them both." "Thanks, Doc." Tia and I walked to Kia's room. "Thank God sissy, she looks just like me. Everybody knows I'm the cuter twin anyway," Tia joked.

"She's gorgeous baby, she looks just like you, when you were born. What are you going to name her?" "I have the perfect name for her, Daddy... am going to name her TaKia Shelenda McNeal." "That's a beautiful name, baby. I know your mom would be extremely proud of you. I know she is smiling down at you girls right now." "Thanks, Daddy. Oh, and while I have you both here, I might as well tell you guys the good news. I'm going to keep her. I know it might be a struggle, but I really need this, I do." "Sure, honey I understand, that's your decision to make. Neither me nor your sister can make that type of decision for you. Not to worry Kia honey we will make it work, between me and your sister that baby will have plenty of love."

Bae-cation: Isis

Our trip was going great, on our first night I won $5 grand on the craps table. I cashed out quick. Mike started teasing me calling me a scary cat because once I won, I quit. I sat around and enjoyed the scenery, well minus the cigarette smoke, that is. Mike bounced around from the Roulette table, to Blackjack, to craps. He was up about $15,000 and he wasn't gambling anything small either. He doubled up and I snatched his ass off the tables before he lost it all back.

I started getting horny, so I whispered in his ear, "Baby, I'm not wearing any panties." As soon as I said that he yanked me by the arm and almost pulled it out of socket. We started getting frisky on the elevator before we got to our room, which turned me on even more. We could hardly get in the room good, before Mike's phone started ringing. I stripped naked. Attempting to distract him while he was on the phone. I started twerking and bouncing my ass in his face.

I couldn't hear what the caller was saying, but whatever it was, it was causing Mike's veins to visibly, protrude through his temples. He must've been agitated because he powered off his phone as soon as the call ended. "Mike, baby is everything alright?" He sighed before responding, "Yeah, Ice everything's good, Ma. What's up?" I could tell he was lying but I didn't want to pry. Instead of nagging him, I went for the stress reliever that never fails. I dropped to my knees, and I started stroking his pole. I went to work until he yelled out in pleasure. After finishing him off, I stood to my feet then I disappeared in the bathroom and let my body sink to bottom of the tub.

When I returned to the room all I heard was snoring. Instead of straddling him, I cuddled up beside him. The next day when I woke up, to my surprise he was already gone. He left me a few thousand on the nightstand, so I decided to go shopping. I freshened up, got dressed, and I went to get myself a bite to eat. After putting something on my stomach I caught a cab to the Venetian. I grabbed myself a canary colored, Balenciaga bag with the matching baseball cap. I also copped my man, a pair of, Balmain shoes with the matching belt.

I still had a couple stacks left, from my winnings that I put away so that I could add to my savings. Before going back to the room, I went ahead and got a massage. The next morning, we ate our breakfast, and we spoke freely. "Baby can we stay a little longer," I whined. "Naw, Ice we have to get back home so I can get to practice and go back to work." I pouted, "Okay." I hate when I don't get my way. Pressed for time we packed quickly, careful not to miss our flight.

I slept the entire plane ride home and I didn't wake up until we landed. As soon as we got off our flight, we grabbed our bags from baggage claim and headed to the arrival area. Mama was already there waiting on us. When we got home, I handed Mama her souvenirs. I guess Mike had to go and handle some business because he barely got in the house good, before he left. I was jet lag, all I wanted to do was jump in the shower and get into bed.

SEVENTEEN

Holler at The Homie: Ghost

As soon as I jumped down, I hit up Greedy trying to check his temperature, but he didn't answer. I decided to hit a few blocks, so I called up cuz and told him to pop out. I blew the horn, when I pulled in front of his crib, and he came right out. I tossed him the loud and a wood as soon as he hopped in. While he was emptying the blunt, I pulled out in traffic and got a quick bite to eat. I placed my order in the drive through, while cuz was still twisting up. After I got me food, I pulled off cautiously, so cuz wouldn't drop any of the buds.

Biting into my sandwich when I got in traffic, and I almost crashed. My phone rang which distracted me. I glanced down, and I saw Greedy's name flashing so I answered, "Yo." As soon as I picked up the phone he started rambling, so I already knew he was lying. Ever since we were kid's I could always tell when he was lying because he talked in circles and started stuttering. I ended the call soon after, but not before telling him I was gone slide. I looked over at cuz, while he was drying off the blunt. "Hold on blood let me bust this move before you flame up it won't take long.

Cuz nodded. I stopped on the low end where Greedy and his crew be posted up. The whole area was deserted. I parked and grabbed my piece before I bailed out. "Be back in a minute cuz." Walking into the spot I and I frowned from the stench. Soon as I hit the stairway, I saw one of the little homies that I helped raise. Chip was a good kid with limited guidance. He was a product of his own environment. His mom's addiction, contributed to his curiosity in the streets. I try my best to steer him the right way. Growing up, black, in America you are born with a strike against you.

His OG was my 2nd grade teacher. She was a beauty before the drugs took over. When I was a shorty, we had an encounter that I would never forget. I don't remember all the details but all I know is while she was performing oral on me the principal walked in the classroom and that cost her job. The next time I saw, Miss Washington I could tell she had been using. It pained me seeing Chip so lost, in a world full of corruption. I make sure I look out for him every chance I get. I throw him a few dollars whenever we bump heads to. In return all I expect from him, is to get good grades and to be a kid. He tapped me on the shoulder letting me know he had some news for me.

"What's the word little homie." "Nothing big dog. Word on the streets Pac Man, Murder, Mono, and his boys got knocked (locked up)." "Word? What they say, went down?" "I don't know man. All I know is the other day, when I cut class, I seen this white van circling the hood parked in front of Turtle's spot. Next thing I know, Joe, some tall dude, pulled up in a black truck, with all black on and a brief case full of money." "Wait man, how you know he had cash on him?" "Because I saw homie stash two, rubber bands full of money in his pants before he ran in the building. After he left, that's when I heard the shots firing. Next thing I know, Turtle and about 6 or 7 others came out in cuffs. Some pregnant bitch came out crying to."

"Word. Little homie, did Greedy, get bumped to?" "Naw, man, he wasn't in the mix. I did see him the other day though with some thick ass chick." "Little homie, you a fool. What you know about a thick bitch?" "Duh, I got eyes, don't I? You know I know what be going on." "Aye, little homie, are you sure Greedy didn't get slammed?" "Come on, man, now you know I know." "And what chick did you say came out crying?" "Some thick ass hoe, that I never seen before. She was a hot little thot (hoe) too."

"Okay little homie, thanks, but what I tell you about ditching school man? That shit, not cool. Ain't nothing out here in theses streets, trust me, my boy." "Big Homie, I know. I was just sneaking to my new chick, Sabrina's crib. These bops (hoe), be on my dick like a condom, ever since you took me shopping." "Little nigga you crazy," I said as I reached down inside my pocket and pulled out two crisps one-hundred-dollar bills and I handed it to him.

"Huh, Little homie, don't let me hear about you skipping school no more, alright. Be smooth. Hit my line." Chip smiled then he stuffed the bills down in his pocket. "Thanks, I got you, Ghost." Chip left. Once he dipped, I continued walking up the stairs. By the time I got to the top I was out of breath. I twisted the knob with my shirt, careful not to leave any DNA behind. The door was cracked which caused some suspicion. I removed my stick (gun) from my waist before I entered the unit.

I smell of decomp was strong, so I covered my nose with my shirt. I shook my head when I saw Tank motionless, with Miss Washington's head slumped over in his lap. I stood there for a minute, then I got up out of that jam. Lucky for me, nobody saw me coming but my little mans. I know sooner or later the place was gone be swarming with homicide. I made my way back to my ride a bit shaken up. I jumped in and peeled off.

We road in silence except for the flicking of the lighter. Cuz flamed up the blunt and passed it to me as soon as I got in. I took a long pull of the blunt and I filled my lungs with smoke. "Yo, cuz you good, bro? What you need a nigga bodied or something blood?" I laughed. "It's all good." We finished the blunt then I dropped him back off at the crib. I still needed to holler at Greedy, so I rolled down on him. As soon as I saw him, he started making excuses about why he had been shortchanging me. I grabbed the money that he had and got back in traffic. I hit up Pop's, but the voicemail picked up, so I jetted to the crib. The way they been posting the hood on the news, I already knew the pigs (police) a be to holler at me soon, so I gave my lawyer a call.

EIGHTEEN

It's Up: Ghost

I been ripping and running so much that I barely had time to eat. I walked in the corner store, hollered at the homie, then I grabbed myself a burner phone. I was finally able to hit up the old man. Soon as Money, jumped on the line, he started talking about, oh girl. He claimed the hoe was pregnant and she just moved in with him. "Congratulations, my boy," I said dryly. "What's, the deal famo? Ghost man, what you jealous, homie you shooting blanks, my nigga, and my bitch pregnant before yours? What your hoe pussy out of commission g?"

Silence. "First off OG, stay out my business and that's on that. My bitch good. You just met that hoe and you already playing house nigga? For all you know that bitch could be an opp." He laughed, but I could tell his ass was offended. "Man, son I love you blood. You the only family I got, but don't fuck with me, homie. I showed you the game and how to get this money. Don't you ever forget that ya-heard." I stared at the phone for a minute because I had to catch myself before I got disrespectful. Homie or not it's up there and it's stuck there. "Yeah man, you right, it's smooth. I'm gone holler at you. Stay sucker free!"

I ended the call and came up out the basement. Then I jumped in the shower and got dressed. I ran upstairs and grabbed my keys. Before leaving out I stood in the doorway watching my baby sleep and she looked so peaceful. I tiptoed in the room and gave her a kiss. She squirmed as soon as she felt my touch, then she pulled me closer. I leaned in and we kissed. Before I was able to move, she whispered in my ear, "Baby let me get that." "Later, I gotta make a move, Shorty."

She sighed. "Baby don't go, stay home with me. Your pussy needs you." "I wish I could, Ma." She cut her eyes at me. "You don't love me." "Man, bitch be cool, stop tripping, damn." She looked at me with daggers in her eyes and she flipped me the bird. "So, now I'm tripping for wanting to make love to my man? You are such a jerk. I'm good though. It's all love, enjoy your night. Gone do you, hope you strap up!" "Shorty, I'm not thinking about no bitch."

"Yeah, alright." I leaned in to kiss her, but she moved. So, I grabbed her face, we locked eyes, and our lips interlocked. Then I left the room, ran downstairs, grabbed my lighter off the table, set the alarm, and I bailed. I hopped in my ride, and I sped off. I'm not gone lie; I was feeling so guilty that I was contemplating on turning around. As soon as I was in traffic my phone started jumping.

"Come play with me, Daddy." I didn't even get a chance to respond she hung up so fast. Ready to bust my load, so I bust a U. I pulled up to the spot, parked and hopped out. Walking in the door, my instrument started jumping. She was sprawled out on the kitchen table, like a feast. I removed the blick (gun) from my waist and placed it on the counter but not far away from my reach. I stood at the edge of the table and removed my member from my jeans.

I signaled for her to devour me, and she did just that. I emptied my load, straightened my clothes, grabbed my gun, and I left how I came. She hollered behind me, "I won't some of that D." I laughed. "Catch you in a minute." "Yeah okay, asshole." "Yo, lock up," I hollered as I walked out the door. I jumped in my ride, flipped on my CD changer, and I got back in traffic. By the time the chorus came on, I had a blunt in the air.

I hit up cuz and I told him I would see him in 20. Then I called my O.G. She picked up on the first ring,

"The Lord is good, son." "Love you OG." She hesitated before responding, "What's wrong baby?" I laughed. "Nothing Ma, everything's good." "Are you sure?" "Yeah, I'm straight." Silence. "Oh shit", I screamed as soon as I felt the sizzle of the ash burning my flesh causing me to swerve. "Hello... hello, baby what happened? You, okay?" Silence. "Yeah, I'm cool, I'm gone hit you back, Ma." I made it to cuz crib in record timing. When I pulled up, he was already on the porch waiting. He hopped in and I passed him the blunt. I glanced over in his direction briefly, "Damn, nigga all that black on, where the fuck you think you going to a funeral?" He laughed.

I maneuvered my way back in traffic. "Shut up man, you gone make me drop the doty (weed)." He passed the blunt back to me then he started twisting up another one. I hit that shit hard and coughed. While we were cruising, I spotted Fly, so I pulled over and he hopped in. I introduced the two before I got down to business. I handed Fly an empty (blunt) and some loud (weed) and he already knew what to do with it. I pulled off and we hit a few blocks.

NINETEEN

Thrown Off: Isis

I don't know what's been going on with my man, but lately he seems so detached. Then to top that off, I've been feeling really nauseated lately. I used to think that I was the rhythm, to his blues but not anymore. It's like we're not on the same beat and whenever I call him out on his shit, he says I'm being insecure. His ass has been gone all day, and every time I call him, I get the voicemail. He knows that ticks me off. Then to make matters even worse somebody has been playing on my phone non-stop all week acting all weird and it's freaking me out. I started, taking some self-defense classes a few months ago, but Mike doesn't know. My FOID card came in the mail the other day and I got myself a baretta, with a leopard printed handle.

I been going to the range lately to release some of my stress. I'm getting pretty good to. I didn't bother telling Mike about my gun because he would probably blow his top. My baby is all about business, not violence. My future, pro-athlete, doesn't do anything except play ball, go to work, and work my last nerves. The doorbell rang while I was deep in thought, so I grabbed my cell and scanned our surveillance camera. I didn't see anyone there, so I ran downstairs. I shifted the blinds to the side, so I could get a better view and I saw a giftbox.

I walked over to the door, and I cracked it halfway. I grabbed the box and locked the door behind me. The box was wrapped neatly but the wrapping paper looked a little weird. I lifted the box and shook it, trying to guess its contents. I started getting excited because I knew it must've been a surprise from my baby. I called Mike on his cell again, wanting to talk about my gift but he still didn't answer. Needing a distraction to get my mind off things so I grabbed my cell and dialed Kia up, but I got her voicemail. When she didn't answer I called up, T. When she picked up the phone, she sounded out of breath. I cleared my voice before I spoke, "Hey, T, where's Kia at?" She hesitated before responding, "Aw, what up Ice? She's in the room trying to get some rest. The baby, been keeping her up all night." Silence.

"The baby...what baby?" "Girl, it's a long ass story." "Well, I got time, so spill the beans."

"Well...um," she said before a brief pause. "I guess you're going to find out soon anyway, so, uh, the baby is hers." She blurted it out so fast that I barely had time to process the information. My mouth dropped to the floor. "Wait what? I didn't even know she was pregnant." Silence. "Nobody did, it was a shocker to me to... It happened that night." I knew exactly what night she was referring to, so I was careful not to be intrusive. "So, what did she have? What is the baby's name?" Silence.

"Well Ice, it's a girl, and her name is, Ta'Kia Shelenda McNeil." Thinking to myself that's one ghetto ass name but I kept that to myself. "Aw okay T, I can't wait to meet my niece," I said right before the house phone rang. "Hold on really quick, T," I said, as I muted my cell. She sighed, "Yeah, alright Ice." I answered the other phone, secretly hoping it was my baby. "Hello." Silence. "Mrs. Isis Montgomery, please." Nervously I answered, "Uh...yes, this is she, how may I help you?" Right then, the phone slipped, from my hand as it came crashing to the floor. I stood there in shock as the room started spinning.

The Twin's House: Tia

Ugh, I can't believe Ice put me on hold and never came back to the phone. That is so rude. I only answered the phone in the first place, because I thought she was one of my dips. I been super annoyed lately, living with this screaming ass baby. I thought me and sis was on the same page, but apparently, she's not since she kept that whining ass baby without consulting with me. This is the most selfish thing that she has ever done. She didn't have any consideration for me at all. Then Daddy and that stupid little nurse, Crystal, Keisha, Kristy, or whatever her name, is, been spending way too much time together, and I don't like it one bit, either.

She may have Daddy and Kia wrapped around her little finger, but not me. I'm not going, I can see right through her manipulative ass. She needs to find some other family to play with. That bitch is not my mother. My mother is irreplaceable. I just don't even care for her ugly ass, at all, period. She will never be accepted as part of our family and I'm standing on that.

Sick to My Stomach: Isis

I snapped back to reality when I heard the operator's voice protruding through the airwaves. The call came from a Detective Douglas. He said it was urgent that Mike contacts him. Apparently, my man is wanted in for questioning. He didn't go into any details. He just left his contact number. I needed something to calm my nerves, so I decided to open my gift. I grabbed the giftbox, a cold glass of milk, and some cookies and I headed to our room upstairs. I plopped down in the bed and tossed the box to the floor. I bit into a piece of the chocolate chip cookie and sipped my glass of milk to wash it all down. My head was pounding.

I sat the glass down next to the plate of cookies that was on the nightstand. I tried laying down, but I couldn't seem to get comfortable, so I tossed and turned. My stomach was in knots. I figured I had a bad case of gas, so I sprinted to the toilet, but nothing came out. I stood to my feet and felt nauseous, so I leaned forward, and I threw up. To get rid of that nasty taste in my mouth, I rinsed my mouth with water and goggled with some Listerine. I rubbed my aching stomach. Then I walked back to the room, slowly.

I grabbed the box from off the floor and I paused. I placed my ear to the box, as I listened intensely for any ticking sounds, but I didn't hear anything. Somewhat relieved, I laughed to myself at my own suspicions, as I thought to myself, I watch too much damn TV. I tore between the wrapping, quickly. As soon as I got a clear visual, the box slid from my hands. I fell to my knees, and I screamed, "Oh my God. No!" I sobbed as I was physically shaken, and my tears started to flow even heavier than before.

Blowing Back: Ghost

We hit a few blocks while the blunt was in rotation. I nudged cuz, "Aye, man hold that shit down," I said as I nodded my head at the law (police) that was slowly approaching. As soon as they drove off, I hit the blunt hard, then I handed it to Fly. "Shit man, that was a close one. I be trying to stay as far away from them people as I can, straight up. The judge told me if I ever stepped foot in a courtroom again, I would never see the light of day. I'm not going back to that hell hole and that's on my dead homies," Fly spat as he took another pull of the blunt before he started coughing.

"Shit, I feel you, homie," said Chance as he lifted his gun. Then he started big teething (talking shit), "I'm gone put a hole in a motherfucker before I let them cuff me." "Facts," said Fly. I shook my head in agreeance. The fire on the blunt went out so I sparked it back up and I took another pull. Sitting on the block cooling, we started reminiscing. "Shit ya'll wasn't on shit if you weren't rocking a first down," I said. Fly jumped right in, "That ain't shit dirty, you couldn't talk that big boy shit without sporting them Ewing's." We all laughed. "Hell yeah." "You a fool with it," Chance said while he was cracking up.

"Peep game though, ya'll ass wasn't on shit if you didn't rock BK's (British Knights) with a fresh ass Used fit, while you were grinding on yo little hoe at the Rink," said Chance. We all laughed at that one. "Aw shit, man hell naw, the Rink. Now you really taking us back. That use to be my spot, man." Chance hit the blunt, before he continued, "Yeah man, back then there was unity." "Hell yeah. You right about that dirty, loyalty to," said Fly. "This new breed of nigga's out here ain't cut from the same cloth. All they know is drugs, card cracking, pulling stains in strikers (stolen rides), gang banging, and shooting guns while missing their targets, no cap," I said as I took a quick hit of the blunt again.

"Cuz, on the real, gangs were more respectful back then, on bro. Now days kids can't even be kids because of all this senseless violence. Now days these kids are in a battle just to live," said Chance. "Back then the streets had a foundation and shit, we were......" In mid-sentence, I was stopped when I heard a loud boom sounding like an explosion that was close by. I lowered the volume on the radio. Click---Click boom! Pop, pop, pop, boom! Boom! Boom! I immediately went into survival mode. I grabbed my loaded 9, from my secret compartment, and I took the safety off. "Fly you strapped?" He held up his piece (gun) and cocked back his slide, before responding, "Always, dirty. I keep it on me." I heard a loud thump hit my rear window causing the glass to shatter. We ducked. "Aw they want all the smoke," Chance shouted before he let down his window and started blasting. "Oh shit, Fly you good? FUCK!"

TWENTY

Blood, Sweat & Tears Cont'd

Nervously, I pulled off. I swerved a bit in traffic almost losing control, but I gripped the steering wheel tightly. I made it around the corner to Fly's crib and I parked. "Pull the fuck back off nigga," I heard one of them yelling from behind. Fly hopped out the ride like he was hunting to kill, and I don't mean the movie with Steven. "Cover me," he shouted back at us. As if on cue, Chance, started letting off rounds making sure Fly made it to his porch safely. I figured he was scared so he dipped. You know you can talk all that stepper, shit, but when it gets real, the scared ones, run. A few minutes goes by, and Fly reappears, blazing, this big ass Jack Hammer (Rocket Launcher). Me & cuz hopped out. Climbing, out the truck, I tossed the lit blunt to the ground ready for whatever. We moved away from the truck as we continued to shoot back.

By this time the city is painted red, even in between the cracks. I shifted my index finger from resting on the trigger of my, "heat," referring to the pistol that I never leave home without. Bullets are flying rapidly. My heart is beating so fast that it might rip through my blazing chest. My nose burns from the smelling of flesh. I wiped my hands on my designer jeans to reduce the moist. In this game we call life, anything goes. There are no rules. Some win and some lose that's the chance you take being made. Aiming, and shooting like the range. Shot's pouring. Pop, pop, pop, bang, bang, bang, boom! I'm sure that I would lose my hearing because of the sounds that are echoing through the foggy sky. It's so, foggy out, that I need night vision on.

Skipping through this smoggy atmosphere is becoming, unbearable. Brains splattering like paint balls. All I hear is onlookers crying and screaming. Others shaking like they have Parkinson's disease, fleeing the scene. Whoever this is, knows my ride because I don't sit on blocks. This personal but I can tell they amateurs though. I'm not about to be another statistic, fuck out of here. I reloaded, and started back yacking (shooting), trying to hit anything moving. Pop, Pop, Pop, Pop, Boom! Boom! Out of nowhere I see Fly's bitch running out in a vest, double breasted, with the prettiest gold toned AK, that I have ever laid eyes on.

I glanced at her briefly and I could've sworn I saw her throw something resembling a baseball in the opposite direction, causing the ground to shake. That gangster shit, on a female does something to a nigga like me. I damn near got my head blown off, staring at LaLa's pretty ass. She smiled. "I like my guns pretty," she shouted in the best Kim's voice that she could muster, while she continued spraying. "Oh, shit!" I heard cuz scream. I glanced in his direction noticing he was laying on the ground and hit. "Man, cuz you good bro? Say something cuz shit."

Blood soaked through his clothes. "Chance, man you good? Get up." He got up staggering. "I'm hardbody. Now I'm gone soak these fools like super soakers," he said with a slight grin. Fly and LaLa were emptying clips before we got split up to. I'm parking niggas, for playing with me. Bullets were thundering, rigorously, ricocheting off trees. "They hit me blood, so now it just got real, my dude!" Cuz voice was a bit weak but firm. I could still hear the venom escaping his lips even through his pain. While in combat, a menacing smile crept, onto his cold face. It was almost like he was getting off, from the gun fight. Death filled the air, shells, and clips, were everywhere. A 357 Magnum tiptoed to my ears.

I moved quick, they shot in my direction, but they missed. I couldn't make out the shooter, but it was something real familiar about that cat. I ducked behind some parked cars praying the alarm doesn't sound. "FUCK!" Bodies are falling like Jenga pieces. Maneuvering through this warfare is becoming more and more of a struggle. Anxious and nervous, my mind is racing. One thing I learned a long time ago, life isn't promised but death is. The truth is no matter how gangster you claim to be, don't nobody want to be carried out by six or tried by twelve.

I know I'm not God and I'm not trying to be, but if you come for me, I'll hurt your soul. If I'm strapped and trust me, I'm always strapped, I'll end, your lease here on earth. Everybody got an expiration date, and when your time is up, poof, just like that you're gone. There is no dodging death. If you take life for granted your freedom will be revoked one or two ways; either by a white sheet, or some uncomfortable silver metal bracelets, choking your wrist. That's just life. Me, I'm just trying stay humble, stack my bread, and disappear.

Gliding through carefully, seeing nothing but bodies. Ketchup colored puddles are splattered all over the pavement. I heard a familiar sounding voice creeping behind me. I stopped dead in my tracks as I was caught off guard, lacking with my magazine empty. "Ghost, nigga you not on shit. (A loud chuckle) You think you a boss? You a bitch ass nigga! You think you run these streets, but I bet you didn't see this coming. Boss up now." As soon as we were in eyesight, and he removed his mask, I paused because I couldn't believe my eyes. "Bro are you serious right now? All the shit that I do for you. I feed you man, I feed your whole family, bro. This how you j-down on me huh?"

He chuckled. "All you do for me... You don't take care me, I'm a man. You not on shit, now fall to your knees, you a bitch! After I end, your pathetic ass life, I'm gone slide on your girl to." Mentioning the wife, made my adrenaline pump even more, so I charged in his direction but was suddenly stopped when a round went off. "You a goner Ghost. I'm gone be the new boss running these here streets and getting my dick sucked like a king by that pretty ass bitch of yours. Now drop to your knees before I splatter your bitch ass."

He continued to aim in my direction. "Shoot then clown! Death don't scare me, while you are rushing me to my casket, your time gone come." While I was slowly stooping down, I swiftly grabbed my other gun from my ankle holster, and I spun around. I raised my gun and aimed in his direction. "Man, don't make me do this, fam. I'm warning you." "Do what? You not gone do shit but meet up with Tank and your Pops in hell. You're done now, Ghost, you're finished," Greedy stated with no remorse, before he fired a round, I ducked but not before getting hit in the shoulder causing me to lose the grip that I had on my gun.

"Shit." I stooped to ground reaching for my gun, but this time it was out of my reach. Then he lifted his gun and aimed in my direction right before being stopped by the bullets that ripped through his back. He dropped to the ground, face first. I heard laughter, in close range. I squinted trying to make out the face. That is when I heard a female voice saying, "I fucking told you to listen." Then that very person stood over Greedy's body and kicked him over to his backside. While he was spitting up blood, he managed to say, "You, conniving little cunt. I should have never trusted you." She laughed. "Is you cool, man? I'm the one in charge. I call the shots you bitch ass nigga," she shouted before she fired three rounds that landed in his face.

She looked up at me, "See, Ghost baby look what they made me do. I did this for us. Now we can finally be a family." I looked at her like she was retarded while she kicked Greedy's lifeless body. "He should've just followed the plan, but no, now look at him. He should've got the bread and gave me my cut. But no, he wanted to wear your crown and sit on your throne. I didn't...I didn't mean for any of this to happen baby. Please believe me. This was supposed to be an easy score, but Greedy's ass got too motherfuckin' greedy." I stood their staring at her delusional ass as I listened to her ranting, without saying a word.

"What's.... what's wrong baby? What, don't I look pretty?" She spun around. "Want me to take care of you like I did at home earlier, baby?" She scratched her head with the handle of the gun while she was looking spacey. I remained silent. "Ghost I love you so much baby. Your bitch, she doesn't deserve you. Don't you see it now? Don't you understand? We were meant to be." With her free hand she reached inside her pocket, pulls out some lipstick and she smudged it all around her lips. "I'm supposed to be your girl, not her. I'm the one that loves you the most."

"Man, what the fuck is wrong with, you?" Silence. "What's wrong with me? For starters that bitch wife of yours, has my spot. That's supposed to be me living that fairytale lifestyle. I need you, me and your baby we both do," she stated. Then she started rubbing her stomach in a circular motion while she held the gun with her other hand. I laughed, "My baby, bitch you sound stupid. Hoe you for the streets?" "Ghost, don't you dare say that to me. Don't you get it? You're my soulmate." "Your what? Bitch what type of dope you been smoking?" "Okay Ghost, that's the way you want to play it? You'll be sorry, they always are. I guess I'll just have to make your little prissy ass girlfriend disappear to, then you can finally love me," she cried.

With shaky hands, she aimed her gun in my direction. "Ghost, baby I tried. I really, really, tried to make you fall in love, with me, but all you care about is her. I'm the one that loves you. Why don't you love me?" Silence. "I could never love a disloyal bitch like you, that fake shit not in me," I stated coldly before the bullets started discharging. I moved and I ducked trying to stay clear. "Ghost, can't you learn to love me?" I shook my head, "Love, bitch you a bop (hoe), ain't no love in this shit for no hoe like you." "Don't say that baby, I know you don't really mean it. You're just upset right now. Please, don't make me do this."

"Man scratch all that, if you gone shoot then shoot." She lifted her gun, then she lowered it, then she lifted her gun again. Then she started letting off rounds, but she missed. Next thing I know, Fly, appeared out of nowhere. "Drop the gun before I end your ass bitch," said Fly followed by a loud thump. I turned around and I saw Fly on the ground. "Shit, get up man," I shouted. "So, Ghost, baby where were we? See baby you need to listen to me. You never listen to me. What about my feelings? I'm begging you, just give us a chance, you can learn to love me. I'll take care of you."

I reached for Fly's gun, but it wasn't close enough. Silence. "Last chance, baby, just tell me you love me, and everything will be okay. We can put all of this behind us and run away together. We can start all over fresh." "Negative." She frowned. "Okay then fuck it...Check mate Ghost, your tired ass game is now..." Right before she had a chance to finish her sentence, I grabbed hold of one of the guns from off the ground. I aimed and lit her ass up, then I completed her sentence, "Over," I said as I emptied my clip completely. Then I redirected my attention on my homie.

"Fly, man get up bro." I kicked him, but he didn't budge. I dragged him near a bush to get him out of harm's way. I reached down and checked his vitals and was relieved when I felt a pulse. Gliding through the streets I moved callously. I reloaded and I stayed vigilant. The shooting seemed to be ceasing but I still wasn't in the clear, so I wasn't letting up. I started to maneuver in the direction of the truck, so that I could bring it around, and grab cuz and Fly. I looked around trying to spot LaLa, but she was nowhere in sight. I reached for my keys in my pocket, never removing my hand from my gun. I hit the alarm button twice, then I heard a loud noise… BOOM! BOOM! I ducked.

Pop, pop, pop, pop. BOOM! A bit rattled, my keys fell from my hand and slid underneath my car. "Shit," I shouted over the noise as I returned the fire. Bullets were dispersing rapidly. I moved quick, dodging a few bullets to the head. That's when I felt a burning sensation, stinging one of my limbs. Hot lava began to trickle down my leg causing me to stagger. Falling to the floor, my gun ejected from out of my hand. "Fuck," I shouted. I hit the ground and began to pray. I flashbacked as I thought about my accomplishments, my life, my family, and my girl. My ego was bruised. I was tired of fighting to survive and tired of this rollercoaster that we call life. A single tear escaped my eyes.

I rolled over to face my assailant. I shook my head in total disbelief. "Damn, Chip, man. You were like a son to me man. Where is your loyalty, homie?" He foamed at the mouth as he shouted back at me, "Your son, my loyalty?" He laughed, "Get out here boy. You don't got no love for me homie. Don't you dare, talk that loyalty shit to me, Ghost. You a clown, you hear me? You a motherfuckin' clown, you did this to me. You took away my innocence and turned me into a menace, a straight savage. Now, tell me this Ghost, how could you call me your son when you didn't raise me? These crooked ass streets made me. I begged you to put me on, so that I could save my mom's, but you didn't and now she's gone. So, fuck you, Ghost," Chip spat.

He lifted his gun and I tried to reason with him, "Chip, man don't do this. It's fucked up what happened to your mom, but once you pull that trigger it's no turning back," I said while I was reaching for my gun. "Man, if you do this shit man, you're no better than I am." He laughed grimly, "I never cared, a life for a life, Ghost, it's up. I don't have shit else to live for anyway." By his actions I could tell there was no pleading my case, but I tried one last time to make amends. "Chip, I got you man. Let me make this right." Silence. "Let you make it right… Oh so now you want to make this shit right huh?" He laughed until he teared up.

"Big homie, you know like I know when it's up there it's stuck there. You taught me, a long time ago, the game is cold, but it got to be played." I shook my head in agreeance and raised my hands high like I was surrendering, but I kept trying to convince him to fall back. "Think about your life little homie. You don't want to do this. Think about your future." He paused, "Future, what future? Enough talking big homie, you said what you said, now adios." I shrugged my shoulders and shook my head to let him know it was smooth.

The next thing that I heard was a loud, BOOM! I looked down and saw a hole as big as a penny in my chest. "See, Ghost, man, you play too much. You shouldn't have forced my hand." I clutched my chest as it heaved up and the blood started gushing out. I slowly lifted my hand as I felt the wetness of the blood in between my fingers. Blood leaked from my mouth to. Chip smiled at as his handy work. He looked at me and shouted, "See you in hell Ghost!" Then he looked up to the sky and started talking to the clouds, "See, Mama I told you, I was a man."

Not much longer after that, he turned the barrel on himself, placing the gun to his temple, as he squeezed the trigger. I watched as the gun tumbled from his hand landing next to his body as he took his last breath. Keeping my eyes open was becoming more of a challenge. I started to flashback on life. My eyes slowly, closed as I started to fade away. I heard sirens approaching. "Sir, sir," I heard a woman's voice yelling. "Stay with me sir. Sir....... Sir can you hear me? If you can hear me, please try and open your eyes?"

I wanted to reply but, no matter how hard I tried, I couldn't. "Clear! He's unresponsive, charge to 200...Clear... Sir stay with us." The heart monitor started to beep continuously. "Last time, clear." I could feel myself, slowly, slipping away. My mind started to race in a slow but steady pace. "Clear," The beeping sounds started to increase. "We're losing him clear. Sir, you look like a fighter, and you have probably been fighting battles all your life. I can tell you have, don't give up sir, clear." As I faded into a dark place a tear slid down my face. "Sir. Come on stay with us sir, clear."

While I was fighting to stay alive, I started reflecting over my life and all I could think of is: "They say jealousy and envy corrupts minds. So much to live for my soul cries. I know life is not promised, but this can't be goodbye. Sin overpowers my good fortune no matter how hard I try. Everyone has an expiration date we are all living on borrowed time. Please, catch me before I... drown." BEEP! "Clear! There's nothing more we can do for him... Clear. He's gone." Flatlined... BEEP! "Call it." BEEP......

Feeling Faint: Isis

After seeing the contents that was inside the giftbox, I fainted. Only to be awaken by the phone ringing off the hook. So much was going on around me that I dreaded even answering the call, but I did. I sat up and reached for the phone. I heard Mama's voice on the other end. "Ice, honey, what's wrong?" Silence. "Nothing's wrong Mama, I'm okay," I lied, as I cleared my throat. I managed to pull myself together long enough to deflate the question. "I'm just tired I guess." She paused, "I love you Ice, see you in a bit." "Love you to," I said before disconnecting the call. My head was spinning. All types of questions were flooding my brain.

Should I call the police? Whose ear is this? Why did they send this here? Is this person alive? Is this my man's ear? Puzzled, I sobbed uncontrollably. Staring into space, half out of my mind and the house phone rings yet again. I ignored the call and turned on the big screen. Then I started flicking through the channels until I saw a news coverage story that caught my attention. "This is Natasha Cumberland, with a breaking news report. Here I am, at the scene of a horrific, crime. Standing in the middle of a massacre in what the city is now calling a "Murder Madness," I am encouraging everyone to lock all doors."

While I was tuning in to the breaking news report my phone started ringing like crazy, this time I answered. On the other end of the receiver was an unfamiliar female's voice. "Hello," I said a bit agitated.

"May I speak to a Miss Isis Montgomery, please?" I paused, "Yes, this is she. How may I help you?" Silence. "This is Mrs. Armstrong calling from Miracles, trauma unit." I hesitated as I took a deep breath, "Uh huh, yes, please go on." "I believe we have you listed as the emergency contact number for a Mr. Michael Johnson. Mam, I think..." Before she could utter another word, I screamed until I was interrupted by her voice. "Hello, are you still there?" Tears bounced off my cheeks.

"Hello, Miss Montgomery are you still there? Hello..." I tried my best to pull myself together. "Yes ...I'm...I'm here. Oh my God. Yes...thank you for calling...I'm on my way," I said before disconnecting the call. My mind went blank, everything after that was pretty much a blur. I grabbed my keys rushing downstairs to the door. On my way out, Mama was on her way, in with her hands full of groceries. She immediately became alarmed as she saw my disheveled appearance and her bags came crashing to the floor.

"Baby is everything alright? What is going on Ice? Is Michael, okay?" I stood there in silence barely able to speak. All I could do is cry. She grabbed me by the hand and without any words exchanged, we exited the house and drove in silence the entire ride to the hospital. Not sure how but I got us there safely. As we pulled into the parking garage, she squeezed my hand. After we parked, we headed straight for the emergency room. We walked through the double set of doors physically shaken and emotionally drained. We approached the information desk in record timing.

I was already nerved up, so I wasn't in the mood for any ignorance, so I cleared my throat, "Excuse me," I said calmly. I stood there anxious and nervous while the receptionist continued to ignore my presence. She didn't even have the common decency to look up from her computer. Instead, she continued popping her gum and gossiping on the phone. Trying to keep my cool, so I decided to give her one last chance before I grabbed her by the throat and pulled her ass from across her desk. So, I cleared my throat again, "Excuse me," I said but only this time I added a little base in my voice.

She finally decided to look up as she ended her call. Threatened by my facial expressions, she refrained from making any smart-ass comments. She cut her eyes sharp before she responded. "Yes, may I help you?" As much as I wanted to bug out, I just bit my tongue. "Mam, do you have a patient by the name of....?" Before I had a chance to finish my sentence, she shoved a clipboard in my face. "Here, you go fill this clipboard out and return it to me, thanks," she said in a ruffled tone. Then she looked around me and tried to dismiss me, "Next."

That's when I became a little more aggressive. I shoved the clipboard back in her face. "Excuse me, I'm looking for a patient by the name of Michael Johnson Jr." She paused as she rolled her eyes, sucking her teeth. "Oh, Lord...Please let my baby be alright," Mama shouted. She snatched the clipboard from my hand, placing it on her desk. It was taking everything in me not to treat this bitch, life but I didn't. She smacked her lips again before she spoke, "Oh... okay sure, let me look that up for you." While we were waiting, I rubbed Mama's back trying to console her.

Then the snotty ass receptionist finally shouted out a room number and pointed us in the right direction. "Thanks," I said through my clinched teeth before disappearing down the hall. The walk seemed like an eternity. Mama stopped, grabbed my hand, and looked me in the eyes before speaking, "Isis, you're like a daughter to me and no matter what happens, you will always have a home with us." "Mama, thank you so much for treating me like your own," I said as I sobbed. We stood there and embraced one another in a hug before continuing down the hall. By now the tears are cascading down both of our cheeks. I was petrified and I could tell that Mama was scared to.

TWENTY-ONE

The Dungeon: Candi

I was sitting around feeling helpless, waiting, for my girl to return. She had been gone for a few hours now. I tried reaching her on her cell, but I kept getting sent to the voicemail. I must admit the plan was rocky, but I still went along with it. We've been dating for a little over a year now and lately I've been considering marriage. We have an open relationship, which is cool to. If we pull this stain off, me and my baby gone be straight. Deep in thought, so I grabbed the remote and started flicking through the channels. I stopped when I saw, Judge Mathis because he tells it like it is. You can always get a good laugh off one of his cases.

15 minutes in passing and a breaking news story interrupts my show. "We interrupt this regular schedule program for a very important announcement. This is Natalie Cumberland here with the channel 3 news. I am here at the scene of the crime in what the city is now calling a "Murder Madness." The news report sounded interesting, so I increased the volume. I listened carefully to every detail. "Police say a shooting occurred on the Chicago's southside, which is believed to be a drug deal gone bad. Authorities say there are 2 victims in stable condition and 2 victims in critical condition.

Montrell "Chip" Washington, ZaKee "Mono" Jefferson, Quantrell "Fresh" Johnson, Benjamin "Greedy" Nichols, and Kiosha Kiara "Kiki" Wilson, the daughter of our very own, Detective John Wilson, were all pronounced dead at the scene of the crime. No suspects have been apprehended."

I fell to my knees as I screamed, "No... No... No!" I became startled by a noise that was coming from the basement, so I dried my face and I walked downstairs. Once I was there, I noticed Money, was squirming as he was slowly regaining his consciousness. "You crazy bitch, untie me, now! Call 911, I need to get patched up before I bleed out you stupid bitch." I stared at him, as if there was a language barrier. Enraged, I grabbed my gun and I hit him upside his head. "Let me go and I'll let you live; you blood sucking bitch." I looked at him and laughed because kidnapping him was personal for me. "First off sir, you're in no position to make any negotiations. If you haven't already noticed, you're not the one in control, I am! If you're looking for somebody to blame, blame your dope fiend, ass mother."

"What did you just say to me, you, scandalous, ass bitch?" "You heard what I said. I said what I said. Your drug addict mother is the reason you're here. That bitch is also the reason that my family fell apart. She is the one that got my dad locked up, and unfortunately you're going to pay for it, so help me God you're going to pay." Silence. "Aw wait, what you didn't know?" I laughed. "Well, let me break it down for you. Your mother's, father, is also our dad."

Angry, Money started fumbling around trying to break free. "You're one sick bitch." "Sick, now watch how you talk to me baby, we're family. I found a picture of my dad and your mom, buried deep in my mother's closet. It didn't take long before Mommy came clean and told me all about our dad. After that I connected the missing pieces of the puzzle and here, we are. You are so pathetic, you really thought I loved you. How could I ever love you? I've had harder orgasms with my toys than feeling your premature penetration. You thought because we fucked and I sucked you up, that I liked you? You a whole clown, you're my cousin, my former lover or maybe my half-brother, I'm really not sure now, I lost track." He frowned.

I bent down so that we were eye to eye. "You discuss me," he said coldly right before his spit landed in my face. Annoyed, I wiped the spit out my face with the back of my hand and I took, the, but, of the gun and I rammed it in the side of his temple. "I hate you Money. I hate you! Oh, and when you get to hell, kiss your mom for me and make sure you tell her I sent you. It's all, your fault, that my girl is dead to, so I have no remorse for you." I blanked out and I hit him with the gun until he was unconscious. Out of breath I grabbed the cash he had laying around and I rushed to the door. I knew that it was only a matter of time before the police caught up with me. I wasn't trying to stick around for that, so I did the dash.

24 Hours Ago: Kiki

Since me and Greedy's shriveled dick ass started dealing I got accustomed to faking my orgasms. After this power move, I'm gone be set for life. I'm only using Greedy's ass to get what I want anyway but this goofy think's we're an idol. His slow, dumb ass talking about leaving his family for me and everything. To seal the deal, I faked a pregnancy, now I really got him eating out the palm of my hands. He thinks the baby is his, but I was already 8 weeks when I told him. Ghost is the father of my child, but I haven't told him yet. I'm just waiting on the right time. I think I'm gone keep this one though.

We gone have a pretty ass baby. I find myself wondering at times, how my life would've turned out had I kept my oldest son, Derrick. Candi's been so extra lately. I think she's catching feelings for Money, it's like she's obsessed with him or something. I don't know what's gotten into her lately. All I know is she better not mess up this plan. I ordered up some gadgets from the spy shop one of which prevented Money from receiving incoming calls. Next year around this time I'll be sitting on an island sipping on a Mai Tai. Me, the hubby, the baby, and maybe even little Derrick and we can finally be a family. I can't wait to tell my baby daddy the good news so he can cancel that bitch he got.

My daydreaming came to an end when I heard my name being called. I frowned. "I'm horny baby, come play with me," Candi whined. "Okay baby here I come," I said in an agitating tone. I was starting to regret ever fucking with this dumb bitch, but I can't cancel her now. I needed her to make this plan work. When this is all over, I plan on dropping this hoe to. "Hurry up Ki," she whined. "Yeah okay, put on that little purple lace thing, that I like to see you in," I said trying to sound concerned. "Ok, baby."

Before entering the room completely, I stopped in the doorway, "Baby did you remember to gag, Money?" "Yes, Ki, now come play in my puddle." I responded with a head nod. For about a week we've been hiding out at Money's crib. Zap's crazy ass been calling me collect, nonstop, so I blocked his ass. While I was walking over to the bed, I stripped naked. I flamed up a blunt and hit a couple times before putting it out. We went at it, like animals. I took her head in my palm and I positioned her to taste my kitty. I hadn't had any since earlier, but that was only from Greedy, so that didn't count. After I got off, I reached over to the nightstand. I strapped on my strap, and I rammed it in her insides until her pussy lips started to swell.

She straddled me, kissing all over my body. While we were in the middle of our heated pleasure, the doorbell rang. I stopped, but she started whining, so I started back up again. Then the doorbell rang again but this time it was more aggressive. I slowed down my motion, then I stopped abruptly. "Baby, no! Don't answer the door. They'll get the message and go away," she whined as she started kissing me again. I smiled, "I'm not going anywhere, you are." She got up, with her lips poked out. I slapped her on the ass, before she walked to the door.

As soon as she left out, I flamed back up. Getting antsy so I hollered after her. "Baby what are you doing? What's taking so long?" Silence. When she reappeared in the doorway she was in tears. "Baby, what's wrong?" By now, her tears are flowing heavy, so I reached for my gun. "Baby, I'm sorry." "You're sorry, for what?" I couldn't even grab my gun fast enough before an unwanted face appeared. "Bitch where is my motherfuckin' money at? You better talk quick before I off this bitch," Zap spat before he shoved her so hard to the floor, that she blacked out.

Nervously I asked, "What are you doing here Zap? I mean baby let's talk things over and work it out," I stuttered. "Bitch say less, run me my bread. Matter of fact eat this dick first before I put a hole in yo head." I raised up from the bed. By now the blunt had went out so I placed it in the ashtray. "Aw wait a minute you wearing straps now, huh? Aw so you big gay around this bitch," he said with a smirk. I removed the strap from around my waist and I tossed it to the floor. "Hurry up hoe I don't got all day. You gone do this motherfucka' or what?" Shakingly, I walked towards him. I didn't utter a word because I already know how short fused, he was.

I unzipped his pants, as I fought back my tears. I fell to my knees, and I put my mouth around his pole. Then I sucked him dry. Afterwards I stood to my feet. Then he massaged my kitty and pointed towards the bed, so I walked in that direction. I put my hands on the bad and I kneeled because I already knew how he likes it. I screamed out in pain as he rammed his rock hard in my ass. Still and all, I threw it back at him. I figured that I might as well get off a nut or two. It didn't make any since letting this big ass cock go to waste. After we smashed, we smoked a blunt while discussing my plan.

Shortly after Candi came to. As soon as she pierced her eyes on us, the look of disappointment appeared on her face. I introduced the two, and I filled her in. I convinced her to have a 3-way with him because I was still trying to get back in his good grace. We played with each other, while he watched, then we let him join in. After our little sex-escapade was over, we got straight back down to business. "Now you know I can make a couple calls to aid and assist," he said.

"It's cool baby that won't be necessary. I got a full proof plan." He looked at me strangely before shoving a phone in my face. "Make sure you always answer this motherfucka'. I would hate to have to pay a visit to your son, Derrick." I nodded my head in, knowing he meant business. I already knew he had connections all over the city. After giving me further instructions, Zap grabbed the back of my neck forcefully and kissed me on the lips. "Don't cross me or that boy of yours, is bodied. Do you understand?" I shook my head while the tears formed, in my eyes.

Candi remained silent the entire time. "After all these years, you still don't trust me, baby. You would actually hurt my son, our son?" "Our son, bitch please. All I'm gone say is try me, and I'll gut you both like a fish!" He stared at me coldly, fixed his clothes, stormed out the room, and he left just like he came. After we heard the door slam, Candi started flooding me with questions, but I didn't say much.

Lord Give Us Strength: Isis

As soon as we got close to Mike's room, we were greeted by his doctor. He said they were only able to remove one of his bullets because the other one was lodged too close to his heart. At that moment I felt numb. With tears, we walked inside my baby's room and tubes were everywhere. The first thing that I did after the initial shock wore off, was check both of his ears to make sure they were attached. I held his hand while, Mama, stood on the opposite side of him, talking to him like he was awake.

I couldn't help but notice the handcuffs connected to his bedrail. Seeing my man like this, really broke me. I told Mama, she could go home, so that somebody could be there when Shayna got in. She talked to him for about another thirty more minutes or so. I left the room and went into the waiting area, so she could speak freely. She joined me soon after. We hugged, "Ice honey, I think you're right. I'm going to go on home. I know my son is in good hands as long as you're here with him." I smiled weakly through my tears.

"Okay Mama, I'll be right here with him. I promise not to leave his side." She smiled, "I know Ice. I always told him you were a good woman and he better not screw things up with you." I smiled slightly, "Aw thanks." Silence. "Ice, baby, give me a call if there are any changes." "Of course, I will, Mama," I said before handing her a couple twenties for her cab fare. We embraced momentarily. Then she disappeared.

I walked back to Mike's room and sat down beside him. I cried until I fell asleep. I woke up the next morning, with a cramp in my neck, to the sound of the nurse's voice who talked me into going home and showering. Hesitant at first, I left my contact information, and I left the hospital. I didn't waste any time coming back. Since my baby's accident, I've been at the hospital so much that I know all the nurses by their names, and I developed a daily routine. I read to him, wash him up, talked to him and prayed with him.

To prevent unwanted visitors, I put a secure code on his visitors list and his recovery process. There were a couple of detectives that stopped by his room quite frequently. They didn't say much, they only left their business cards. Surprisingly, his Pop's hadn't even bothered getting in touch with us. The Twins, his coach, Mommy and Daddy stopped by to check on him to. I was so stressed out that I cried myself to sleep every night. I only wish that this was all a bad dream.

The Escape: Candi

Heading out the door I heard helicopters that sounded like they were circling around the house. Nervously, I rushed, out the door, with a duffle bag full of large bills in my hand. Exiting the door, I was nearly near blinded by the bright lights, which strained my eyes. "Shit," I shouted while I was squinting. I searched for an exit, but I was surrounded. Then I heard the words that everyone feared, "Freeze! Show me your hands, put down your weapon, get on your knees, now!"

I paused briefly, "Okay, okay, I surrender," I said as I threw my hands up in the air. "I'm lowering my weapon now. I don't want any trouble," I shouted. Before my weapon was completely lowered, I started firing shots. "Oh fuck," I heard one of the officers yelling. I spun around trying to get away. "Get down on your hands and knees, now!" I continued shooting until I was stopped by the bullet that struck my arm. Still contemplating my next move, my weapon fell from my hand. I saw the two burley officers rushing towards me, so I started to run. I didn't get very far before I felt a sting in my thigh causing me to fall.

"Oh shit." While I was on the ground we tussled. It took a few of them to hold me down and cuff me. "Let go of me, stop…wait. No, I'm not going back! Let go of me," I screamed. While I resisted arrest, I was approached by one of the officers, who looked kind of familiar. "Candice is that you? What are you doing here dear?" As soon as I recognized his face, I lowered my head. "I love her so bad sir. I really did love her. This plan should've worked, she promised me it would work. I'm sorry, I'm so…so sorry."

He stared at me with the look of confusion on his face. "What plan are you talking about Candice? If you love my daughter the way you say you do, tell me what happened, please. Help me solve her murder, please," said Detective Wilson. "With all due respect sir, I can't. I'm not saying anything without a lawyer present. Forgive me sir but I can't go back to that psych ward, I just can't." Next thing I know I'm being shoved in the back of the police car. I saw the other officers rushing inside the home, they searched inside the premises and found Money, in the basement, gagged, restrained, and covered in blood. Nothing left for me to do accept admit defeat, so I stared out the window, feeling helpless as they hauled me away.

Shocking News: Nurse Kristy

I noticed heavy traffic, at the start of my shift. I sat down in the lunchroom eating the cold cut that I prepared. I bit into my sandwich while I checked my emails on my phone. Suddenly, my sandwich came tumbling down when a picture of my son's biological mother, was plastered all over the news. According to the news article, she was pregnant at the time of her murder. Apparently, she was the daughter, of a Detective Wilson. Although the young girl was partially the reason for my divorce, I still by no means wished any harm on her or anybody else for that matter.

I decided to give my ex-husband, Jake a call. His response was cold and shocking even for him, "That dry pussy hoe got what she deserved." I looked at my phone because I couldn't believe what I was hearing. Silence. "What are you sounding all sad for. Kristy, you hated the hoe to." Outdone, I didn't bother feeding into his negativity. "Well, I was only calling you just in case you wanted to take Derrick, to say his goodbyes to his mother."

He laughed, "The only mother my son knows is you. My son will not be anywhere near that funeral. That deceitful, bitch lucky somebody got to her before I did." To make light of the situation I tried to change the subject. "So, how's Derrick doing?" "He's doing okay. Why don't you just ask him yourself, this is your weekend right?" "Yeah, it is my weekend." "What time will you be here to pick him up, Kristy?" I paused. "6.

I'll be there at 6 Jake. Well, I must go I'm being paged. Talk to you later," I said as I ended the call. Before returning to work, I picked the sandwich up off the floor and tossed it in the trash. After that conversation, I hated that I even tried to reach out to him.

TWENTY-TWO

By Your Side: Isis

Still praying for a miracle, it's like my entire world has been shifting upside down. I found out later, that the ear I received, belonged to Mike's, Pop's. From what I've heard he was so badly beaten, that, he had a closed casket funeral. Mama and I paid the entire cost. I had never seen so many people at a homegoing service before. I could tell by the amount of the people that showed up he was loved. I knew the bond, that him and my baby shared so I sent a beautiful flower arrangement in Mike's honor. Mama, Shayna, and I all attended the service. I still didn't know how I would break the news to my baby when he wakes up.

We got word that some of Mike's other close friends like Greedy was killed but we didn't attend his funeral. I didn't care for him to much, I always got snake vibes from him. My stomach was feeling queasy, I had been running back and forth to the bathroom all day. The last time that I went to rinse my mouth, I could have sworn I heard mumbling coming from out of Mike's room. I haven't been able, to sleep much so I figured it was all in my head. While I was looking in the mirror at my disheveled appearance, I heard what sounded like some mumbling again. This time the sound was louder than before. Then I heard a gentle, whisper that sounded like my name was being called, and it scared me.

"Ice," the voice said. I froze momentarily. Then I sprinted over to my baby's bedside teary eyed. "Oh my God. Yes baby, I'm here," I said frantically. He smiled weakly, as it pained him to talk. "I'm sorry Ice," he said, in a gentle whisper. He tried to move his arm, but he couldn't because of the restraints. I grabbed his hand and I kissed it. Then I pushed the red alert button signaling for the nurse. Anxious, I removed my hand from his and ran to the door. "Wait, one second baby," I hollered back at him. I rushed to the hallway towards the nurse's station. "Nurse! Nurse! Nurse! Come quick."

I rushed back to his room and moments later, one of the nurses came dashing in. She clutched her chest out of amazement. "He's a fighter," I said proudly. "He sure is." Tears slid down my cheeks. The nurse smiled warmly, while she checked his vitals. "I see you're back with us sir. How do you feel? You gave us all quite a scare." In a tiny whisper he spoke, "I'm smooth." She smiled and then she turned in my direction, "Let me page the doctor."

I nodded my head and she left. Then I refocused my attention back on Mike. "I love you baby, don't you ever scare me like that, again. You better not..." Before I could finish my sentence, my nausea overpowered me, so I covered my mouth and sprinted to the toilet. When I reentered the room Doctor Brownstone was already in there. He looked at me and said, "You don't look so good. Are you okay?" I hesitated, "Yes, Doc I fine, it's probably just something I ate. I'm okay just take care of my man." Doctor Brownstone, summoned for me to step out of the room. "I'll be right outside that door, baby," I said to Mike before walking into the hallway. He smiled weakly.

I watched the birds feasting while I was staring out of the window. I called up Mama, "Mama…Mama… he's awake." "Praise God," she screamed loudly. 20 minutes later her and Shayna appeared. They walked in smiling, as they cried tears of joy. We hugged briefly. Shortly after Dr. Brownstone joined us. "Hello, you all have a fighter in there," he stated reassuringly. We remained quiet as we listened carefully as he spoke, "Michael will make a full recovery with the help of physical therapy that is. We recommend that he stays in the hospital for another week just for observation. Do you have any questions for me?"

I looked at Mama and then Shayna before I replied, "No, Doctor B. We don't have any questions. Thank you for taking care of my…." In midsentence I grabbed my mouth and I rushed to the bathroom. Before leaving the hospital, the doctor recommended that I allowed them to run some test, on me. Annoyed, I agreed but only because Mama insisted. The nurse led me to another room, checked my vitals, and did some blood work. I hated needles with a passion, so I was none too happy about this.

An hour later she reentered the room with a gigantic smile on her face. I immediately got up and started gathering my things so that I can go. "See I told you it was nothing to be worried about Miss. Montgomery," the nurse stated. "That's great, did you bring me a script to be filled so that I can soothe my stomach?" She paused. "Miss. Montgomery, I am pleased to announce that you are 8 weeks pregnant." In shock, I stared at her like I was waiting on a punch line. Notably frustrated I screamed, "I'm what? There has to be some sort of mistake."

"No mistake, Miss you are 8 weeks pregnant," she reiterated. As soon as that news resonated to my brain, I fainted. When, I came to, Mama, Shayna, and my overbearing parents, were all hovering over me smiling. "Congratulations Ice. I am so happy I am going to have a little niece or nephew," Shayna said. "We love you Sunshine," said Daddy. Completely stunned I cried. All I could think to say was, "How could this have happened?" My mother's response irritated me the most, "Well Ice sweetheart, have I ever told you the story about the birds and the bees?" Everyone laughed except me. "This was not a part of my plan. I was supposed to get my degree first, get married, and then have a baby."

"It's okay Sunshine. God doesn't give you anything that you cannot handle. You know things don't happen when you want them to, they happen when they are supposed to," said Daddy. Then I turned to face him, "How can you say that to me Daddy when I can't handle this? My man was shot and now I'm pregnant. This is just too much for me." Mama and Shayna tried reasoning with me to. "Baby everything is going to work itself out. Mike is going to be so excited when he hears

the news."

"No, Mama you're missing it. You are all, missing my point. What about school? Ever since I was a kid, I have had my life mapped out. Now my life is ruined." "Ice I'll be here to help you anyway that I can, sis." I smiled, "I really appreciate the love and support from each one of you. I just need some time to think. Mama you say that Mike will be happy when he hears the news, but how can you be so sure? Look at us, we're a mess right now. I don't want anyone telling him either. This news needs to come from me and me only. Do you guys hear me? Promise me?"

In unison they agreed, "Okay, we promise." Frustrated and feeling alone, I shouted to the top of my lungs, "Everybody out!" No words were exchanged, everyone did as I asked and one by one, they gathered their belongings to leave. Feeling down I cried myself to sleep. When I woke up in the middle of the night, I really needed to feel my man's presence. I stood to my feet, closed my gown tight, and I snuck downstairs to his room. I held his hand while I watched him sleep. I leaned over and I laid my head on his arm and I cried some more. I guess he felt my presence because he woke right up.

He spoke softly, "What's wrong, Ma?" "Nothing Mike, nothing." "Ice, please baby talk to me," he said calmly. "Michael, baby. Oh, my God, baby I'm..." I paused. "What is it, Ice tell me?" Nervously I continued, "Baby, I'm... I'm (sniff, sniff) I'm... pregnant." "You're what," he said with a slight grin on his face. "You heard me Michael, I'm pregnant and I'm scared to death. I don't know what to do." He frowned. "What do you mean you don't know what to do? You not killing my seed, that's unforgiveable Ice." I sat there unresponsive. "You hear me Ice?" I nodded.

"But Mike, we didn't even plan this. We're not ready to be parents." "Shorty, I almost died but for some strange reason, God spared my life and gave a sinner like me, a second chance. So, now, I'm living every day like it's my last. Life is short, Ice. You're here one day and gone the next." "You're my wife, it's only right that you have my seed. You have to have Michael Jr." I shook my head up and down but I was petrified in the inside. "I love you baby." "Love you to Ice." I could tell that the medicine must've been kicking in because he kept on nodding in and out. I stared at him until he drifted off to sleep. Then I walked back to my room.

Detective Wilson

There were still no leads on the investigation leading to my little girl's death. When I arrived at the scene, blood was everywhere, and she had already taken her last breath. It had been years since the last time that we spoke. Truth is she, blamed me, for her mother's incarceration. It ate me up inside, knowing that my child's mother, was in jail for murdering one of my lovers. In hopes of catching, my daughter's killer, we tracked down her good friend, Candice by the signal on her phone. When we arrived, Candice seemed loopy.

After we checked the home that it appeared she we found an earless man being held captive. All the evidence pointed back to Candice, but it wasn't really adding up. She couldn't have apprehended the victim alone. I was fishing for answers, trying to figure out what role my daughter played in all of this. I will not rest until the perpetrators are captured. I didn't waste any time burying my daughter either. Once word traveled to the prison systems, her mother hung herself. Now I have both of their blood on my hands.

My head was starting to hurt, so I popped 4 pain pills and I washed it down with some Jameson. Captain had me on administrative leave, because of the conflict of interest to the case so I did my own private investigating. My partner filled me in regularly on any leads. I sat around in sorrow, drinking away my pain until my phone rang. It was my partner calling informing me that my prime suspect, had just woke up from a coma. Douglas suggested we paid him a visit first thing tomorrow morning. If Captain had gotten word that I was somehow involved in this investigation he would have my badge, but that's a risk that I am willing to take for my little girl.

Questioning

The nurse came in, handing me my discharge papers, which I gladly signed. I called Mike's lawyer and filled him in just like I was instructed. I still hadn't gotten the courage to tell him about his Pop's passing. While I was sitting around talking to Mike, Detectives Douglas and Wilson barged in. "Miss, do you mind stepping out of the room," one of them asked. I stood up to leave, but Mike grabbed me by the hand and stopped me. "Anything you have to say to me you can say in front of my wife, we don't have any secrets." I smiled at his gentle gesture, and I sat back down.

"Your wife, huh," Detective Wilson marked, as he was reeking of liquor. "Yes, my wife, I didn't stutter," proclaimed Mike. Then the other one intervened, "Okay, well Mr. Michael "Ghost" Johnson, it's been a while sir." As soon as they addressed him as such Mike gritted his teeth and I frowned. "Excuse me, who is Ghost? My baby's name is Mike there must be some sort of mistake." I turned to face him, "Michael baby, what are they talking about, why are they calling you that?"

Before he had a chance to answer me the mouthier one responded, "Yea Michael why are we calling you that?" "Baby we'll talk later," he said dismissively. "Yea Michael, I mean Ghost we sure will." I slid my hand from his. When I heard the name Ghost, for some reason or another I got chills down my spine, and I tuned in even more. I heard rumors about some guys by the name of Money and Ghost being ruthless, kingpins but I didn't pay it any mind. Detective Douglas continued, asking question after question and surprisingly Mike stayed calm.

I overheard one of them, claiming that they were allegedly responsible for the biggest drug ring in the city. I sat there in silence as I was barely able to breathe. The more they talked the more I felt like I was in love with a stranger. They asked about his involvement in the murder of a Kiara Wilson while showing us pictures of her. The pictures that I saw on the news of her, looked like the girl that crashed my birthday party, but I wasn't for sure, so I didn't utter a word. They told Mike that since Money was dead, he has two options either give up his connect or face kingpin charges.

Surprisingly, Mike seemed unbothered by their allegations. "Connect...Only connect I know is the board game, Connect Four. I think we're pretty much finished here gentlemen. Good day, oh, and by the way if you have any other questions for me, please feel free to contact my lawyer." Then I handed the detectives our lawyer's business card. They smiled arrogantly. "Sure, we'll be in touch. Oh, and by the way please don't even think about leaving town," Detective Douglas stated firmly before uncuffing him from the bedrail, and they left. After they were gone, Mike started grilling me.

"Yo, Ice, man...what do they mean Pops dead? What the fuck is going on?" I lowered my head as I searched my soul for the right words to use, "Baby I hate that you found out this way, but yes Michael, he's gone." "Naw, man famo can't be done checked out on me like that." "I'm sorry baby but Mama and I took care of his arrangements. You would be proud, we put him away in style." "Thank you, Ice. Baby, I don't know what I would do without you, being by my side." I snarled at him then I stood to my feet and walked to the door. Mike called after me, "Ice, where the fuck do you think you're going?" Silence.

"To get some fresh air Michael, I can't do this with you, right now. I just can't. It's like I don't even know who you are anymore." "Baby don't do this, please sit back down so we can talk." "Nah, I can't. I wish that I could, Michael but I can't. Too much damage has been done and to many lies has been told," I said, and I left. Walking down the hall I could still hear him calling after me, but I didn't stop.

Check Out: Mike

The nurse came in with my discharge papers. Shayna came to my room and wheeled me to the exit door. As soon as I saw Ma's car, I became eager. As we drove to the house, I remained silent and in deep thought. I heard Ma and sis talking but I tuned them out. The news about Pop's getting bagged, was really weighing on me. I needed to make a few calls, in the morning to put this contingency plan into motion. First thing first, I needed a haircut asap, I'm looking like teen wolf or something. I was looking forward to starting my therapy so that I can regain my strength to. When we got to the house Shayna helped me to get in the door. I smiled as soon as I smelled the scent of a homecooked meal. Mad and all Ice was still like my personal chef.

She had even fixed up one of the guest rooms on the first floor for me. My mini fridge was stocked, and she had me some blunts rolled up in the ashtray waiting for me to. I know that she's mad right now, but I hope she doesn't do anything stupid like abort my child. I heard a knock at the door, so I yelled, "Yeah come in." As soon as the door swung open Shayna appeared in the doorway. "You good bro?" "Yeah, Shay I'm straight come in." "Just checking in on you, big head."

I laughed. "Everything, smooth sis." She hugged me and she started to cry. Then she stood up and playfully punched me in the shoulder. "Ouch! What was that for?" "Don't ever scare me like that again." I smiled. "I won't, not to worry, I'm not going anywhere." "Promise," she said as she held out her pinky. "Yeah, I promise. What you been up with you?" "Well, I guess I've been okay. Don't be mad bro, but my grades been slipping like crazy since you got shot." "Now, we can't have that." "I know bro-bro. If you stay out of trouble, I can stay focused." "Yeah, you better."

"Love you bro. See you later," she said before she left back out the room. "Yep," I hollered. I laid back down, grabbed one of those pre-rolled blunts and flamed up. I let the smoke hit my lungs, while I was deep in thought. As I inhaled the dope, I started flicking through the channels. I couldn't sleep so I called Ice's phone, but I only got the voicemail. Twenty minutes later I heard her walking in the house, lit. I knew she had to have been drinking because it sounded like she was bumping into everything, so I yelled out to her, "Ice, get the fuck in here!" She walked in, with plenty of attitude, "Aw, hey Ghost, what's up fam." I nearly jumped up out the bed before the pain knocked me back down.

"Ice what the fuck is you doing drinking, and you pregnant with my seed?" "First of all, you got some nerve. Stop tripping, I might not be pregnant for long anyways," she slurred. "Bitch you mine forever and who is fam? Ice you better stop playing with me!" "Mike, I'm exhausted I don't want to fight. I'm not in the mood for this." "Yeah, alright Ice," I said before she staggered out the room. Stressing, I rubbed the side of my head and then I flamed back up.

TWENTY-THREE

Making Moves

The next morning when I woke up, Ice was already gone. I had a lot of errands to run so I couldn't worry with that right now. I called Shayna up and had her chauffer me around town. First stop was the barbershop. After I got lined up, I went straight to my therapy session. Therapy went better than I expected, but I was kind of sore afterwards. As soon as Shayna picked me up, she started ranting about her new boyfriend. "Oh my God bro just wait until you meet him. You gone like him." "Yeah, that's cool Shay as long as you stay a virgin until you're 30."

She laughed, "Mike really, 30?" "Yeah, I think 30 is a good age." Pulling back up at the crib, I noticed those same detectives from the other day sitting around lurking. I started to tell her to re-route, but instead I had her pull on the side of them. "Follow me gentlemen." I already knew they didn't have anything on me, otherwise they would have already booked me. When we walked in the house, I never took my eyes off them. They questioned me for about 30 minutes before they left. About an hour later Ice, decided to show face and Shayna left out. Ice spoke dryly so I did likewise. I tried making small talk to avoid confrontation. "Hey Ice. How my two babies doing?" "Excuse me, your who? I'm fine thanks for asking and the other one will be gone in a couple days, so you don't need to worry about that." I flamed up a blunt and watched as she stormed off up the stairs.

I'm Grown: Shayna

Man, I love my brother, but he be so extra sometimes. I'm a grown ass woman and he be trying to dictate my life like I'm a child. I am fully capable of making my own decisions. I mean he acts like he's my father damn. I don't know what he gone do when he finds out how heavy me and my boo been rocking. I met my baby Hakeem through my homegirl Tommie. I think they call him some crazy ass nickname like Zap or some shit like that. One thing I know for sure is that I like him, and I like him a lot.

My baby's fine ass is roughly about 6 feet tall, and he has muscles in all the right places to. His dreads swing to the middle of his back which are wildly untamed, but I like his rouged look. He spares no cost when it comes to me either, the boy breaks bread. We only been dating for a few months now, but he's already, talking about moving in together. I'm kind of skeptical because I don't want to be moving too fast. While we were sitting around waiting on Tommie's date to pull up, I confided in him about what happened earlier with bro.

"Man, baby I was so freaked out today when I pulled up and the detectives were surrounding the crib," I said as I exaggerated trying to make the story sound more interesting. "Word," he said as he listened in content before Tommie entered the room. "Hey girl hey," I said to Tommie, taking my attention off Hakeem. "Hey," she replied dryly as she sat down and started flicking through the channels. "Any word from your boo-thang girl," I asked her as I glanced down at my watch. "Dang girl you thirsty, he'll be in a minute."

Then I redirected my attention back at Hakeem because clearly, she wasn't in the mood and quite frankly neither was I. Right before I had a chance to speak, Hakeems phone rang so I started playing a game on my phone. "Aye yo, let's bounce." I really wanted my boo all to myself, but Tommie insisted on her and her guy friend tagging along. We drove separate cars and dinner went better than I thought.

Me and Tommie had a couple of Margarita's that were strong to. She and I laughed it up while the guys talked business. After dinner we said our goodbyes and went our separate ways. The night was still young so me and my baby decided to catch a late-night movie. The movie was hilarious, I laughed until I was in tears. I started feeling my drink so I dropped some popcorn in his lap on purpose, so I could see how well he was hanging. As I grabbed the popcorn kernels from his lap, I felt his manhood jump and boy was it huge.

After the movie let out, I pulled back in front of Tommie's crib to drop him back off. "So, what's good? You coming home with me tonight?" I paused. "I really do like you Hakeem and..." Before I had a chance to finish my sentence, he interrupted me. "I like you to Little Mama, so what's the problem? We both grown, what you trying to send a nigga home with blue balls?" Silence. "Hakeem, you're moving too fast. I'm just not ready to take it to the next level I hope you understand."

He looked at me and smiled then he kissed me on the cheek. "It's cool Shayna, I'll yield." As badly as I wanted to straddle him, I knew that it would be best if I made him wait. "Okay thank you Hakeem, I'll talk to you tomorrow." He kissed me on the cheek before he got out my ride. I checked my mirrors and I sped off. As soon as I got in the crib I went straight to my room, but not before I heard Mike's ass calling after me. He has always acted more like a father figure than my big brother. "Shayna get in here."

I walked in the room and as soon as I opened the door he started tripping. "Shayna, where have you been?

Who you been out with this late?" I sighed, kind of irritated because he was blowing my little buzz. "Damn, bro if you must know I was out with my home girl, Tommie from school." He stared at me as if he was searching for answers. "Yeah, okay Shay." I wasn't too sure if he believed me or not, but I left before he started doing the most. As soon as I got upstairs, I slipped out of my clothes, jumped in the shower, threw on my PJ's and laid down. Just as I was about to get comfortable in bed, my phone rang, and it was Hakeem, so I answered.

"What's up Ha?" "Nothing much, baby. I just wanted to hear your voice. What you got going on Ma?" "Shit really, just getting ready, for bed." "Aw, yeah. Okay cool. You gone dream about me?" "Yes, baby for sure." "Yeah, okay cool, I'm gone hit you tomorrow." "Hey Ha, we still on for tomorrow?" Silence. "What kind of question is that? If I said I got you, then I got you." "Okay cool, can't wait." (yarning) "Good night, sweet dreams." "Goodnight, Ha."

Falling for Him: Shayna

I went straight home after school excited about my date with Ha. As soon as I walked in door, I jumped in the shower, and got dressed. I was trying to look effortlessly cute, so I threw on a pink tightfitting jogger set that my sister-in-law had copped me, so you already know it was designer. I matched my outfit with my McQueen's and tings. I sprayed every inch of my body with some smell good and I started feeling myself.

While I was humming, that Ric Ross song, "Bag of Money," Ice, crept up on me and scared me. "Hey sis, where you headed looking all gorgeous?" I paused. "Oh hey Ice. Nowhere really just downtown, for a little minute, with some friend's, why what's up?" Silence. "Some friends huh? What friends is that?" Irritated I rolled my eyes. "Man, Ice what's with the third degree? First bro, now you to. Damn you supposed to be the cool one." Ice looked at me strange, "Yeah okay, my bad I was just checking on you miss attitude. I see you on one, so I'll fall back boo."

I paused. "Naw, it's cool Ice, if I tell you something you have to promise not to tell." A bit hesitant she answered, "Okay, girl what's up? You know I got your back, I wouldn't betray you. But let me ask you this sissy, are you pregnant?" "Girl boom, no I'm not pregnant Ice," I said as I looked around for some wood to knock on. "Let me find out you trying to pour salt on me Ice." "Well, if you're not pregnant, then what's up?" Silence. "Nah Ice it's nothing like that. I'm just going shopping with this new guy that I been seeing for a couple of months now. I really like him, and I think he might be the one."

"Oh, so you do, do you?" "Yeah, I really do." "Well, when am I going to meet this fella?" Silence. "Uh, maybe today." "Today." "Um yeah, he'll be here in a minute." "Aw, so you think you're slick huh. You waited until your brother went to therapy to have oh boy come and scoop you up?" I smiled, "Well you know how he is Ice...please don't tell him." "Okay Shay, I got you." The doorbell rang and I started getting nervous. "Sis, can you check the camera and buzz him in the gate please." Ice glanced at her phone. "Sure thing, I got you. By the way if your brother hears of this, I plead the fifth," Ice said as she went downstairs to open the door for me.

I checked myself in the mirror, making sure everything was in place. I heard them downstairs getting acquainted, so I took my time. "Hey what's good. I'm

Hakeem, Shayna, here?" Silence. "Yes, she is. She'll be right down. May I offer you a cold beverage while you wait?" "Uh, yeah a beer if you got it." "Uh, okay well let me go and check to see if we have any in the fridge," Isis said as she disappeared in the kitchen and opened the fridge. She hollered back at him, "Sorry, we're all out. Can I get you something else Hakeem?"

Startled by his presence, she jumped. "Yes, you can." Ice smiled awkwardly, "Aw hey, you scared me. I thought you were still in the living room." Silence consumed the room. "So, your name is Isis, right?" Feeling a bit uncomfortable she answered, "Uh, yeah." "This is a very nice crib, that you have yourself. Do you and Shay live here alone?" "Uh, no I stay with my husband and he's the police." "Aw, okay really? What district is he working out of?"

"5th precinct, why'd you ask? "Just making small talk." Then he reached down and grabbed her by her waist side, but she removed his hands quickly. "Wait a minute. What do you think you are doing?" She stepped back out of his reach. "Shayna's my sister, and I'm a happily married woman?" Hakeem looked at her kind of eerie, "Are you really happy Isis?" She paused. "What kind of question is that? Yes, Of course I'm happy and you're making me feel very uncomfortable." Walking in the kitchen, I could feel the unwanted tension in the air, so I broke the silence. "Hey guys. What are you two talking about? Were you guys' chit chatting about me?"

"Aw there you are Shay. We're not talking about nothing." Silence. "Uh…Okay Ice." "Hey, baby. You're looking mighty sexy right now." I blushed. "Aw, thanks baby, you don't look so bad yourself." On our way out the door, he kissed Ice on the hand, real gentleman like. "Nice to meet you, um, Isis, right?" "Yeah, you as well Hakeem. Shay call me," said Ice as she snatched her hand. "Okay got you. See you later sis," I said as we headed to the car.

At the Mall: Shayna

While we were out blowing cash, a few hoes tried approaching my man, but he dismissed them. Money wasn't an issue at all that day. He copped me a bad ass orange, Fendi bag. That bag ran him for about $3,700. I think he spent about 6 or 7 bands, easily on me. I didn't have to come out of my pocket for nothing. Every item I grabbed he paid for without a question. He was like the man of my dreams. I had never been spoiled by any man other than my brother. After we finished shopping, we ate at a quaint little, Italian restaurant. Later, that night, we rolled around just enjoying each other's company.

He didn't even try to get fresh with me, after dropping all that bread (cash) and that was impressive. After we hung out, he took me back home, like the gentleman he was. "I would invite you in baby, but my brother be tripping." "I understand Lil Mama, it's all good." He kissed me one last time before I got of his ride, and he drove off. I punched in the keycode then I walked up the driveway. I had to stop a few times because my bags kept slipping from my hands. When I finally got in the house, I sounded the alarm. Then I rushed up to my room so Mike wouldn't catch me.

I was excited, so I called Ice. "Hello," Ice answered. "Hey sis, where are you? Where's Mike?" "I'm down the hall from you Shay and Michael's downstairs," "Are you, okay? What's up?" I smiled. "Girl nothing, I just wanted to tell you how my day went with my boo, that's all. I didn't really want nothing." She paused. "Aw that's all? Shay I'm super exhausted can this wait until the morning?" I looked at my phone and I frowned because that was not the reaction that I was hoping for. "Alright sure Ice, goodnight." That conversation kind of rubbed me the wrong way. If I didn't know any better, I would think that she was hating. I shrugged it off and went to sleep.

Dodging Sis: Isis

The next day I left out earlier than anticipated for my daily run. I was really trying to dodge Shay because I still didn't know how to break the news to her about her guy. My day is always pretty much the same. I get up, wash up, get dressed, drink my protein shake, and go for a jog. Afterwards I sign in and complete my online coursework. I had been doing a lot of thinking about volunteering at a law firm lately to. After finishing up my homework, I cooked dinner and then I checked on Mike's stubborn ass.

While I was in the kitchen cooking Shay came in. She looked so happy that I couldn't bring myself to telling her about her boyfriend. I reasoned with myself that maybe I had misinterpreted his actions. Besides that, if Mike ever got word of this, it would be a mess. So, to avoid all the drama, I decided to forget the whole thing ever happened. Besides I don't have to be around him like that so it's no harm no foul.

It's Lit: Shayna

The weekend came, and it was finally my baby's birthday. He was throwing an, all white, birthday bash, on some big ass yacht. That shit gone be rocking to. Hakeem sent a driver to pick me and Tommie up. I had to be cute so, I wore my all white, strapless, tight-fitting dress, with my mint-colored laced Dior's, identical to my clutch. I wore my hair pulled back in a fish tail ponytail which made me look exotic. I knew I must've been looking nice because as soon as I came downstairs, Ma and Ice started clapping. "Thanks, ladies."

"You're welcome, super star." My smile expanded because it really meant a lot hearing those words coming from Ice. "So where are you going all dolled up, Shay?" Hesitantly, I answered, "Aw nowhere spectacular Ma, I'm just going to a party with my girl Tommie." I didn't want to go into any specifics with my her because she would only worry and tell my brother, but I filled Ice in earlier on the details. I let them snap a few flicks before heading out the door. I got to the end of the driveway, and I feasted my eyes on a champagne colored, stretched Escalade truck.

As soon I was near, the driver opened my door, and the first face that I saw was Tommie. She looked nice in her white linen pants suit with her two-tone bustier and platformed heels. We gave each other an approving smile before we popped the cork to the champagne bottle. She poured me a drink and we made a toast. Arriving to the party fashionably late, and all I heard was the sounds ripping through the speakers. The name Zap was written in bold, red letters on the side of the boat. As soon as we boarded, I scanned the room for Ha, but I didn't see him anywhere.

I was getting mad action to, but I didn't want to come off as being disrespectful, so I kept my cool. I was sitting around enjoying the tunes when Tommie got up and excused herself. While I was waiting, patiently for her to reappear, a light brown guy with long cornrows approached me. He seemed flashy yet smooth, he had three or four chains wrapped around his neck, that were full of ice. He had green eyes that looked like they glow in the dark. He had gold fronts but surprisingly he looked good with them. I looked down, noticing his diamond AP, which was impressive to.

He looked at me and smiled but I shied away. "Damn, Ma you fine." Before I had a chance to reply, Tommie came up out the cut. "Yo, I don't think the birthday boy would appreciate you shooting your shot at his girl." I looked at her and frowned, because she was doing too much, but I didn't say a word. "His girl, huh? Well, he needs to keep his bitch on a leash then," oh boy said as he looked at me with lust in his eyes. Refusing to lose my cool, I just laughed.

Next thing I know, Tommie's drink was landing in his face. Stunned by her actions, he balled up his fist, to strike her. "You're lucky you affiliated, but you better watch it because you won't get another pass," he stated coldly. He smiled, as he reached for a napkin and wiped the contents of the drink from his face. Then he turned to face me. "My apologies Miss lady. Zap that's my man's, but if he fucks up come holler at me. They call me Sticks, Ma," he said with a smile.

He could tell I was unimpressed by the way that I frowned. Then he shoved his business card directly in my face, but I let it hit the floor. Shortly after that he disappeared in the crowd. As soon as he was out of ear sight Tommie started grilling me. "What was all that Shayna? You into rappers now, too?" With my face all twisted up, I said, "Rappers, what are you talking about?" Silence. "Yeah, alright, Shayna don't forget who you came here with," Tommie said as she sucked her teeth like she was checking me. To avoid causing a scene, I didn't even respond.

Not much longer after that I saw Paco, Tommie's, date from the other night in the crowd. He stopped and spoked to me, but he didn't even acknowledge her. I could tell something must've taken place the way her face scrunched up when she saw him. There were a couple fat guys trying to holler at her, but she shrugged them all off. I stood up and walked towards the bar and saw my cousin Chance. He was looking like a boss. I hadn't seen him in years.

As soon as he saw me, we hugged. I looked around and made sure Tommie wasn't around before I told him what went down with Mike. I didn't want her all in my family business, besides that I wasn't really feeling her tonight anyways. Cuz was shocked by the news. "Who you here with Shay?" "My home girl, Tommie. You're not going to tell Mike, are you? You know how he gets." "Naw, it's cool baby cuz, I got you. You're all grown up and you still scared of big bro, huh?" I shrugged my shoulders, and we shared a laugh.

"Well, I'm about to cut out. So, tell your brother, I said to hit my line Shay." "Okay, I got you cuz but don't rat me out." He laughed. "Rodger that, later blood." After the bartender refilled my drink, I walked back over to my seat and sat down. I was staring in my phone looking on social media when my baby walked up looking like he had the key to the streets. He wore some, all white, Off-White distressed denims, with a blue and white Vlone button up. The sole of his shoes was red, and he was icier than a freezer, so I already knew how he was coming.

I could tell he had his dreads freshly done to. "Hey, you." I smiled, "What's up Ha?" He looked me up and down. "You, Ma, you. You look mighty edible over there," he said as he licked his lips. I blushed. "Where, Tommie at?" "Not sure baby, me and her got split up. I was too busy trying to find you." "Well, now that you found me, what up?" I stood to my feet and whispered in his ear, "Whatever you want to be up," I spoke seductively as I wrapped my arm around his. Then he led me in the back in a secluded section of the yacht.

I was sipping, gracefully while nodding my head to the sounds. Fireworks were twinkling in the sky. The air was perfect, and the mood was just right. While we were laughing and talking, I became distracted when I noticed a group of girls surrounding some guy that looked to be of importance. He drank out of an Ace's bottle and his demeanor screamed money. The women flocked to him. He had a young and rugged look about himself. He had tattoo's everywhere, including his face. Ha noticed my distraction and excused himself.

He swindled through the crowd, making small talk with a few, as he headed to the bar to get us another bottle. While I was holding on to the rail, I continued to admire the ocean and its beauty. I glanced from the water to the sky when suddenly, I felt a hand touching mines. I smiled, before I spun around because I loved my man's touch. To my surprise, it was dude that was drinking on that gold bottle. His smile was flawless, minus the gap in between his two fronts. He was quite handsome, light brown, and clean shaved.

His voice was raspy, but he spoke clearly. "What's up Ma, I'm Lucky and you are?" I was hesitant at first. For a moment I had forgotten all about Ha. Then I cleared my throat, "I'm sorry but I'm already taken," I said as I moved my hand from his and turned away. I could tell that he wasn't used to rejection. "That's fine Ma, who isn't. Call me when your problem not around," he said arrogantly. Then he slid his card underneath my palm before he walked off. I couldn't help but to smile.

As soon as I turned around, I noticed Ha was headed back. Thinking fast, I slid the number in my bag.

"Baby, I missed you. What took you so long?" He glanced at me then he darted his eyes at dude. "You missed me huh?" "Yeah, baby I missed you." He smiled slyly, "It's all good. I know they want what they can't have," he said before he kissed me. I guess that was his way of marking his territory and letting dude know I was off limits. I had a little buzz from the champagne. I called Ma and scripted her telling her I was spending the night with Tommie, but I was really planning on staying with Ha's fine ass. The party ended around 4 or 5 in the morning. Once all his guest were gone, Ha and I stayed on the boat. We talked and we sipped champagne all night long.

Ha shared intimate details on his troubled childhood, which truly broke my heart. The more he opened up to me, the closer I felt to his soul. That was the night I finally decided to share my world with him. I felt so connected to him, I just couldn't resist. That was the night that I gave him a piece of my pie. That was the night that we first made love. I'm know virgin, but he really took his time with me. That night was magical. From that day forward I yearned to be in his presence and to feel his touch. That was a night that I will live to cherish forever.

TWENTY-FOUR

Months Later: Ghost

I was almost back to my old self, and it felt pretty good. The physical therapist told me that I was progressing faster than she anticipated. Ice ass been moodier than usual so despite her abortion threats, I know she's still pregnant. She finally stopped questioning me about my nickname which was good. I had another week left before I was cleared to drive so Chance slid on me and we chopped it up in front of the crib. We talked about the night of the shooting, and he told me that he had gotten shot in his shoulder and his foot. He was shot in the chest to, but the vest stopped the lodging of the bullet.

"Man, blood I'm not gone lie to you, Ghost. Moms must've covered me with her angel wings, straight up." "Yeah man, we definitely caught a blessing that day. I thought I was gone, man." "Yeah, man word." "That was one crazy ass night. We lucky we made it out that jam alive, on Shorty." "You ain't never lied cuz. Ghost, man that was like a scene out of a gangster movie. I saw your boy Fly get hit a couple times to, but his bitch ran up and she started blasting going crazy fool. She stretched oh dude." "I haven't gotten around to hollering at them either, but I'm gone check Fly's temperature one time and make sure they straight."

"Ghost man, his girl a beast, though blood. I wish, my B.M. (Baby mother) was a goon like Shorty, straight up. No, fuck that, she would probably shoot my ass, for cheating, I take that shit back." "Hell yeah, Chance you a fool." Silence. "No, but seriously, cuz you know how scorn women be, she a mess around and shoot me in the dick." We laughed. "Man, cuz why, the fuck those trolling ass pigs (police) called me by my nickname in front of my bitch." "Get the fuck out of here. Swear." "Hell yeah, the bitch been in her feelings ever since. She been talking really greasy threatening to kill my seed." I hit the blunt and passed it to cuz.

"Damn, man that shit fucked up, boy." "I told her ass, that shit is unforgiveable, ain't no coming back from that." Silence. "Wait Ghost man, so, your girl pregnant?" "Yeah, as far as I know she is." "That's what's up, congratulation's man, many blessings cuz." "Thanks blood." "Oh yeah and um I heard about your boy Money getting smoked. My condolences fam, I know he was like family to you." I grabbed the blunt from Chance's hand and I took a hit.

"Man, hell yeah...thanks man." I started cough uncontrollably while I was hitting the blunt. "Slow down Ghost man, shit." I laughed while I was still choking. "Fuck you cuz...Aye man I had to check that nigga Money before he checked out. But yeah, it's fucked up what happened to him to him though." "Damn, man thought that was your boy, can't trust nobody." "Yep, it's smooth but, oh yeah how was that party last night? Everything check out?" "Aw yeah, everything was straight." "Alright man cool." "Aye yo Ghost man, I'm gone holler back fam I got to go grab your little cousin something to eat." "Okay man, I'll hit your line when I put everything in motion," I said to him before I jumped out his ride and walked in the crib.

Mood Swings: Isis

It's only been 4 months and I'm already big as a whale. I'm so over this pregnancy thing, I feel hideous. Mike's lying ass, keep gassing me up, telling me how beautiful I look and that makes me so mad. I'm even moodier than usual. Every little thing that Mike does, aggravates me except for when he rubs my stomach and my feet. That always puts me to sleep. Sometimes I wake up in the middle of the night, having one of my weird cravings. My hormones got me so emotional, that I cry at a drop of a dime. Ma and Daddy stops by often to check up on me. I don't know what's been going on with Shayna because lately she's been missing in action.

On stressful days I go to the range and practice my skills. I'm even started my own, mini gun collection, that don't nobody know about. I didn't want Mike tripping, but I keep my pink Taser C2 on me. I had a taste for some pizza, so I ordered a shrimp pizza with extra anchovies, pineapples, and onions. An hour and some change later my delivery finally arrived. I waddled to the door anxiously and I buzzed him in the gate. I paid for my food, and I slammed the door in his face. I hurried to the kitchen while the food was still hot because I was starving. Halfway into my meal and Mike brings his raggedy ass in wreaking of weed.

"Look at my babies." I rolled my eyes. He came in, kissed me on the forehead, then he leaned down and kissed me on my belly. He stood to his feet and wiped the marinara sauce from the side of my mouth. "You want some baby?" "Naw, bay, ya'll go ahead. I'm tired I'm gone head on up to the room and jump in the shower. Want to come?" He looked at me and winked his eye, letting me know he was horny. "Sure, baby I'm right behind you," I managed to say with a mouth full of pizza. "Okay Ma." When I got in the bathroom, he was already in the shower. I brushed my teeth quickly and rinsed my mouth before I joined him.

I stripped down to my birthday suit. I hopped in the shower and his face lit up with glee. He grabbed me, pulled me close, and planted soft wet kisses all over me. He lifted me up carefully leaving my back against the faucet then he ate me up like a meal. I squirmed as I felt his moist lips on my pearl, while the water tickled all my spots. He tasted me until I couldn't take it anymore. Then he lifted one of my legs and he slid his member inside of me, while he bit down on my neck passionately. The deeper he dug inside of me, the more I cried out in ecstasy. I kissed him long and hard as he made my cookie's cream and we both came.

Afterwards we took turns washing each other up. When we got out of the shower, I dried him off and I dropped to my knees, no words were needed. I swallowed his remote while I glided my hands up and down his hard. I kissed his thighs as I played with his bottom bags. I bobbed my head up and down, matching my hand gesture. I continued that routine until I heard my baby yelling out in pleasure. "Shit." I slurped it all up in one gulp. I stood to my feet and kissed him on his cheek. When I turned around to head to the bedroom, he grabbed me by the arm. He kissed me one last time and we walked in our room. We cuddled the rest of the night. It felt great to feel wanted, appreciated, and loved. "I love you," I said in a gentle whisper before I dose off in his arms.

What A Night: Shayna

Me, and the bay been hanging tight, since his birthday. We did everything together. I barely even saw Tommie anymore other than class. I been meaning to call her, but I never got around to doing so. She was acting so funny the other night that I barely said two words to her now. Last time we spoke she seemed distant, and she kept throwing shade. I figured she was just jealous, so I fell back. I found myself thinking about Hakeem day in and day out. Lately, he's really been pushing the issue of us getting a crib. I told him I needed to finish school first and he agreed but I could tell he was salty though.

I think I finally met my match and boy does it feel good. We talked about everything. I didn't keep any secrets from him. I wanted him to learn the real me. He had been asking me all week what I wanted for my birthday. I couldn't think of anything, so I told him to surprise me. I know I'm going to have to think of an excuse to tell Ma, Mike, and Ice because they are going to assume, I would be spending my weekend with them. It's my birthday and I just wanted to do me for once. I did agree to letting them take me out to dinner because I wanted my gifts. The rest of the weekend is reserved for Ha. Ha had already slipped up and told me he had us some front row tickets to one of Tyler's plays.

He even threw me a couple grand a couple days ago so me and sis went shopping. She had already told me she was gone buy my birthday fit, so I had that covered. All that was left for me to do is to grab my shoes, my bag, and my accessories. She got me this fire ass, fuchsia Halston jumpsuit that hugs all my curves. "How would you like to pay for this ladies, cash or credit," asked the cashier. Isis laughed, "Cash sweetie, we don't do credit." I smiled. "Happy birthday little sis, that's from me and your bug ass brother." Ice peeled off all hundreds from in between two rubber bands like it was nothing. "Oh, and keep the change, you work on commission right." The cashier's mouth dropped.

"That's what I'm talking about sis; everything you do is like a boss. I want to be just like you when I grow up. That's why I hope everything works out with me and my boo." "Shay you're being silly, this little change is nothing and always remember anything a man do is extra make sure you always have your own. Now never mind that it's your birthday, baby." I was looking around the store when Ice called me on the other side of the room. "Shay come here really quick, you have to check out these, bad ass pumps. These shoes would go perfectly with that salt shaking ass fit you just got."

I rushed over trying to see what the fuss was. "OMG (Oh My God) Ice, I saw these same shoes in a magazine on Mary last week. These bitches a hit. How much are they?" She looked at me sideways before she spoke. "Just see if they have your size, boo. We don't price items. Bosses do what they want others do what they can." I shook my head and smiled. After the sales associate came back, with my size, I tried the shoes on, and they fit me to perfection, so I had her to box them up. While we were walking back to the register this pretty ass Balmain clutch was calling my name.

"Excuse me Miss let me get that bag to," I said as I pointed to the manikin that was holding it. Lucky for me it was the last on in stock and I caught it on sale. I was good though I had been saving the money Ha had been giving me, plus, I had been cuffing a few hundred's off back whenever he leaves his money out. I looked over at sis then back at the register. I counted $2,500 and I handed it to the cashier. It felt good not having to ask Ice for anything. Quite as kept, I admired Ice, she is a lady with substance, and she keeps all my secrets. She really is the only one that I trust.

She stays fly to, even on her bad day she can put a pretty chick to shame. "Thanks Ice you always come through in a clutch." She smiled, "Girl please it's nothing." After I got my change from the cashier, we left the store and headed home. I must admit I was exhausted, but I couldn't wait to get my day started. As soon as we got home, I hopped in the shower. Ma and Mike had to work overtime so they told us that they would meet us at the restaurant downtown, which was fine for me. Isis got ready quick.

She looked radiant letting off a slight glow. She had on a bad ass tan colored pants suit, with Louie wedges, and her cylinder, shaped LV bag. She wore her hair pulled back in a ponytail with a swoop in the front. Her diamond stud earrings complimented her features to. I was applying my makeup when I heard her yelling my way. "I see you, Shay-Shay, come through sis, yes!" I smiled. "What…This old thing, Ice," I said as I spun around. Then I gave myself a once over in the mirror and I started making my cheeks clap. Then we both fell out in laughter. "Girl let's go; you are too much for me. You know we have reservations downtown and traffic is going to be crazy right? I grabbed my, "spend-the-night-bag" and we headed out. Ice hit the alarm and we hopped in our separate cars. Pulling off I trailed her to the spot, and we valeted. Then we strutted in the door like we owned the place.

TWENTY-FIVE

Birthday Delight: Shayna

This is going to be the best birthday ever I can feel it. I just wish I could've invited my man. When the greeter seated us, the first face that I saw was Ma. Now, of course everyone is here except for Mike's, late ass. To kick off the celebration, I ordered myself a Hennessey long island, Ma order a glass of wine, and Ice ordered a virgin daiquiri, while we waited on bro. We sat around shooting the breeze. Ma spoke first. "So, Ice, how do you feel? It's almost time for you to have my grandbaby." "Well Mama, actually I was terrified at first but now it's growing on me and I'm actually excited. I'm going to have a baby girl by the love of my life, which is such a blessing."

"Ice baby, I want to thank you for coming into our lives and helping to change my son for the better. I am so thankful that you and that stubborn son of mines are finally giving me a grandchild, I couldn't have asked for a better daughter-in-law," Ma said to Ice as she became teary eyed. "Yeah Ice, my niece is going to be spoiled rotten just like her Mommy." "Isn't that the truth." We laughed. Two drinks later, and in walks Mike. Now I must admit, Mike was looking spruce like it was his birthday. He had on a tailored made, navy blue Armani suit. His belt, shoes, tie, and handkerchief were made by Louie. As soon as he sat down as if on cue, the waiter approached our table with a bottle of Clicquot and 4 champagne glasses.

I smiled. We sat around talking. I looked up and saw Ice, grab Mike's hand and she placed it on her belly. She spoke with glee, "Baby do you feel our daughter kicking me?" Silence. "Yeah, of course I feel our son, footprints." We shared a laugh, then they got into a playful gender debate but nothing to serious though. I cleared my throat trying to redirect the attention back on me. "Sorry birthday girl, we'll behave," said Ice. "Yeah, my bad sis. Here," Mike said as he shoved a gift box in my face. When I looked inside, I saw the most, elegant, silver, Gucci bangle, watch, that I had ever seen. Underneath the face of the watch it was engraved, "Much love sis, from Ice & Mike." That right there brought tears to my eyes.

"Thank you both so much. It's beautiful, can one of you guys put it on for me?" "With pleasure Shay. Now you can stop asking me to borrow my watch, girlie," Ice said playfully as she reached down and snapped the watch on my wrist. We laughed. "I guess," I whined with my lips poked out. "Just playing Shay you already know the vibes." Moments later, Ma hands me a card, along with a larger gift box. Enclosed was an engraved jewelry box that read, "Love, Hope, Life, and Eternity, you are the best part of my very being."

Inside of the jewelry box was a pair of yellow gold, diamond, tear drop earrings. "Aw Thanks Mommy," I said tearing up. "Aw man y'all got a gangster crying," I teased, and we laughed. "You are very welcome my precious little angel." Then Mike's ignorant ass interrupted, "Yo man, what's with all of the waterworks is this a birthday celebration or a funeral?" I wiped away my tears and playfully punched him the arm, "Shut up Q-tip head." We all laughed again. Mike grabbed his head with a look of confusion on his face. "It's ok baby, I love your Q-tip head," said Ice as she kissed him on his forehead. "Uh, yuck, get a room."

Ma smiled as she enjoyed the atmosphere. The waitress reappeared and took our orders. When she walked away, we continued our conversation. That night we ate good, cried, and had a good time. The dinner prepared by the chef was scrumptious. The waitress offered us dessert, but we declined. While I was glancing down at my watch in amazement, Kels appeared out of nowhere, with a microphone in hand. I smiled as he sang the song, "Forever." By now, everyone in the restaurant had their eyes glued on us. Mike, hands Ice a single white rose. Then he looked her in the eyes.

He grabbed her by the hand while Kel's hummed the rest of his tunes. Then Ice spoke, "Michael what is all of this?" Ignoring her question, he reached down into his pants pocket, and he pulled out a tiny black box. Then he got down on one knee. "Ice, I was incomplete until I met you. Baby let's make this official, will you be my ride or die, and marry me?" By now the entire restaurant is snaping flicks and recording the entire engagement. There isn't a dry eye in sight. Ice sat there, as she clutched her chest. Tears rolled off her face.

She looked up at him and looked all around before she screamed, "Yes." Mike smiled. Then he placed a gigantic, rock on her finger and they shared a kiss. Mike stood to his feet, he looked around the room and he shouted, "A yo, she said yes, my girl said yes!" He lifted his champagne glass with glee. Everyone clapped in unity. "Congratulations, Mike and Isis," Kel's said. "It's a fiancé," I shouted with joy as I raised her hand showcasing her ring. "I love you baby. I love you so much," she said as she cried.

They embraced one another as they kissed passionately. Shortly after the waitress reappeared with a slice of strawberry cheesecake and a lit candle. They sang happy birthday to me, I smiled, and I made a wish. Ma was crying so hard that we could barely understand what she was saying. "Congratulations you too. I love you both," Ma sobbed. "Thanks Mama." Kels, tapped Mike on his shoulder. "Congratulations again, Ghost hit my line with the wedding details." "Thanks, my boy. Gotcha." Then Kels walked away.

While I was admiring Ice, I heard a commotion, so I turned my head for a split second, trying to see what the uproar was. It seemed to be some sort of disturbance coming from the front of the restaurant so being the noisy person that I am I tuned right in. High off love, Mike and Ice were staring into each other's eyes. Ma watched in amazement as she looked at the lovebirds. While I was watching the drama unfold, some big burley dude stormed through the door, demanding to be seated. "Check the roster again," he demanded.

To avoid confrontation, the manager intervened, "Sure sir no problem, sir. Your name is?" He looked down at the clipboard then back at the man. Nervously he spoke, "Sorry sir, I do apologize but you're not on the list for this evening." That's when everything unraveled. The next thing that I know that same guy who barged in, sent the greeter flying to the other side of the room. Mike looked up, he stood to his feet, and reached for his gun. "Fuck." Mike cursed himself when he realized he had left his gun in the car. Next thing I know one of the guys shot in the air which got everyone's attention.

Everything else after that, was pretty much a blur. All I know is three men, that I had never seen before, rushed, straight to our table. The restaurants, security guards tried their best to stop them, but they were shot in pursuit. Mike felt helpless without his gun. Everybody was screaming and panicking. By this time gunshots were spraying in every direction. Pop…pop…pop…Bang…. BOOM! Mike tried covering Ma and Ice by hovering over them as he hollered for me to get down. I ducked as I tried to hide underneath the table. Then I heard one of the unfamiliar men yell in Mike's direction, "Get at me nigga, you know what it is." Mike ran towards them, but he paused when he upped his pipe (gun).

Mike looked back at Ma and Ice. He saw blood and he panicked. He felt around on his person before rushing towards the assailants. I came from underneath the table for a minute to look around. I saw Ma and Ice and I waved them over. But they didn't move so I made a dash for the door. As soon as I reached for the handle, I was stopped, abruptly, when I felt somebody grabbed me by my hair, and slung around placing a bag over my face. I panicked. The man who captured me, tossed me over his shoulder and yelled, "We got her."

"Help, Mike please. Help." Mike ran in their direction ready to risk it all. "Man, put my motherfuckin' sister down, man." Seeing Mikes bravery gave one of the customers the boost of courage that he needed, so he charged in their direction before being hit by multiple bullets. A gun was pointed in Mike's face. "Gone play hero Ghost, you gone wake up in a casket for sure." I heard a man with a deep sounding voice say. Mike stopped dead in his tracks. "Yeah, that's what I thought, pussy." "Mike please help me. I'm scared Mike please." "I'm gone see you soon, clown. You trying to play God? You know it's, up, right? Yo, tell your family to make funeral arrangements," Mike shouted.

He paused. "Only funeral being held will be yours pussy," said dude before exiting the door with me on his back, unwillingly. Mike ran back towards Ma and Ice, "Ma, Ice baby are you okay?" Seeing blood soiled on their clothes caused Mike to be alarmed. Mike looked up and screamed, "Somebody call the motherfuckin' ambulance, we need some help now please!"

Outside: Shayna

As soon as we got outside, I felt a breeze followed by a loud noise, resembling some gunshots pop...pop.... pop...pop. I tried to bite a plug out of dude arm who had me. "Shit," he yelled when my teeth pierced his skin. I kicked and scratched him util he put me down. He placed a metal object on the back of my head and forced me to walk in front of him. I elbowed him and I ran. I heard car horns honking as I was running in what I believe to be the street.

"Watch where you're going stupid bitch," a passerby shouted. I yanked the bag off my head, and I kept running before I tripped and broke one of my heels. I got up and started running again. "Help, somebody please help me," I screamed. I turned around for a minute, and I was yanked by my hair. Then I heard the same voice from earlier say, "You a dumb ass bitch." Then he backhanded me something serious and I fell to my knees, crying hysterically. One of the guys placed another bag over my head. "No, please let me go. No." Then he lifted from the ground with my feet dangling in the air.

I was kicking, scratching, and screaming until I was thrown in the back of somebody's smelly trunk and then they sped off. I overheard various voices talking, none of which I recognized. I heard one of the men asking another, "Well what are we going to do with the little bitch?" I couldn't hear the response all I know, is, whatever the guy said was amusing to the rest of them. My hands were still free, so I removed the bag from my face. Then I fumbled around in the trunk trying to find anything that I could use as a weapon. They must've been some amateurs because on the crime shows I watch they always tie up their victims' hands.

While I was rumbling around in the trunk, I came across a spray can, that I knew would somehow come in handy. Thank God, I had been sneaking around smoking weed with Ha, because I keep a lighter on me. A feeling of guilt entered my mind. I could only imagine what my man must be thinking after I stood him up. We came to a complete stop, and I kicked off my shoes when I heard the car door slam.

While I was getting into motion, I heard footprints that sounded like they were heading my way. Then one of them lunatics said, "That's one pretty little bitch. I think I'm gone fuck her before we off her." They laughed. As soon as the trunk door opened, I squeezed the button on the spray can while my lighter was sparked, and I lit him and one of his friends up. I heard them screaming in agony. The mixture of the chemicals irritated my lungs causing me to cough but it also made a torching effect. I looked around and I hopped out of the trunk. Then I sprinted. "Oh, shit, my face." "You're one dead ass bitch," the other one shouted. I ran, trying my best to get away.

Unbelievable: Mike

20 minutes passed, and the ambulance finally arrived. They hauled off the wife, Mama, and the others who were injured. I was halfway out of my mind when one of the officers approached me, "Sir, did you get a look at the perpetrators?" "No officer it all happened so fast. I couldn't get any visuals. I think I'm still in shock," I lied because street business is street business. "Well sir, we are here to serve and protect. We have some of our best men, out here on the prowl looking for the assailants as we try to bring forth justice." "Thanks."

My pride was crushed. I couldn't believe somebody had the audacity to come in my city and fuck with what's, mines. I was staring into space, trying to think of a master plan. The officer continued asking questions as if I was at fault. I know that I need to check on Ma, Ice, and the baby but I have some unfinished business to handle first. I need to make some calls. After the slicks (police) were out of eyesight, I left out of the restaurant. I jumped into my ride and spent off.

I had some of my homies, grab Shayna, Ma, and Ice's cars from the lot. Luckily, I had a copy of all their key's. I had them drop off the cars to one of my homies lots that was close by. I couldn't take a chance letting anybody know where we lived, especially after all this fuck shit that's been going on. I went straight over to my man Chop crib, to grab some burners (burn out phone). I couldn't get rid of the other line yet in case any of the family called. I used the burners for outgoing calls only.

Soon as I grabbed the new line, I hit up the team and demanded an emergency meeting, they already knew, that it had to have been urgent. I gave them the time and the Lolo (location) before ending the call. I stopped on the block and grabbed a couple quarters of that strong (hydro) because I needed to calm my nerves. Then I ran into the corner store and grabbed a few empties (blunts). I twisted (rolled) one up, as I rode in silence, without even so much as the music playing. I hit the blunt hard and headed over to, the hospital.

I walked in and went straight to the information desk demanding to see my girls. Then I turned around and I followed the signs to the chapel that was down the hall. I needed God, now more than ever. It had been years since I stepped foot in a church. I talked to him for about thirty minutes or so. It was like a burden had been lifted off my shoulders. I parted with my faith a long time ago when I was forced in the streets after my dad split. I been trying to stay out the way but now these clowns are forcing my hand. They are about to unleash a monster that I had buried away. They don't won't these demons inside of me to hit these streets.

Running for My Life: Shayna

I don't have a clue where I am. All I know is we're somewhere close to a cemetery, which freaks me out. I always hated cemeteries since I was a kid. The area seemed woodsy which reminded me of one of those scary ass Jason or Freddy, flicks. I ran into the woods, hoping to make it to the other side of the road. The more that, I ran the more hopeless, that I became. I tripped a few times over leaves, sticks and unknown objects. I even fell, twice, one of the times I scraped my knee and my hand on what felt like a log.

It was dark out now, so it was kind of hard to see clearly. I heard one of the kidnapper's footsteps, so I picked up my pace. I ran faster, until I found a big enough tree to hide behind. I tried to slow down my breathing patterns so they wouldn't hear me. I peeked my head around the tree as I heard one of them yelling closely after me, "Come on out, I won't hurt you." I covered my hands with my mouth to try an escape the sounds. "You're really starting to piss me the fuck off. Keep playing and I'm gone burry your ass alive." Petrified I cried. My heart was beating extremely fast.

As soon as I thought the close was clear I made a dash for it. I ran as I tried to wipe away my tears, which caused my eyes to burn. Blurry vision and all I continued running. I heard another voice yelling, but this time it was different than the one before, "Come on out. It's okay Shay. We're not going to hurt you." Him calling me by my name scared me even more. I hid behind another tree trying not to be seen. I wanted so badly, to call Mike and Ha. I know that one of them would save me. I cried my eyes out unsure of my fate. While, I was spacing, out, I nearly fainted when I felt an unfamiliar hand grab my arm forcefully. "Got her," he yelled. It took everything in me to hold myself up as my knees started to buckle. I felt weak. With the little strength that I had left, I screamed, and I tried to fight my way free, but he was too strong.

I figured it was now or never so I bit him as hard as I possibly could. My bite must've stung him because it caused him to unhand me, and he used his other hand to cover up the gash on his arm. "Ah! You crazy ass, nutty, bitch," he shouted. I spit out his flesh and I started back running again. I didn't get very far before I ran into another one of the assailants. He grabbed me up, in one, swoop and threw me over his shoulder. I continued screaming, kicking, and biting him wherever I could, but he just wouldn't let up. Instead, he hollered, "Not this time bitch." I cried out, "Please let me go. What do you want from me?" No response. Once we were back to where we started from, they placed another bag over my head. This time they gagged me only leaving me enough air to breathe.

Can't Catch a Break: Mike

Tears slid down my cheeks, as I started to pray. I stood up, wiped away my tears and headed towards the receptionist desk. She was finally off the phone when I made my way back. She typed something in the computer and handed me a slip with some room numbers written on it. Then I disappeared down the hall and hopped on the elevator. I stopped at Ma's room first which made me want to punch a hole in the wall. Seeing my mother, the woman that gave birth to me, hooked to all those tubes, was killing me. The doctor came in immediately asking me who I was, and I told him. "We've done all that we could do except for surgery to prevent the hemorrhaging. We need your consent to try and save her damaged organ."

I found out that Ma had got shot in her stomach and because the bullet had not lodged in a bone, it traveled piercing her kidney. "Where do I sign Doc?" He handed me the consent form and I signed it before he walked away. "I'm so sorry Ma. I love you," I whispered in her ear. I stayed with her until she was hauled off for surgery. I left but not before leaving my number with her nurse. Feeling defeated, I glided my feet down the hall, and hopped back on the elevator heading towards Ice's room. As soon as I got to her door, I was greeted by one of the nurses who had just finished checking her vitals.

"One moment sir, I will page the Doctor for you." When she reappeared, she was accompanied by a surgeon. She introduced herself as Doctor Romero, "You are Mike I presume." Nervously, I answered, "Yes mam." I had a puzzled look on my face wondering how she knew who I was. "Your wife asked for you when she came in complaining that she had some abdominal discomfort." "Is my baby, okay? Please tell me my baby is going to be okay Doc please," I said as I searched their faces for answers. She paused. "You are the child's biological father, correct?" Silence. "Yes, yes, of course, I am. What kind of question is that?"

"Sir I regret to inform you, that your wife miscarried. We ran some test, but we were unable to locate the heartbeat of the fetus. Removal of the fetus was the only option, to save your wife's life." It was at that very moment that I could no longer hold back my tears. Life's rollercoaster seems to be spiraling out of control. I couldn't understand why my life was full of such turmoil. I wiped my face as the pain was eating me up inside. While I was deep in thought, the doctor walked away. I snapped back into reality when I felt a hand resting on my shoulder which happened to be Isis's nurse. "Sir please try to pull it together for your wife." Silence. "Yeah, okay." I wasn't trying to hear none of that, somebody is going to have to pay for this in blood.

TWENTY-SIX

Where Am I?

They took me inside of some building that was totally out of my element. The placed reeked of stale urine. The smell was so bad that I had to fight back my urge to throw up, it sickened my stomach so. They took me up some stairs, threw me in a room and locked the door. There was a voice coming from the other end of the wall yelling for help which scared me even more. The room was cold. I sat there as I cried, rocking back and forth. I heard two male voices, that sounded like they had entered the room next door. I heard a woman's voice crying out, "No, please stop. I'm sorry. I didn't say anything I swear. Please don't hurt me."

Silence filled the room momentarily. "Shut up bitch you're lying," I heard a male say followed by what sounded like a slap. Then I heard a loud thump. "No, no, please I told you everything that I know. No...I'm begging you... Please don't kill me. I'm sorry. I'll do anything." A counted a total of 5 gunshots that were fired causing me to jump almost out of my skin. Afterwards, I didn't hear another peep from the female's voice. Shortly after that, I heard some heavy footstep's that seemed to be approaching. Then I heard a male speaking with a Caribbean sounding accent, "Grab the girl." The door opened and closed quick. My skin started to crawl, and I flinched when he grabbed me.

Play Time Over: Ghost

I called up my savages and everybody showed up, ready. I even had a cleaner close by for human disposal. "Play time over, anything goes. If anyone wants to bag down, now will be your chance, no hard feelings." LaLa, was the first to speak, "Man fam you already know how we bumming. Let's do this Papi," she smiled. I nodded in acknowledgement. I introduced the team, LaLa, Seven, Pac Man, Fly, Murder, Chance, Trig, Popeye, Snake, and Chase. "Yo, they shot my OG, killed my baby and kidnapped my little sister. I'm out for blood. Any questions?" Silence.

Murder asked in his Bronx accent, "Yo you got the drop on them Ghost?" Hesitantly I replied, "Soon, everything will unfold." I handed them each burner phones (untraceable cell phones) with all their numbers programmed and I told them their roles. Scanning the room, I asked again for reassurance, "Any questions?" "Nah," everybody said one by one. "Okay cool, I owe y'all one." On our way out Seven yelled back at me, "Let me find out you done got soft bro." We shared a laugh, but I felt like I was dying in the inside. "Negative cuz, you already know what the fuck going on," I told Seven. After the meeting everybody left but Chance.

When I looked up at him, he had a look of worry all over his face, so I asked him, "What's the word blood?" "Man, Ghost I don't know if this is helpful or not but remember when you put in that order, the other day." I paused, "Aw yeah, yeah, yeah. You talking about that move, right? What happened with that?" Silence. "Well, shit I ran into Shay-Shay little ass that night to." "What? Man, why you just now telling me that?" "Damn, cuz, she told me not to say nothing. I didn't want too backdoor her. Shit man, I should've said something. She was with some funny looking ass bitch with a boy ass name. I think that hoe name was Bobby or Tommy or some shit like that."

"Bobby or Tommy huh, I got to ask Ice if she knows anything about her." We gave each other a pound and we went our separate ways. I was sitting back in the trap trying to put a plan in motion. I figured this was the best spot for us to meet since nobody new about it except for Pop's. I kept a few dollars stashed in the safe but nothing to major though. I even had a secret button hidden in the wall which led to the gun room in the cellar. The lab contained all types of heavy artillery like I was preparing for war. I locked up the spot and hopped in my ride. I flamed up a blunt and I sped off.

In Transit: Mike

In route to the hospital with my sounds blasting. I parked in the lot and jumped out. I alternated from room to room. Half out of my mind when the Doc reappeared, telling me the OG's surgery was a success. Shit was crazy so I got a room at a nearby hotel. I didn't even go to the crib to grab myself any clothes, instead I went to one of the stores in the hood and grabbed a couple fits. I went to my room, and I jumped in the shower. I laid down, but I was restless. A few hours later I hopped up, got dressed, and went back to the hospital. I stood in Isis's room watching her sleep. When her eyes opened, I was the first face that she saw. I stepped out into the hallway, and I called up her folks.

Then I walked back in, and we talked. When her parents arrived, I could tell her mom had been crying. I ran script on her folks telling them she lost her balance and fell. I could tell they didn't believe me though. They tried convincing her to move back home but she wasn't having it. "Ma and Daddy, I love you both, but my home is with Michael now. He's my man and I'm not leaving him unless Jesus calls me home. I appreciate your concern though." Silence. "We love you, Sunshine. We just want the best for you."

"Thanks Daddy, love y'all too. I'm getting pretty sleepy, so I'll call you guys tomorrow." They gave her a kiss and walked out the room. "I'll be back baby," I said to Ice as I hurried trying to catch up with her parents. While we were heading down the hall to the elevator, Mr. Montgomery pulled me to the side, "Son you say you love my daughter, right?" Silence. "Yes, sir without a doubt. I would give my life to spare hers." "Well, if you love her like you claim you do, why won't you let her come home with us? Let us take care of her. You both are still young, why not give each other some space and then reunite later?"

"With all, do, respect sir, Ice makes her own decision's. I am not at liberty to decide that for my woman. But I can tell you this sir, I love her with every breath in me." Silence. "Okay son, I understand. I know in my heart that you'll make the right decision." Feeling the tension in the air, Mrs. Montgomery, gave me a hug and they left, but not before she was able to say, "Michael, son, take care of my baby." I smiled, with confidence, "Always, mam always," I said right before the elevator doors closed shut. Talking Ice's parents made me realize just how close I came to almost losing her and it sickens me.

Why Are you Doing This?

The strangers touch creeped me out. Nervously I asked with my voice cracking, "What do you want from me?" One of them laughed. The other answered, "I want you," he said with this sexy ass accent. Demented by his comment I asked, "What do you mean you want me?

Why are you doing this?" Next thing I know, one of the guys tied my arms and my feet with what felt like, rope. "Enough of this. Where does Ghost keep his stash at?" Silence. "Huh? What? Who is Ghost and what stash are you talking about?"

Unimpressed by my response his hand landed on the side of my face. "Don't play dumb with me bitch, you know who Ghost is.," he said aggressively. "No, I swear I don't know anybody by the name of Ghost?" He slapped me again but this time it was even harder. "Bitch, stop playing. You starting to piss me the fuck off," another voice said angrily. Silence. "Just tell me the truth and we'll let you live. Where does your brother keep his money at?" I paused. "Wait…what, my brother…what money?" He slapped me again. "Ouch, stop hitting me. Wait please stop."

"You know what be going you slut." Then he slapped me multiple times. After the last strike, the guy with the accent spoke up. "You heard what happened to the other whore in the other room didn't you? Do you want to be silenced to?" "No, no. Please I will do anything just don't hurt me," I cried. "Now that's more like it. Tell us what we want to know, and you might make it out of here with the use of your limbs," the voice spoke coldly. By the sound of his voice, I cried even harder, "I don't know anything, I already told you that."

This time he grabbed me by my throat and slammed me on the ground. "Do you want us to kill your family?" "Wait, no, please. Leave us alone." "Let me end this bitch now, boss," one of them said. "Man, fuck you," I shouted. Then somebody grabbed me by my throat, this time they strangled me until I nearly passed out. "Enough," a male yelled as the grip, on my throat loosened. I could tell that the one with the accent must've been the one calling the shots.

"Just wait until my boyfriend and my brother get a hold of you, just wait. You're going to be in big trouble." Then the voice spoke coldly, "Bitch shut up your brother, not getting active. And who the fuck is your boyfriend?" I cried, "You don't know him, because if you did you would be scared. He's a real man, just wait until he finds out what you did to me." They laughed at my expense, but I continued. "Just wait you'll see." Then I heard one of them saying, "Ooh your man. I'm so scared I'm shaking in my boots," he teased.

Then the one with the accent spoke, "Silence," he screamed. "Remove the bag from her face so we can see eye to eye." As he removed the bag from my face, I kept my eyes closed because in the movies they always killed the victims after they showed their face. My eyes were shut tight until one of them men grabbed my face forcefully. "Open your eyes little bitch," he spat. "No, I'm begging you please." Then he squeezed my face even harder. I opened my eyes slowly trying to get readjusted to the light. Once I was able to see clearly, I started hyperventilating and I almost had a panic attack. "You... Oh my God, you're behind all of this? How could you?" He smiled, "What's the matter Shay? You're not happy to see me? Surprise."

As he spoke, I wailed. "How could you do me like this, I trusted you?" His laugh was vicious. "This business, baby. Don't, sit here like you're so innocent, in all this bitch. All the money you done skimmed from me," he said as he laughed. "What money are you talking about baby? How dare you accuse me of stealing from you. I would never cross you like that. You have to believe me baby," I lied. Then he struck in the face and gave me a busted lip. "Cut it out, stop playing."

We Need to Talk: Ghost Speaks

The closer I came to Ice's room, the more nervous that I became. I thought long and hard about my conversation that I had with her dad, and it was pondering in my head. I didn't know what to say. I didn't want her to think that I was abandoning her, but at the same time I didn't want to put her in any more danger. Although me and her people don't see eye to eye, one thing for sure, she is our common denominator. I walked in and I stood by her bedside. "I need to holler at you, Ma," I spoke with a level of urgency in my voice. "What is it, Michael?" She looked up at me with a look of terror in her eyes.

"Baby, what's wrong? Talk to me you're scaring me." I paused, "Baby, I don't know how to tell you this, but..." "But, what Michael, baby you can tell me anything you know that." I lowered my head before I spoke, "Our, baby, didn't make it, Ice." "What...what do you mean Michael? Don't say that baby." I reached down and grabbed her hand, but she yanked away. "Michael, don't you dare say that to me, don't you dare," she cried. "Ice baby, I love you more than life itself. Our baby, she didn't make it." Silence.

"Stop saying that, please. Nurse, nurse," she screamed. "Michael what do you mean?" "Baby you had a..." The nurse rushed in. "Mrs. Montgomery please calm down. How may I help you?" The nurse looked at me and I gave her a nod. "Mam, when you came into the hospital you were complaining of having abdominal pains. They were mild at first but later they became more severe." Silence. "Yes, go on." "Well mam, it saddens me to inform you that the fetus didn't survive."

"Oh, my God, Michael what happened? Why? Oh God why?" The nurse left. Then I held Ice as she cried uncontrollably, and I felt like I was drowning. "Ice baby, it's going to be okay." She stopped rocking and she jerked away from me. "It's going to be, okay? What do you mean it's okay? Michael, nothing about this is okay. That baby is a part of me, a part of you, and she's gone. It will never ever, be okay. This is all, your fault Michael. This is, all, your fault! You did this, I thought you loved me but all you seem to do is hurt me."

Her words pierced my heart. I rubbed her back trying my best to console her. "Baby, we can try again. We're going to get through this." "No, Michael we can't. What do you mean we can try again? How, can you say that to me after what just happened?" Silence. "Baby I know this isn't the best time, to be saying this but your parents want you to come home, but this will be temporarily though just until you heal. I think it's a good idea, too."

"Wait a minute what did you just say to me Michael? Aw so let me get this straight. So, first I lose our baby, now you're kicking me out of our home like I'm disposable. You know what Michael you're a piece of work, you're a real piece of work. How dare you turn your back on me at a time like this Michael? Shame on you." "Baby I'm doing this for us." "Right, Michael, right. That's your favorite line. You say that you're doing this for us, but you're really only doing this for you because you're selfish Michael you're selfish." I opened my mouth to talk but no words seemed to formulate so I just hugged her, not wanting to ever let her go and I continued rocking her. She tried shoving me away, but I wouldn't let up.

Crushed: Shayna

Through teary eyes I spoke softly, "I don't understand, Ha how could you do this to me? I thought you really loved me." "Love, man get your stupid dumb ass out of here." Then he laughed before continuing, "Yo clown ass brother thought shit was sweet because I was locked down for a minute, banging my bitch, and counting my bread. These, my blocks, don't shit move in my city unless I say so. I give the orders. I'm big boss in these streets and that, bitch he clipped was one of my hoes to. Now tell me where your brother keeps his bread, before I dead your ass."

Spit formed in the corners of his mouth as he shouted at me. I could tell he meant business to. "I…. I don't know Ha." "Bitch you thought I fucked with you because you threw that tired, ass pussy at me?" He laughed. I was mortified while I was being disrespected by the man that I once loved. I tried my best to plead with him, "Please Hakeem just let me go. I won't tell anybody. Don't do this, please. I love you." "Bitch you don't love me. You love my bread." "Well yeah, I loved the fact that you were spoiling me and spending time with me. You're acting all brand new now, but I didn't hear you complaining when you were licking on this pussy and eating my ass."

My comment must've struck a nerve, because the next thing I know, blood was flying from my lip. As soon as he was close enough to me, I spit in his face. "You stupid bitch," he shouted. He removed the spit from his face with his shirt. Then he grabbed a handful of my hair, "Bitch where that bag at? I'm not playing around." While he was yelling and screaming one of his boys was aiming a gun in my direction. At this point I was just over it and something came over me. "I'm not telling you shit, go to hell, you goofy."

Then I hawked up as much spit as I possibly could and it landed dead in his face again, "Nigga, fuck your limp dick ass." He wiped his face, but I could tell by his expression that he was blew. "Shut up, you bitch. I should end your ass right now," he screamed. "Go ahead, kill me and my brother won't give you shit but a toe tag. You disgust me, I can't believe that I fell for you." I laughed. I could tell he was big mad because the grip that he had on my hair tightened before he released me. "Fuck you bitch."

"Awe, naw Ha, don't you remember we already played that game with your shriveled dick ass." "Bitch keep playing and I'm gone off your whole family and make you watch." "Man, I'm sick of this call that nigga Ghost. Let that clown know what time it is." Silence. "Well Ha, what time is it?" He slapped me again. "Keep playing hoe and its gone be a closed casket funeral. On Shorty, I'm not one of them."

Calm Down: Mike

Ice was so upset with me, that I felt guilty and stayed the night. The nurses were accommodating to. "Mike," Ice called out. "Yeah, baby I'm here." "Can I ask you a question?" "Sure, baby, what's up?" "Do you still love me?" "Always and forever, Shorty." I was finally able to get her to calm down, so I lied and told her I was going to the vending machine. Once the coast was clear, I hopped on the elevator and snuck to Ma's room. When I peeked in, she looked so peaceful. I sat near her bedside, and I talked to her like I was expecting an answer.

"Ma, I'm sorry. All I wanted to do was make you proud and to provide a better life for us. Now, I'm on the verge of losing everything that matters the most. Ice is mad at me, and I don't know how to fix it. I hope she don't leave a nigga. She's a good girl Ma, so pure. All you ever wanted me to do was to follow my basketball dreams but somehow along the road I got tangled in this street shit. Ma, I need you please wake up. Wake up Ma. I love you, OG."

I raised, up from my seat. I kissed her on the forehead, and I headed down the hall. I stopped in the bathroom and splashed some water on my face. Then I left out and jumped on the elevator once again. As soon as I landed my phone rang, so I stopped dead in my tracks. I glanced down at the ID and noticed it was an unknown call. "Yo," I answered. The caller on the other end had some sort of accent but I didn't recognize the voice. "If you ever want to see your sister alive again, I'm gone need what belongs to me $100K in unmarked bills." I paused. "Man, who the fuck is this playing on my phone?"

He laughed, "Playing, Ghost, play time over run me my motherfuckin' bread or this bitch gone, get it!" I became defensive, "Man who the fuck is this?" I was trying to catch his voice, but I couldn't. Then the caller said to me, "Who I am is not important but getting me my money is. I need that 100 bands like yesterday. You got a week." Silence. "Are you crazy? I don't have that kind of cash. Man, how am I supposed to know if she's still breathing anyway?" My voice was projecting, causing people to stare so I knew I needed to calm down.

Silence. "Pretty face, speak," he demanded. "Hello, Mike (sniff, sniff), I'm sorry, my boyfriend is crazy," Shayna said. "Bitch this not the fucking love connection, quit talking all that boyfriend shit," the caller said as he snatched the phone from out of her hand. Then I heard what sounded like a slap. "Ouch," Shayna screamed which made my blood boil. I punched the wall next to the elevator because I couldn't stand hearing my sister cry. "You'll get your money nigga. Just don't hurt her.". The caller laughed, "Well, now Ghost that depends on you. I need's my motherfuckin' cut! You have exactly one week. Just follow my orders and everything a run smooth. No police, no funny business or the bitch dead."

I stepped to the side where nobody could hear me. "If you harm my sister, on my soul, homie, you the fuck dead! You can cancel Christmas, homeboy." "Nigga is that a fucking threat?" I laughed, "Check my file, I don't make threats, it's a promise," Then I ended the call. I hopped on the elevator, fuming. I needed to make some moves and fast. When I reached Ice's room, she was sleep, so I left. Before leaving the hospital, I called her parents and arranged for them to pick her up f and they agreed. Then I hopped in my ride and twisted one up. I flamed up my blunt and I rolled to the hotel in silence.

Before going to the room, I called up the guys and arranged for another meeting. While I was trying to piece together the puzzle, my sisters last comment replayed over again in my head. I circled the block a few times before entering the hotel lot just in case I was being trailed. I sat in the car for a minute while I finished up my blunt. That's when it clicked in my head that if anybody knows who her boyfriend is, it would be Ice. As much as I hated to get her involved, I'm going to have to chop it up with her. I tossed the finished blunt to the ground and I hopped out. I walked to my room, slid the keycard in the door, grabbed my gun from my hip and entered. I scanned the room, for safety precautions. Once I made sure that the coast was clear, I put my banger (gun) underneath my pillow. I opened the fridge, and I downed a water, and it was lights out.

Let Me Go: Shayna

"So, let me get this straight, I never meant anything to you, this was all about money?" Silence. "Don't just stand there Hakeem, say something, answer, me." He laughed. "You heard of the saying money makes the world go round?" "Well of course Hakeem...Yeah." "Well, on foe nem' grave, whoever said that shit was motherfuckin' right." "Why won't you just let me go, Hakeem? What have I ever done to you to deserve this? Are you that heartless?" "I don't give a fuck about no heart, bitch it's all about them Benjamin Franklins." "Okay then Ha, I get it, so it's fuck me, right? Well, I have to go the restroom. Can you untie me Ha please?"

"If you have to pee then by all means... go right ahead." He slid a bucket in my direction with his foot. His entourage laughed. "Hakeem what am I supposed to do with that? Are you kidding me right now?" I darted my eyes down at the bucket then back at him. "Bitch, I don't play what's wrong with you? We'll give you some privacy but make it quick." "Hakeem. I need a little help please." "Oh yeah." He walked towards me and adjusted my clothes. "I hate you Hakeem," I whispered in his ear. He looked at me and laughed then he exited the door.

I held my urine in until I felt like my bladder was about to explode. I stooped down, and I cried as the urine, started to cascade down my legs. I sat there in my soiled clothes feeling violated. I couldn't believe that I had slept with such a monster. The stench was unpleasant to even my nose. I felt so much hate in my heart for Hakeem at that point. I have never wished any harm on anybody, but he hurt me so bad that I wanted him dead. I can't even begin to imagine what my brother must be thinking of me. This is, all, my fault. I hate to have brought such havoc to my family.

I wondered what gave this goofy the impression that my brother was caked up like that. He does alright for himself but he's only a realtor. He doesn't have any ends like that. Then the question kept pondering in my head, why does he refer to my brother as Ghost. I pulled myself together as best as I could. I scanned the room in search of some sort of escape exit or a weapon, but the room was empty. I tried to remove my arms from the rope. I tugged on the rope until my arms bled, but I couldn't break free. I hate it here.

It Just Got Real: Ghost

Before the meeting I somehow found the time to stop at the hospital. I didn't want Ice to be alarmed when she woke up and she didn't see me there. The last thing that I wanted to do is to cause her anymore pain. To my surprise when I arrived those same nosey ass detectives, appeared to be leaving her room. In passing they looked at me in disgust as they shook their heads. I frowned but I didn't say a word. Then that Wilson character looked at me and called me by the street name, "Ghost," as he was mugging me. I turned to face him, when I heard my name being called, out of habit.

It was almost like he could see right through my soul or some shit. I didn't let that bother me though. I had too much other shit on my mind, instead I nodded at, and I kept it moving. When I walked in her room, to my surprise, she was sitting up crying. Then out of nowhere she grabbed the vase that held her flower arrangement and aimed for my head. I had to move quickly so I wouldn't get hit. "Baby what's wrong." Through tears she spoke, "You Michael, you are what's wrong! Stay away from me you creep, stay the hell away from me." I was confused because I still didn't even know what I had did. "Is it, true Michael?" "Is what true baby?" "Is it true that you aren't who you say you are?"

"Baby nobody's ever who they say they are." "What is that supposed to mean, Michael? I mean excuse me, should I be calling you, Ghost? So, is it true what they said about you? Are you some sort of assassinating king pin?" Silence. "Baby you know me. What type of questions are these?" Annoyed, I frowned. I walked towards her to try to calm her down. "What did they say to my Ice?" Silence. "That's not going to work Michael, so stop calling me that." "What?" "Stop calling me your Ice. They told me all about you. They told me that you and Money were notorious criminals. They also told me that Mama, Oh God, Michael, Mama, was shot and asked me was I aware of Shay-Shay's disappearance. Is all of this true?" Silence.

I wasn't sure how to respond so I was careful when I chose my words. "Yes and no." "Yes and no, what does that even mean Michael?" "Yes, baby Ma did get shot and Shayna is missing. But no, I'm not some sort of thug king pin, you know me baby. I need you to believe in me Ice, like you always have. You're the one for sure thing in my life. Just give me a little more time and you'll understand everything. I'm a businessman, I do what doctors do, Ma. I simply handle business transactions."

"What does that mean, Michael? You know what, I can't with you right now, I just can't!" "Ice, we'll chop it up later. Right now, I need you to focus on healing. By the way, baby what did you tell them anyway?" "I didn't say anything other than they were lying and if they have any further questions, they will need to contact our lawyer." I smiled at that very moment because that right there is true loyalty. "Good girl. I'll handle the rest." "Michael I'm scared."

"Don't, be, Ma, I got you." "So, do you really own those buildings where I pick up the rent money from or is that a lie to?" Silence. "Yes, Ice of course I do, I co-own them. I don't lie to you. Those are me and Pops cribs. How do you think I keep you in all that designer shit you like? Everything I do is legit Ice, trust and believe me baby." "Michael, I love you and I want to believe you but right now you're making it hard. I don't need all those material things if that means you jeopardizing your freedom. All I need is you and we can figure everything else out together."

"We, gone be good, they just mad because I'm young and I'm clocking more cash than they see annually. We, straight over here." "How is Mama doing?" "She's good. She hardbody she'll come around." "That's good Michael and where is Shayna?" "I don't know yet baby. That's what I'm trying to figure out now. Oh, yeah that reminds me, baby I have an important question for you, and I need you to be straight up with me." "Sure, what is it now Michael?" "Baby, do you know anything about Shayna having a boyfriend?" Silence. Hesitantly she answered, "Huh? A what? A boyfriend baby, that's insane. I don't know anything about that. Why do you ask?"

"Damn, okay baby, I was just hoping that you knew something." "Well Michael baby…" Before she could finish her sentence, we heard a knock at the door. It was the nurse coming in hand her, her discharge papers. She could tell we were deep in conversation, so she left the paperwork on the table, and she left back out. "Now what were we talking about, Michael?" I gave her ass, the look like you know what I just asked you. "Aw, uh…yeah well why would he have her Michael?"

I could tell by her facial expression that she instantly wanted to retract her statement when she noticed that she had gotten caught up in her lie. "What do you mean, why would he have her? Aw so you do know something huh Ice?" "Now, Michael I never said that baby." "Aw, so it's like that, Ma? So, now, we're keeping secrets huh, Mrs. tell me everything because it's healthy for our relationship, on that Oprah, shit?"

I smiled. "Come on now, I know you not talking playa. Mr., I have more identities than Jason Borne. Oh, and are you the father, like you're a Maury's guest?" We both fell into laughter. "Truce, Ice baby I don't want to fight. Seriously though if you know something it's urgent that you let me know. I won't get mad?" Silence. "Well," she said hesitantly." "Well, what Ice? Talk to me baby Shayna's life depends on it." "I kind of know a little bit about a little bit." "Okay Ice, spit it out I'm listening." "Don't get mad Michael, you promised."

"Now baby, why would I get mad, unless there is reason to?" She paused, "Well Michael baby, Shay did bring him by the house one afternoon, when you were gone to therapy." "What! Shayna did what Ice? So, wait let me get this straight. Shayna had some clown ass nigga, in my crib and you allowed that shit to go down?" "Michael, now you said you wouldn't get mad." Silence. "I'm not fucking mad (gritting my teeth) this is just unbelievable, un-fucking believable Isis." "I didn't tell you because I knew how you would react, especially after he kind of hit on me."

Silence. "What! So, some strange nigga, hit on my wife in our house, that is dating my baby sister, is that right?" "Uh…Yes, Michael it really wasn't that big of a deal though." "It really wasn't that big of a deal, really, Ice? Okay it's smooth we'll have to talk about this later because now you starting to make me angry acting like a dingy ass blonde. I see we need to discuss boundaries and some ground rules. So, do you by any chance remember buddies name?"

"Oh, uh yeah I believe his name is Hasean, or Henry…no, no uh, hold on give me a minute let me think. (Pause) I got it baby, I got it, his name is Hakeem. Yeah, that's his name Hakeem." "Hakeem huh, thanks Ice, I'm about to go make a run. I'll hit you later." "Wait, baby wait, did that help and where are you going?" "I'll fill you in later and yeah that helped. Oh, and Ma's in room 5234." "Thanks Michael. I hope she's okay." "Yep, I do to. I'll let you know how everything goes with you and Shay's lover, though."

"That's not funny Michael, you got jokes. Wait a minute how am I getting home?" "Oh yeah, your parents gone come and scoop you." "My parents, you called my parents Michael?" "Yeah, baby, I had to. I gotta make a run but keep your phone on Ma. I'm gone hit you in a minute," I said then I left before she started throwing sharp objects at my head.

TWENTY-SEVEN

Savage: Ghost

I sped out the lot, amped up. I was already late for the meeting, which is unlikely. I stopped on the 9 and grabbed some loud (hydro) and a box of jacks (blunts) from the gas station to. As soon as I got to the spot, I threw the smoke at Chance, and he started rolling up. I didn't waste any time I got right down to business. I explained the ransom. Chance and Seven said together they had $25 bands on it. I had already withdrawn, $50 from one of my offshore accounts and Fly and LaLa said they had the other $25 bands (thousand), so we were straight. "Man fam, love my dudes," I said to them.

"Man, we family, you would do the same for us, blood. It's nothing," said Seven. "Facts cuz," I shouted. Chance didn't waste any time, he jumped right in, "Man who we need to body (kill)?" "Man cuz, I wish I knew," I said as I looked around at my team. I didn't want to be backdoored, so I didn't mention anything about what me and Ice discussed earlier. Then Snake spoke next, in his "What you want to do, son?" "We gone wait it out fam."

"Don't worry we gone get your sister back unharmed and those clowns gone pay," said Trigg. "I know man, I know." We put a few blunts in the air. Shortly after the meeting was adjourned, I pulled Seven, Chance, LaLa and Fly to the side. "Let me holler at ya'll a minute." I filled them in and told them who I suspected captured sis and as a team, we devised a plan. The others were like pon's on my chess board, these are my key player's and I'm the knight. "Aye y'all some real ones, for this one straight up, I just want to say thank you for being down." They smiled and nodded in my direction before they left. I stayed behind, and sat around deep in thought, while I domed a blunt.

Out This Jam: Isis

Soon as Mike left, the nurse came in and released me. I stopped in Mama's room before I left. Seeing her on a ventilator, brought me in so much pain. I talked to her for a while and told her that I loved her before I left out. I caught a cab ride to the crib. I had to get up out of that jam before my parents arrived. I needed to go home and soak in my own tub. I also wanted to grab a couple items from the house. After bathing I got dressed. I grabbed my duffel and filled it with my necessities. I locked up the house, hopped in my car, and I sped off. As soon as I parked my car and my parent's crib, my phone rang. I looked down at the caller ID and saw that it was my mother, so I answered.

"Hello." Silence. "Isis, where are you?" I laughed before I answered her because she is so dramatic. "Girl, come get the door." "Hold, on for a minute honey." Silence. "Honey, Ice is here, (sniff, sniff) go let her in for me," Ma shouted to my dad as she disconnected the call. As soon the door swung open Daddy gave me hug. "Hey Sunshine," he said before he turned and walked away. I smiled. "Hey Daddy." Then Ma walked up, and she hugged me to. Then, I heard Daddy hollering back at us, "How long are ya'll gone stand in the doorway? Ya'll letting all the bugs in."

I closed the door and I stepped inside. I walked upstairs and to my surprise, my room looked exactly how I left it. As if on cue Smokey was standing there purring, waiting on me. I stooped down and rubbed him on his head. I couldn't believe how good it felt to be home. I lifted Smokey and I pressed my nose against his. "Isis," Ma called out to me. "Yes Ma." "Come on down and have a glass of warm milk with me. That is still your favorite right or are you to grown for that too?"

I smiled, "Yes, Mommy, that's still my favorite." "Well, hurry up, and join me." "Yes mam, here I come." I ran down the stairs and joined her at the kitchen table. "How have you been holding up, Sunshine?" "I'm okay Daddy." He grabbed me and he squeezed me tight. Then he whispered in my ear, "You will always be my Sunshine no matter how old you get."

Sitting Duck: Ghost

I sat around anxiously, waiting for the phone to ring. It had been hours since we spoke, so I hit up the wife, "What's good Ma, you straight?" "Yea, baby I'm good, just missing you that's all. I'm not doing nothing, just sitting around talking to my parents." "Okay cool. Love you." "Love you back baby." I called Chance and Seven and I told them we needed to link. If these clowns still moving how they use to, I know exactly where they keep their stash at. The Hakeem, that I use to know was known in these streets by the name Zap. He was as grimy as they come to.

When he got slammed (locked up) his crew was big on trying to take us out. Pops tried to convince me to body them, but I didn't want that blood on my hands. As soon as cuz came through, we put on our vest, and our gloves and we loaded up. I didn't even bother to hit up the others. We stopped at one of the spot's, in the hundreds and I paid a cluck (hype) that went by the name of Sleepy, a twenty piece, just to knock on the door and act like he needed a hit. He agreed without hesitation and had cuz meet me around back. Knock. Knock. The person on the other side of the door slid open the peep hole just slightly. "Yeah."

"It's me man, it's me, Sleep," he said while scratching and squirming. "Sleepy gone head on, ain't no credit happening man. I already told you that," he said as he laughed. "Aye man, I need to stand. I'm sinking like quicksand, so I'm trying to get right man," Sleepy rhymed. "Gone head on Sleep them tired ass tunes ain't bout' to get you shit here man." "Naw, man. I got doe, my brother. I'm on the floor man, I need a hit man." Sleep lifted his hand and flashed his twenty-dollar bill. "Aw, okay Sleep. You should've just said you was holding." As he started to unlock the door, I kicked it in sending him flying to the other side of the room.

Then I paid Sleep and he disappeared. I scanned the room and peeped what looked like it had to be $20,000 rolled up in rubber bands that was laying on the table. "What the fuck," the guy said as he reached near his waist searching for his gun right before I shot him in his wrist. "Shit. Oh shit," he screamed. With my gun drawn aiming at his head I asked, "Where's the girl?" Silence. "What girl? Man, I don't know nothing about no girl." Unsatisfied with his answer I put a hole in the wall inches from his head to let him know I meant business. "Damn man, what the fuck! I don't know shit about no girl." "The girl your boss, is holding hostage, is my sister nigga. Now where the fuck is she?" "I don't know nothing man. You got to believe me."

"Aye man my beef not with you so I'm gone give you one last chance to make things right." "Thank you, man." "Now, last chance, where is the fucking girl at?" "I swear to God, on my kids' man. I don't know, man...I don't know," he said sounding shook. "Man fuck you and them kids. Ain't no sense in you calling God, he can't save you now," I said before letting off another round near his head. BOOM!

"I don't know anything about no girl. I swear," he stuttered. "Aw, okay you don't know huh?" I raised my gun, but this time I pointed it at his head. "I really don't know shit. Please man, I got a family man," he pleaded as he held his hands up. I aimed and I squeezed the trigger. Pow, Pow, BOOM! "Shit! That's my thigh you psycho." "Yeah, and your head is next, now stop fucking playing with me and tell me what I need to know." "Man, I can get you money, man, just don't kill me man please. Please just let me go. I don't know anything about no girl, on my soul."

"Man, fuck yo soul, where the fuck the money at Joe?" He hesitated, "Uh it's in... the...uh... freezer downstairs man. It's a few bands on the table next to the dope to. Please just let me go, man. I got a family man, 3 kids and a wife," he said. "Tell me where the girl is, and I'll let you go." Silence "I swear man, I don't know, man. If I knew I swear to God, I would tell you." While he was pleading for his life, I heard a loud bang, which sounded like a gunshot, so I kept my hand on the trigger. Then Chance and Seven appeared in the doorway dragging a body in the kitchen. "How many in here?" "Including me and Crip that's now dead man 10," he said nervously. "Last time, or you're next. Where are they keeping the girl?" "Okay, okay, just don't hurt me man. I'll tell you everything that I know..." In midsentence he was stopped by a bullet to the head by one of his own guys.

"I knew we couldn't trust him," I heard the unfamiliar voice say. My heart started pounding. Then dude showed face and he aimed at Seven and I upped it on him. "Where's the girl?" He laughed, "Nigga fuck you. I'm not telling you shit fuck that whore," he spat. "Fuck this Ghost shoot this clown cuz," said Seven.

"Man, nigga you shoot me, I'm gone pop him, no cap."
"Last time man where the fuck is the girl?"

"Fuck that hoe," he spat. Then I shot him in his neck causing him to drop to floor and his gun slid from his hand. He grabbed a hold of his neck that was oozing with blood. "Fuck you man, I'm not saying shit," he spat with blood leaking from his mouth. Seven lifted his gun and put a bullet in his skull. Chance ran over and grabbed the guns from the floor. Then we headed down to the basement. "Duck man," Seven shouted. Boom! Click, click! BOOM! We ducked right on time because oh girl was packing heavy artillery.

Chance saw a shot and he took it, and he filled her with led who was holding the 12 Gage. "Anybody else want some?" Silence. The basement resembled a meth lab. Drugs were everywhere, cooked, and raw. All the women were naked apart from the gloves, and the mask they wore. Some of the laborers were pregnant to. Despite the commotion they continued working. "Scram hoes," I shouted but they kept on working. Click, click, BOOM! Seven, fired in the air.

"You, either get out now or your family is gone be making funeral arrangements," Seven shouted aggressively and they scattered like flies. Then we grabbed the cash, and we jetted out. When we got in the front of the house, I grabbed the gas can, I struck a match, flicked it, and watched the firework explosion. Then we sped off. Nobody said a word as we headed over to another one of his spots.

When we got to the trap it pretty much went the same way. Fleeing away from the scene, we rolled in silence apart from the music that was playing. Then we went back to the spot. We burned our clothes, hopped in separate showers, and we changed. I made a mental note to bathe with bleach later. After we got dressed, we met back up in the living room and we smoked. "Man cuz, if you don't hurry up and pass that shit," Seven said to Chance. "This that shit man," said Chance while he choked. I laughed. While we were blowing, we took a couple shots of Jamison.

I led them down to the dungeon and showed them my secret gun collection. I could tell they were impressed by my assortment. "Cuz, you a motherfuckin' fool," said Chance. Seven agreed, "Yeah, man, you got that shit, down here." I smiled. "Man, beloved I thought you were getting soft on me," Seven laughed. "Never that, my dude, on God. Never that. I'm still a beast." The room was sound, weather resistant, and bullet proof. "Fam welcome to my bat cave," I said proudly, and we all laughed. Since those were my brothers, I let them pick out their guns and we disposed of the other ones. Then we ran the guns back to my office and locked them away. After that we ran the money through the money counting machine and we split it three ways. We threw another shot back and they dipped. I was just sitting around playing the waiting game. I already know that it would only be a matter of time before Zap got word about us hitting up his traps and he gone feel that heat.

One Last Time: Zap

I was furious after getting a call from Debrika's thick ass. I'm thinking the hoe was calling because she was trying to swallow my kids instead, she was calling telling me that one of my spots had been hit (robbed). For the life of me, I couldn't figure out who the hell was gully enough to pull a move like that. The money that I stole, was untraceable. There were no witnesses except for a corpse and the crazy ass bitch that was committed.

Fucking with my bread is deadly. Not even twenty minutes passed before I got another call from another one of my hoes saying somebody had hit up another one of my spots. Shit just wasn't adding up.

I hadn't robbed anybody since I hit up Money and that boy was left stinking. I got the pigs in my pocket, so I don't see how this shit went down. I unlocked the door where Shayna was being held hostage, and I slammed the door so hard that it woke her up. "Get the fuck up." As soon as I entered the room I frowned, "Bitch you smell like shit." I hit up Chopper and told him to grab a bucket of warm water. 10 minutes later he returned with a bucket full of water, a towel, a garbage bag, and some dish washing liquid.

"Get undressed bitch, you smell like shit." "How am I supposed to get dressed Ha? I can't," she said as she attempted to lift up her tied arms as far as she could. "Oh yeah I almost forgot." I turned towards the homie. "Aye yo, Mouse untie this hoe. Everybody get out," I screamed, and they scrammed. I watched as she applied the soap and rinsed her body. I could still see her beauty. The sight of her was turning me on. Mouse shouted from the other side of the door, "Boss you straight, in there?"

"Yeah, slime. I'm good. Go next door and grab me a towel, that jogger set and a pair of them brand new boxers off the table." He did what he was told, and he knocked when he came back. I cracked the door just enough to reach my hand out, careful not to expose her. Then I snatched the items from him and slammed the door in his face. While my back was turned, I felt her tiny hand squeezing my dick. "What's up Ha, don't you want me daddy?" The way she said that to me got me an immediate arousal. I didn't reply. She nibbled on my ear while massaging my manhood.

I couldn't resist her touch, I turned to face her, and I pulled her closer. I smacked her on the ass. Then she turned around and started bouncing on my hard. I massaged her clit while I enjoyed the show. Then I stuck 2 of my fingers in and out of her ocean causing a stream to flow. Her towel slipped to the floor exposing her grape size nipples, so I popped one in my mouth like a tic tac. She moaned sweet moans. She lifted my head and we kissed. Then she ripped open my shirt and lifted my tank showcasing my chest. She kissed my neck, and my chest as she unbuttoned my jeans.

Then she dropped to her knees as my pants fell to the floor. Anticipating the warm feeling of her mouth on my pole, I leaned my head back. She teased my head with her tongue and hummed on my balls. I grabbed a handful of her hair as I rammed my joystick further down her throat. "You like that daddy?" "Hell yeah," I screamed. She made slurping noises as she talked dirty to me. "Oh yeah, bitch. Take this dick," I shouted.

"You like this shit, don't you baby?" "Right there...I'm about to cum," I whispered barely able to catch my breath. Her mouth on my pole felt so good. Then I jumped and I screamed when I felt her teeth sinking into my member. "You bitch." I grabbed my dick and I fell to the floor as the pain shot through my entire body. She stood over me and she laughed. Then she threw the remainder of the water in my face. "Aw, shit. You're one dead ass bitch!" "Fuck you, Ha," she said as her voice trembled.

I tried to stand but the pain was too severe, so I staggered back to the floor. Seeing me at my weakest she ran towards me and hit me in the head with the bucket. I could hear the guys on the other side of the door trying to get in, but the door was locked from the inside and I had the key. "Boss you good?" I reached for her leg, and she kicked me in my chin. "Shit, you sneaky little whore." Then the door came tumbling down and the guys stormed in. "It's about damn time."

They looked at me then back at her. "Don't just stand their you morons, do something. Grab the bitch." They charged at her and roughed her up. Smack...smack. "You're one stupid bitch," one of the guys yelled. Smack... smack. "That's all you got. You hit like a girl," she teased. Smack...smack...smack. "Hold on man. I told y'all I need the hoe alive until we make the drop. After that she's trash and I don't care what you do with bitch." "10-4 boss, copy that," one of the guys said. A few of them tried to help me up, but I snatched away. "Get off me you fag.

I don't need your help, fuck off," I shouted as I stood to my feet and adjusted my drenched clothes. "After the bitch get dressed tie her ass back up. Keep an eye on her she's a slick one to," I warned. "Copy that boss," said Chopper before I slammed the door and I left. I needed to get up out of these wet clothes.

TWENTY-EIGHT

The Drop: Ghost

Zap, finally hit my line and gave me the directions to the drop. "Once my guys make sure that paperwork good, I'll let this hoe go," he stated coldly. The more he spoke, the madder I became. "How I know she's alive?" I heard some noise in the background. "Talk bitch," he shouted. Silence. "Hello, Mike is that you? I'm sorry. I am so sorry," she cried. "Everything is going to be okay sis don't worry." Then I heard a loud noise that sounded like a smack. "Ouch, you piece of shit," she screamed. "Chill man, you need to fall back Zap."

He laughed. "Ghost, I'm calling the shots remember that shit." Silence. "I'm warning you Zap, man, don't hurt my sister. Yo beef is with me not her, man." "Fuck out of here, my beef is with you and this hoe. You keep playing and I'm gone grab yo bitch to." "Nigga, you bet not play with her." He paused. "Or what?" Silence. I didn't even respond. "Yeah, Ghost just like I thought. You'll get a call with further instructions. There will be a map taped to the payphone two blocks from the drop. It will have a circle around the location. That's exactly where I want you to send that sexy little bitch of yours. And tell that hoe to wear something revealing to," he said as he laughed.

My adrenaline was pumping. I just wish I could reach my hand through the phone and strangle the life out of this nigga. "Zap, man keep my bitch out this fuck shit, ya heard!" "Let's just say that hoe is collateral just in case I smell some funny shit because we all know how you like to play hero. If you try anything Ghost, I'll kill both these hoes. Remember nigga playing with fire a get you burnt. Got it?" Silence. "Yeah, I got it." "Fucking clown," I mumbled. "What was that nigga?" "Shit, Zap man, I'm gone see you." "I'm glad we understand each other. I'll be in touch," he said before the phone went dead. After that call, I hit up the team. Then I called my wife and told her I needed to holler at her. I didn't go into any details though. All I know is I'm gone get sis back even if it's the death of me and that's my word.

Lunch Date with My Baby: Isis

I been slow dragging ever since I left the hospital. Ma has been, waiting on me hand and foot. After breakfast, Mike called and said we were meeting for lunch. That worked out perfectly because I missed him like crazy, besides that I was still eating like I was eating for two. Other than going to the hospital to see Mama, I had been confined to the house, so I could use some fresh air. Prepping for my date, I grabbed my teal colored, fitted, Shane Justin, jumpsuit, and my Balmain sneaks with the matching fanny pack. On my way out the door I told, Ma that I was going to see Mike.

He had made reservations at one of my favorite sea food joints, so I was geeked. When I walked in my baby was waiting patiently for me, which was a first because the boy is always late. He was looking all delicious like something off the menu to. "Hey baby," I said as I greeted him. "What's up, Ma?" "You said you needed to holler at me, so shoot," I said as I sat down. "Ice man it's like this. I don't know how to tell you this, so I'm gone get straight to it. Oh boy who got sis said to send you to grab her, or she dead," Mike said just loud enough for me to hear. I paused, "What?" Silence. "Now baby I wouldn't be coming at you like this if there was any other way. Shay's life depends on it. If you not down, it's smooth I'll just have to try and make other arrangements."

I lowered my head I wasn't even sure how I was supposed to react to something like this. What came out of my mouth next, shocked even me, "I'm down. What you need me to do baby?" He smiled. "Man Ice, that's why I love the fuck out of you girl straight up. Baby I have to warn you though, the man is off." "Duh Mike, he kidnapped Shay, I know his ass retarded." Silence. "Baby, I know this is a lot for me to ask of you. You a real one though. I don't know how I can ever repay you for all that I've put you through."

I smiled. "Marry me, when Mama wakes up, and we'll call it even. Oh yeah and you know this gone cost you a new bag, some jewelry or something," I said before I playfully punched him in his shoulder. He laughed at my comment then he shook his head. "I love the shit out you girl, you're my bitch for life." "We locked in. You're my dog for sure," I said as I gave him a wink. Mike filled me in, on what was expected of me. I was nervous, but I knew that it had to be done. I ate, while Michael pretty much just played in his food.

Then he looked up from his plate, "Love you Ma, I got to go make a run, but we gone make this marriage thing happen after all this is finally over. Just be patient with me and I got you. I'm gone put another baby in you to and we gone be straight." He looked down at his wrist, to check the time. "I like that watch," I said jokingly." "Yeah, I bet you do. My wife copped it for me a minute ago, don't tell her I was here with you though, she might kill me," he said playfully. I laughed at his humor. He stood to his feet, kissed me softly, handed me a phone and confiscated my other one. I didn't ask any questions. Looking in his eyes, I could tell this was weighing on him. I hated seeing my man like this. I just hope and pray that we get through this, and we all come out of this alive.

Feeling Defeated: Ghost

So much was going on around me I haven't really had an appetite lately. Before I slid on gang nem, I stopped at the hospital to check on my mom's. The lot was crowded I was barely able to find a park. I hit the blunt one last time, tossed it to the ground, and I hopped out. Walking into the ER, I headed straight to her room. I talked to her for about thirty minutes or so, hollered at her nurses then I was out. When I made it to the spot, I noticed that all the guy's cars were already posted.

Nobody was sitting in their rides, so I figured one of my cousins had let everybody in. As soon as I walked through the door, the loud (weed) hit me. "What's good," I said and gave everybody some dap. "So, y'all ready to do shit?" No words were exchanged, all I heard was everybody cocking and loading their pistols. That was all the confirmation that I needed. I paused, and took a deep breath before speaking, "Is, there anybody that want out? This gone get messy, on Shorty. So, if you not feeling this shit, it's smooth. Just leave your weapons on the table and bounce. No hard feelings." I grabbed the blunt out of cuz hand.

"We done came too far to back down now, homie," one of the guys said. "Let's body these clowns, blood," shouted Seven. "Yea let's show them who run these streets, no cap," said Chance. I passed him the blunt and he took a long drag and smiled right before he started choking. "Everybody, know what to do right?" "Yep," they said almost in unison. "Ya'll got y'all new phones and tossed the other joints, right?" "Hell, yeah nigga, we're not new to this," shouted Seven.

"Let's do this shit," I said as I grabbed my pistol off the table and checked my clip (magazine). "Aye man, thanks y'all, this loyalty shit goes a long way." "Aw, man blood, here you go getting all sentimental on us again, should we get you a tissue or something famo?" "Fuck you Chance, like I was saying, once this shits over, I got something for y'all straight up." "Man fuck it, they got my little cuz let's send they souls to an early grave." "You my dog Ghost, you bleed I bleed," said

Fly. I smiled. "Let's finish these bitches off. I'm still mad a bitch broke a nail last time, feel me," LaLa said with a smile. We grabbed our vest, our gloves, and our guns and we split up. Time to up the sco (score).

Back Against the Wall: Isis

I didn't want my parents worrying about me, so I called them up and told them I was staying the night with Mike. I had a little time to blow so I headed to the hospital, to check on Mama. I stopped at the gift shop first and grabbed some fresh flowers and a teddy bear before heading to her room. When I walked in, I replaced the dead flowers with some fresh ones. I talked to her until, her doctor walked in and provided an update.

Once he left the nurse came in and checked her vitals to. I left my cell number with her in case of an emergency. "Oh, it's Isis, right." "Yeah, that's me," I said puzzled. "Your husband was here earlier, and he left your contact information." "Aw, okay thanks." She jotted down something on her chart, then she left. I turned around facing Mama, and I talked her ears off until I felt my phone vibrating. Then I kissed her on the cheek, told her I love her, and I eased my way into the hall. "Hello," I answered nervously. "Yo, you ready Ice?" Silence. "Ready for what?" Silence. "It's time," the caller said before ending the call.

Let's Go: Shayna

"Yo, is she ready?" I heard Zap asking one of his goons. "Yeah boss." "Well grab the bitch and let's go," Zap demanded. I flinched when one of his boys grabbed me.

"Where are you taking me?" Silence. "Hello, do you hear me talking to you? Excuse me where are you taking me?" Silence. "To hell," one of them yelled and laughed. "Gag that bitch. I'm sick of hearing her voice. I swarmed trying to break free, "Let go of me you creep, let me go!" He wouldn't let up, so I bit down in his skin, but he still didn't budge. "Fuck…you're one stupid bitch."

He backhanded me. I scratched and kicked, but I still couldn't get away. Smack… smack… smack. "Be cool, now. I'm trying not to hurt you." He grabbed me and tightened the zip ties on my hands. Before leaving out, I heard, Hakeem yelling at one his guys. "Damn, you didn't put a bag over the bitch head." I hurried up and looked around to familiarize myself with the area. "Damn, if you want something done right, you got to do it yourself." Hakeem walked towards me and placed a bag over my head. Then he threw me in the back of the trunk, and they pulled off. I was trying not to panic but I was freaking out. Fearing for my life, all I could do was pray.

Boss Up: Ghost

We were three cars deep, but I rolled solo and domed a blunt to the face. When I got to the drop, I jumped out and left the car running. Then I tossed the two duffel bags inside the truck. I drove two blocks away as instructed and I stopped when I reached the payphone. The phone rang and it was one of Zap's guys on the other end of the receiver, "Yo, the map is taped underneath the payphone. Send yo bitch to that spot that's circled. I heard you gotta fine ass hoe to me and her gone have a little fun." Then he laughed and I got the dial tone. It took everything in me not to bug up.

I slammed the phone down so hard that I almost broke it in two. I grabbed the map and scanned it, then I hopped back in my ride. I texted the Lolo (address) to Ice and the guys they already know what time it is. I hit a few extra blocks for reassurance. I kept looking out of my rearview mirror making sure I wasn't being trailed. I pulled in the alleyway where I had one of the guys, waiting on me there. We switched rides and I dopped. After I left the alley, I headed straight to the spot. I'm flying that motherfucka' to I can't wait to meet up with Zap and watch him take his last breath.

The Trail: Swamp

"How we looking my boy? Is the count right Swamp?" "Yeah Zap, everything counted, boss. We gone, be the new kings of these streets now right Z?" "We? Naw nigga me, fuck out of here." "Well, yeah okay, then, boss, I guess." "You still have eyes on him, right?" "Of course, Z, we not letting up. Aye yo boss?" "Yeah, what up?" "That nigga Ghost, just went inside of club Paradise. What you want us to do?" "What you mean what I want ya'll to do. Follow him, you idiot. What am I paying you for? Whatever you do, don't let that nigga out of your sight, not even for a shit. As a matter of fact, you said my count right, so gone head dead his ass and I can keep both these hoes. Oh, yeah and Swamp make sure he knows that I sent you." "Copy that boss."

"Now hurry the fuck up I got a plane to catch nigga. Handle that and run me my bread (money) before both of y'all ass be joining him," Zap screamed in the receiver before he disconnected the call. As soon as I got off the phone Turtle started asking me a hundred and one questions. "What did he say man?" "Turtle man be cool man, you thirsty. Zap said he left me in charge. He also said to whack (kill) that nigga Ghost and go in his pockets for all our troubles. Then he said he was gone bless us with a few of those bills once we got back to the spot, feel me," I lied. "Word, Swamp, that's why Zap's my motherfuckin' boy." "Man quit dick riding, get off Zap's dick." "Dick riding, how nigga? I'm just making sure this move goes smooth. Kayla ass been hounding me about getting us a crib. If everything official, we can finally get the fuck up out her mother's garage, cause she's a straight, bitch. If she wasn't my shorty's grandmother, I probably would've offed her ass, a long time ago." "I feel you Turtle, man, I feel you."

They Don't Want No Smoke: Seven

Soon as I got to the club, I heard the bouncers hollering talking about they had already reached the capacity. I laughed and I walked straight to the front. I handed the bouncer a couple hundreds, then he slid to side without even searching me and I walked right in. Scanning the room, I could see they had some bad ass hoes in this joint to. I grabbed a table closest to the stage and them hoes started flocking to me like they could smell money. A couple of the bitches offered me lap dances and I agreed, shit fuck it. Enjoying the show, I started throwing money at them like it was nothing.

Still in character so I ordered up one of those gold bottles. I wasn't into it with money so why not spend that shit? When the bottle girl walked up, she was topless with some booty shorts on that got my attention. She placed my bottle on the table in a bucket of ice and I peeled off 10 crisps, one-hundred-dollar bills. "Can I get you anything else," she asked sexily. "Yeah, come back in 30 minutes and let a nigga get them lips." She looked at me, and darted her eyes on my pants, and she smiled. Then she licked her lips, seductively, "Okay Daddy."

Looking around and I spotted those two clowns in the corner, so I sent them over a bottle of Hen and three hoes to their table to keep they ass distracted. I stopped the hoes from dancing on me so I could run and take a leak. When I got back to my section the hoes didn't waste any time grinding and bouncing, they ass on me. I sat back down, popped my bottle, filled my cup, and I downed that shit. I watched the show intensely as I started throwing money in the air like it was going out of style. 5 or 6 songs later and they were still at it.

I downed another glass, and I smoked my cigar. I gave them each a couple hundred then I dismissed them all. Not much longer after that the bottle girl reappeared so I sent those clowns a couple shots just to get their attention. Then I yanked her by the arm and whispered in her ear, "You want to make a couple extra dollars?" She didn't hesitate in replying, "Hell, yeah Daddy. I'll be right back, let me tell the other barmaid to cover me." "Cool." I looked over at them goofies and I raised my bottle in acknowledgement. It was dark in the club, so they still thought I was cuz, which was all part of the plan. When oh girl came back, I told her to follow my lead. "Daddy, do you want to go to the back room with me?"

Silence. "Naw, Little Mama, I'm straight. Just keep up." "Okay Daddy, whatever you say. What's your name, Papi?" I smiled. "Yo, they call me Zap," I lied. "I like that name boo. So, Zap are you going to zap me with your magic wand," she giggled. "Yea Ma, right in your mouth," I said with a slight grin. By her facial expression I could tell that my comment had turned her on. She followed me to the men's room. I walked to the third stall, and she wasn't too far behind. As soon as I closed the door to stall, she sat on the toilet seat, and she didn't waste any time going to work.

With my back against the door, she let me feel her tonsils. While she had her mouth on me, I reached in the upper decker part of the toilet and pulled out my silencer and I screwed it on my piece that I stashed when I went to take a leak. She was sucking every inch of me, "Shit baby right there," I hollered trying to gas her up. Right before I was about to release, I heard the door open and close. Then I heard two guys talking loudly about cuz on speaker phone, so I became alert.

With my free hand I stopped her, signaling for her silence and adjusted my clothes. Then I turned around to face the door for precautionary measures. "Nigga you not a motherfuckin'...." I cracked the door and eased out of the stall unnoticed leaving her behind. Before he could finish his sentence, I cracked him in his head with my gun. He reached for his piece (gun), but he wasn't fast enough, and I lit his ass up. Then he fell to the sink and dropped to the floor. While the commotion was going, on she yelled from the stall, "Baby is everything alright?" "Yeah, Lil Mama, give me a minute. Stay put." "Uh...okay baby," she stuttered.

Then the other dude rushed in. He saw his boy sprawled across the floor filled with bullets and he charged at me, so I upped it on him, and I filled his ass with led to. I dragged them to two separate stalls, I holstered my gun and I walked back in the stall to join oh girl. I dropped my pants, and I let her finish me off and she took my soul. I shook the remainders in her face, and I gave her a few hundred for her skills. Without so much as a word I zipped up. I wiped the beads of sweat off my forehead and I threw my hoodie over my head, and I left. I unlocked the bathroom door, and I exited the club, unseen like I was never there. I jumped in my ride, I squirted off, and I hit up Ghost.

The Call: Ghost

I received an alert on my phone and it was a text from Seven which read, "The party's on, we st8 (straight). What's you lo (location)?" Seeing his text brought a smile to my face, I responded quick, "My nigga. See you in a minute." Then I sent him the address to the spot. My heart was pounding. Ice hadn't texted me yet, which was blowing me. I downloaded a tracker to her phone, and added one to her car, just in case. My phone rang twice, so I knew that that was her signaling her arrival. Then she called back but she didn't say a word. I circled the spot a few more times, before pulling in. I was trying to time it perfectly before I came in blazing. Before I hopped out, I checked my clip, I was locked and loaded.

Bubble Guts: Isis

My stomach was in turning in knots, I was a nervous wreck. Before getting out of my car, I called Mike. I couldn't even begin to imagine what was going to happen next in this vacant hotel. I erased all the numbers from my call log and cuffed my phone in my bra like Mike told me to do. Then I said a silent prayer. My palms were sweaty, but I was trying to play it cool. I entered the room with the key in hand that was left for me. When I turned the knob the first face that I saw, was Hakeem who was pointing a gun at Shayna's head.

"Hey," I managed to say nervously. He smiled. Shayna looked was petrified. "Hey yourself Isis. Bring your sexy ass over here," said Hakeem in a tone that made me even more uncomfortable. I walked in his direction slowly and he grabbed me by the wrist. Then he tossed Shay to the side, and she fell to the floor. I managed to smile but I was screaming inside. With the look of lust in his eyes he started touching my face like we were distant lovers. I cringed from his touch.

He forced his tongue down my throat and I felt so violated. I noticed a couple guys standing around the room with their guns in hands. I scanned the room silently searching for an escape route. While he was grouping me, I could hear Shayna whimpering in the corner, which broke my heart. I was caught off-guard when he started feeling on my breast, so I jumped. "Bitch what the fuck is that in your bra?" Silence. "Answer me, bitch." "Huh, ugh nothing. It's just my push up wire," I stuttered. He reached inside my jumpsuit and found the phone that I had stashed. Then he yelled into the receiver, "Ghost if this you and you try to play hero both these hoes' dead. I'm not playing around. You hear me nigga, these bitches are dead," Zap yelled into the phone before he ended the call.

He looked at me and he screamed so loud that spit flew from his mouth landing in my face, which grossed me out. "Who was that bitch? Answer me." "Nobody. That was nobody," I stuttered. He slapped me. Then he grabbed a handful of my hair roughly and kissed me. I hesitated then he held a gun to my head forcing me to reciprocate. He started talking to me like we were an idol which further creeped me out. "Baby soon as the guys get back with this bread we gone run off and make a move. You need a real boss, to take care of you. You understand?"

I wanted to throw up from his comment, but instead I played the role. I shook my head up and down like we were on the same page. "Yes, I completely understand." "I'm gone spoil the fuck out of your fine ass girl." I stared at him in disbelief, while he talked with no substance. I glanced down at sis, and she was still crying. Ignoring Shayna's presence, he kissed me on the nape of my neck. Then he bit down firmly but not enough to draw any blood. I'm not gone lie, it made me feel some type of way. He signaled his guys to wait outside which caused me to draw suspicion.

Then he tugged on my clothes. We tussled momentarily as I tried to remove his hands, but he was too strong. "No, Hakeem, please stop. No, I can't!" Shayna cried even harder. Hearing her cry made him mad, "Stop all that whimpering you conniving little slut," he spat. He turned to face me, "Bitch, what the fuck you mean stop." He tugged on my jumpsuit again but this time he was more forceful than before. "No, please stop, I can't," I pleaded.

He slapped me again. Then he unzipped my jumpsuit. I kicked and I screamed but he only became more aggressive. "Stop fighting me baby. Tell me you want this dick," he demanded. With tears streaming down my face I cried, "No, please I can't." He slapped me once again but this time he aimed his gun at my head. "Bitch, tell me you want this dick." Silence. "I want... this dick," I said dryly. Smack, smack. "Bitch, say, that shit, like you mean it, before I put a hole in both of you hoes heads," he screamed.

"I want... this dick," I said a little less dryer than before. He pushed me down on the bed and slid my jumpsuit down to my thighs forcefully. Then he slid down his shorts exposing his erection. He grabbed my hand and glided it up and down his shaft forcing me to jag him off. "Wait," I shouted trying to buy myself a little more time. He paused. "What the fuck is we

241

waiting on bitch?" Slap. "Ouch. Wait please. Hakeem, wait…I'm bleeding, my menstrual just started," I blurted out, clearly lying. He laughed, "A little blood won't hurt the pole. I don't mind running a red light."

He smiled and started tugging away at my panties. "Wait, no wait," I screamed nervously. "Now what bitch?" I paused, "Where's the condom?" "Oh shit, good looking out, boo. Let me grab one." He placed his gun on the nightstand near the TV but not long enough for me to grab it. He reached inside his pocket and pulled out a condom. He unsnapped my bra with one hand, and he sucked on my nipples. "Nice breast." Silence. He played with my princess parts as he kissed my bare skin. Then he pressed his mouth in my creamy spot, that only Mike has ever explored.

Tears began to form. I tried pushing him away, but he forced himself on me. I was outraged and turned on at the same time. I closed my eyes as I imagined Mike's hands being the one that was touching me. I arched my back as I smeared my cookies, all over his face. My cookie creamed multiple times. "Mike," I moaned in almost a gentle whisper as the tears streamed down my face. "Ooh Mike," I screamed but this time I was louder than before. He stopped. "What did you just say bitch? I know you didn't just call me that weak ass nigga's name," he screamed. Then he grabbed me by the throat and strangled me.

I clawed my nails in his hands trying to get him to release his grip, but he didn't. My eyes started to roll in the back of my head as I was running out of oxygen. "Hakeem…stop…please," Shayna screamed. "Shut up bitch," he spat. He removed his hands from my throat. I coughed as I gasped for air, and I rubbed my hands on the side of my sore neck. I looked up at him nervously. "Taste this pussy," I said to him trying to distract him.

Shockingly, he went right to sucking on my pearl. Moments later, I jumped from the loud noise that I heard when Hakeem fell to the floor.

I looked up and saw Shayna standing over his body with a blunt forced object. I readjusted my clothes, because it was only a matter of time before his boys came towering in. I scanned the room for my phone, but I didn't see it anywhere. "Sis, we have to get the fuck up out of here and fast," I screamed. Shayna stood there in shock, "Ice is he dead?" I looked Shayna in her eyes. "Shay I'm not sure, but we have to go before it's too late. We have to move quick!"

Lights Out: Ghost

I sat in my car blowing (smoking) waiting for the guys to pullup. 10 minutes later, they were pulling up, and shutting down their engines. They hopped out of their rides and jumped into mines. We finished the blunt that I was smoking, and we hopped out ready to blick (gun) the place down. I had, Seven outside, casing the joint. We got to move quick before word got back about his boys and that missing ransom money but it's up.

Hostages: Isis

As soon as Hakeem fell to the floor, sis kicked him a few times. His guys must've heard a noise coming from the room, and they rushed in. When they eyed, their boss on the floor, they reached for their guns. One of the big burly dudes, tried to charge at me but I was too quick. I grabbed my 22, from my ankle holster, I aimed, and I shot him in his neck. He grabbed hold of his neck where the bullet had pierced him. He mumbled something underneath his breath, but I couldn't make out what he was saying. They started shooting in my direction, but I ducked. "Grab that gun Shay," I shouted as she stood there. By now his other guys are shooting at us to so I fired back. Then I shot another one of them in the thigh causing him to drop to the floor.

"Shay, grab that gun and shoot that motherfucka' now!" "What Ice?" "Bitch shoot." I kept squeezing until the clip was empty. The initial shock had finally worn off. "I knew you had a wild side Ice," she said, and we both laughed, "Shay kick that other gun away from his reach. Hurry quick and find my phone." My eyes stayed glued on the door while Shayna kicked the guns and searched for my phone. I grabbed one of the guns from the floor.

"I don't know Ice; I don't see it anywhere sis." I took my eyes off the door for a moment and glanced at Shayna, "Hey Shay I'm sorry about how Hakeem disrespected you. You deserve better. I would never do anything to hurt you or to jeopardize my relationship with your brother. Oh, and Shay let's keep this between you and me, you know how your brother is." Then I refocused my attention back on the door. "It's okay Ice you didn't have a choice. He's just an asshole that's all," she said as she kicked him in his side but this time he grabbed her by the ankle, causing her to trip and she fell. "Oh, shit."

Hearing Shayna scream got my attention and I turned, back around. Then I pointed my gun at Hakeem. "Let go of me you psycho." "You heard the lady, let her go Hakeem. I'm not going to ask you twice." "Man, fuck you bitch." Silence. "Wrong answer!" BOOM! I let off a couple rounds and shot him in his hand causing him to lose the grip that he had on Shay. "Oh shit, you crazy ass bitch." I laughed. Shayna kicked him in his face as she stood to her feet. "Mrs. Bitch to you, you clown. Now how many out there?" Silence. He hesitated, "5 maybe 6, I think." I let off another round and shot him in his other hand. "Ah shit, okay, okay. I'll tell you what you want to know just don't kill me shit. It's 6 of them," he blurted out. I smiled. "Now was that so hard Hakeem?"

I raised my gun higher, and he shielded his face. "Don't shoot me, I got a wife and kids." "Well tell me what I need to know, and you'll make it home to your family alive." Silence. "Where are your guys posted, I need specifics?" He paused. "Some are by your car and some…" I looked away for a moment and when I turned back around Hakeem was standing on his feet with his arm around Shayna's neck and a gun pointing at her head. "No more, Mr. nice guy." He smacked Shayna in the head with the but of his gun.

"Hakeem, I'll blow your fucking head off, let her go, now." While Hakeem and I were going back and forth I heard one his guys screaming in agony. So, I pointed my gun in his direction and I spoke calmly, "Let her go or your boy a get it." Hakeem looked at me and laughed, "My boy. Fuck that nigga," he said before he raised his gun and shot dude in his head. I jumped at the sight of the blood. Then I refocused my attention back on him, aiming in his direction. "Do it Ice," Shayna shouted. "Yeah, do it and I'll shoot both of you hoes." "Ice fuck him, do that shit sis." "I don't know about this one Shay, I don't know," I said nervously.

I couldn't get a clear shot because her face was too close to his, so I didn't squeeze the trigger. "Drop the gun now bitch and kick it over here to me if you want this bitch to live," Hakeem threatened. I held my hands up to surrender and I slid my gun to the floor. Then I kicked it towards him. "That's a good girl," he said with a smile on his face before slamming his gun across Shayna's face. Then I charged at him like I had superpowers. "You are a sick piece of shit."

We tussled. Then he knocked me to the floor. Next thing I know I heard a loud knock at the door. "This is the police we have you surrounded, come out with your hands up," I heard a male's voice say. "Never, fuck that I'm not going back in," he screamed. "Help, please help," I screamed. Still aiming at Shayna's head, Hakeem yelled, "You will never take me down without a fight." I moved to the side of the room and the door came crashing to the floor. When they entered the room, their guns were drawn, just like they did in the movies.

"Let the girl go if you want to see daylight ever again," one of the three uniformed, officers yelled. Their hats were lowered so I couldn't see their faces clearly. Outnumbered he pushed Shay to the side with his gun still in hand and I waved her over. "Ladies, please follow this officer to safety as we apprehend the suspect," one of the officers said to us. We did what we were told. As soon as we got outside, I immediately became suspicious when I didn't see any police cars. The officer that accompanied us, instructed us to wait in the room next door and he left. The walls were thin so we could pretty much hear everything. I heard a male's voice who sounded like my man, saying, "Toss that motherfuckin' gun to the floor, nigga, if you cherish your life." "Fuck that, I'm not tossing shit," Hakeem spat angrily.

Silence filled the air while sis and I were huddled in the corner fearing for our life. Then I heard Hakeem yelling, "Oh shit... You're one clever motherfucka. Ghost is that you, nigga?" Silence. "Damn right it's me." "You a clown you not on my level and that bitch you got pussy is whack sauce to." Suddenly I felt faint, and my heart dropped to the floor. I listened carefully word for word not missing a beat. I was terrified as to how my man might perceive me after hearing that. "Lying ass nigga, my bitch not going. She wouldn't dare let a low life like you hit."

"If that's your word, how you think I saw her tat, that said, "Mike's Ice," on her breast? On the guys that hoe was begging for this dick," Hakeem lied. "Negative, nigga, fuck you." "Man, I got to give y'all credit though, dressing up like cops. That was a smart move, but you still a bitch." Next thing I heard were gunshots. "Cuz, we got this go check on the girls." "If this goofy even blinks wrong shoot him in his head. Oh yeah and call my exterminator and tell him 30," demanded Ghost. "Aye yo Ghost man, how'd you know I was here?" "To be aware is to be alive. Before you got knocked (locked up) we tried to buy this shit hole from you and fix it up, but you wouldn't budge."

"Damn, Ghost man I didn't even touch your bitch. You gone let me go right man? You know I gotta family." "Nigga fuck you and your family." Me and sis was still in the corner balled up. Shayna asked nervously, "Ice, what was that?" "Girl I don't know your guess is as good as mines." Boom! Boom! Click, click. Boom! Shayna screamed from the noise of the gunshots, so I covered her mouth not wanted to be recaptured.

Elimination: Ghost

I headed towards the door and four armed men rushed in and started spraying (shooting). I ducked and I returned the fire. I peeped Zap, trying to reach for his gun, so I hauled ass and kicked the gun from out of his reach. Then I grabbed his ass by the throat and put my gun to his head. One of his boys shot Trigg's nephew Murder in the chest but it lodged in his vest. I saw the look of death in his good eye. He was blinded in the other from being stabbed when he was locked up. Murder emptied his clip on the heavyset guy that shot him and left more holes in his body than, swiss cheese.

I kept my gun drawn on Zap. Seeing Murder, clip his boy caused his other soldiers to fall back. Zap, hollered at his henchmen, "Do something. Man, what I got y'all on payroll for?" "Zap you assured me that nobody would get hurt," one of his boys said nervously. He clearly wasn't built for this. "Nigga fuck all that, shoot him and I'll pay you double." The guy raised his gun in my direction and Popeye let his gun go. "Go check on the girls. Me and M got this broski," I said to Popeye. As soon as he grabbed hold of the door, he was stopped as the bullets ripped through his flesh, and he fell to floor. "You a... bitch," Popeye said before he closed his eyes. Angrily, Murder started shooting and he silenced the shooter permanently.

"Shit man. Popeye get up...Popeye," Murder shouted. Silence. "M, go check on the girls, my dude." "You good Ghost?" "Yeah man, I'm straight." "Aye Ghost, man, your bitch gotta a mouth on her man, I see why you keep her ass around," Zap teased. Then I slapped his ass across the head with my gun, knocking his tooth loose. He laughed, then he spit his tooth from his bleeding mouth. "Keep my wife name out your much. On Shorty I don't play about her."

"Your wife huh? Not that same hoe I hit till she bled." "Zap fuck you." "What you jealous? Jealousy doesn't look good on you Ghost," he spat. I continued hitting him with my weapon until I felt something cold on the back of my head. "What Ghost you thought you had this shit," Zap spat. The feeling of defeat was evident, but I was taking his ass out with me.

Pull Through

"Baby, I love you. I'm sorry for skipping out on you and the kids. This should be me, laying here in this hospital bed not you. I never wanted to leave you, but I didn't have a choice. Maybe one day you'll understand, or maybe you won't. How is Mikey and my Shay-Poo? I know they're all grown up now and they probably hate me. Baby, please wake up. You have to pull through. I will never forget how beautiful you were when we first met, I felt like I was the luckiest man in the world. Baby, please open your eyes." I turned to leave but just as I was pulling on the door to leave, I heard a voice say in a tiny whisper, "Michael...Michael...is that you?"

Caught Lacking: Ghost

I wanted to wrestle him for the gun, but the odds were against me. "Step away from Zap, and put your gun down, Ghost. Do it now!" Hesitantly I complied. Zap grabbed one of the guns from the floor while I was being held at gunpoint. Two guns were drawn on me. Zap was aiming in front of me talking that big boy shit, "What's up now, Ghost? You ready to join your homie?" "Man, nigga fuck you, you a pussy. You'll see my Pops before I do, on bro nem." "You know what Ghost it's a shame you didn't join the winning team a long time ago. You wouldn't be on the losing end now," spoke Zap.

"Zap, real talk homie, I don't take L's. I only fuck with winners, and that's that on that, feel me?" Boom. Click. Click. BOOM! I ducked quick as the bullets started flying. Fly and LaLa came in and lit that place up. The vibration from the gun play was deafening. "Bout time, damn," I told Fly. "Early never late," said

LaLa before shooting Zap in his thigh. I needed Zap alive, but his boy not so much, so they shot his ass up. "Don't do it," I told Zap when I caught him positioning his weapon towards Fly.

I grabbed my gun and I spun around. Then I aimed at Zaps head. Murder heard the commotion, so he ran in the room. Zap saw he was outnumbered, so he lowered his weapon and placed it on the bed. "Put your hands up," Fly spat. "Yeah, Punta keep them hands up where we can see them," said LaLa. Zap lifted his hands slowly. We left the room with Zap walking in front of me with my gun aiming at his head. "Fly you and LaLa, make sure the girls straight, get them out of here."

"You sure dirty? We can always walk with you for reassurance," said Fly. "Yeah, you sure Ghost?" Without a response, I struck Zap in the back of his head. "Yeah Fly, it's smooth. Me and M got it from here," I said. "Alright dirty, love," Fly said before him and LaLa turned and walked away. "So, where my money at nigga?" "Man, Ghost what money?" "Don't play dumb with me you bitch ass nigga! Where is the money, you cuffed from my Pops?" "I ran through that shit man it's been gone, but if I tell you where my stash at, you gone let a real nigga live?" I laughed.

"Negative, clown you might as well save your dignity. You're a goner either way, but if you don't want me to pay a visit to your kids and your moms you better start talking." "Man, Ghost man. Leave my shorties and my OG out of this street shit. They are innocent, man, have a heart. This is between me and you man, straight up." I laughed and I nudged M. "Wow, you hear this clown fam? So now it's between us, huh? Fuck out of here, it's up and it's stuck. Now walk nigga."

Murder laughed. "Man, Ghost, man on my soul you have to believe me man, I just wanted my guys to rough you up a bit. I didn't mean for them morons to pop your O.G. Your sister, man that bitch had to be snatched to show you I meant business." "Zap, watch your muthafuckin' mouth, disrespecting my blood." Silence. "Oh, and that little pretty bitch of yours was just an added bonus." Before I had a chance to react to his comment M, hit him across the head causing him to stagger. Then M pounded him until he passed out and we had to drag him the rest of the way to the car.

While we were walking back to the car, I saw Snake laid out on ground riddled with bullets. When we spotted Zap's car, I was relieved. I knew it had to be his ride because the license plate read, "187 Zap." We dragged Zap to the car, and I had M keep an eye on him while I grabbed his keys and his phone from his pocket. I unlocked the door and M sat him in the car, on the driver's side taping his hands to the steering wheel. I dialed up Fly making sure my people were straight. He told me everybody was good, so I disconnected the call.

By the time I got off the phone, Zap was coming too. "If you don't want your family to meet you in hell you better start talking nigga. Where the fuck my money at?" He looked around, startled. I had never seen him this shook before. M laughed. "Uh, let me think," Zap said. "Let you think...the survey says that's the wrong answer," M shouted as he hit Zap across the head. "Ouch shit." "Okay man, okay. Some of the money is in the trunk. Just leave my family out of this. I don't care what you do to me, but whatever you do please don't hurt my son, I'm begging you. On my life man, leave them out of this Ghost, man, straight up."

"Nigga fuck yo life, I never cared. You killed my seed ain't no pardoning that. I don't give a fuck about your family. I got people outside your crib right now waiting on my call." "Wait Ghost, I'm sorry... please don't do this man. Can we just talk this out man to man?" Me and Murder started cracking up laughing. "Aye, Ghost, him sorry, him just want to talk. He won't do it anymore," said M as he mimicked Zap. Then I laughed again. "See Zap, your ass play too much, but say less." "Ghost man please man, I'm begging you please leave my family out of this." "Yo M man pop the trunk," I said completely ignoring Zap's comment.

It's Me: Michael Sr.

I rushed over to her bedside. "Yes, my love it's me," I said as the tears escaped my eyes. Then I ran back to the door, and I yelled, "Nurse! Nurse! Come quick. Come quick." One of the on-duty nurses rushed in, "Yes, sir how may I help you?" "My, my wife, she's awake. She's really awake." She paused. "Oh my, this is a miracle sir. Let me page the doctor now," she said before she turned around to leave. I rushed back to her bedside, and I grabbed her hand. She opened her eyes partially and said, "Michael, is that really you?" I smiled. "Yes baby, it's me." Silence. "Oh my God, it is you. I can't believe it's you, I..." Before she could finish her sentence, her body started to shake in convulsions and her heart monitor started to alarm. I panicked, "Nurse! Nurse, hurry please...nurse! Do something nurse! Something is happening to my wife. I'm begging you please hurry, nurse?"

See You in Hell: Ghost

M popped the trunk, and I grabbed the duffel. I felt something vibrating in my pocket, so I reached down and pulled out Zap's phone. I glanced at the screen and saw Debrika's name flashing across the screen with an emoji, so I answered while on speaker, "Yo." "Zap I'm scared. Why haven't you come to get us yet? Where are you, we're all packed and ready to go? Junior, is antsy, he won't sit his ass down he keeps saying my Daddy this, my Daddy that." Silence. I placed the phone to Zap's ear, "Brik, baby I love you and I'm sorry. Kiss Mama and junior for me."

"Wait Zap, baby, what do you mean by that? Hello…Baby, why are you talking like this? What is happening right now?" Silence. "Hello… Zap, baby please." I snatched the phone from Zap, and intervened, "He's a little tied up now Brika. As a matter fact though, I haven't felt those pretty lips of yours on my dick in a couple months now. What's up?" Murder laughed. "You son of a bitch," Zap yelled as he started squirming trying to break loose. Silence. "Hello…Oh, my God, Ghost, why are you doing this. Zap baby it's not what you think," she stuttered. I laughed.

"It's business Ma, this shit is never personal, feel me?" "Bitch, you were fucking this nigga to. Bitch you better hope they off me, because if not, you done," Zap spat. "Aw shit, Brika he didn't know you was for the streets?" "Fuck you Ghost…fuck you," she cried. I looked over at M and gave him a nod and he already knew what to do. He picked up his phone and made a call while Zap continued to struggle to break free. "Oh my God, baby I'm so sorry. I never meant to hurt you. You gotta believe me Zap baby. Our family means the world to me. I never wanted you to find out like this. I was drunk. I love you though and only you, Zap. You believe me, right?" Silence.

"You whore," Zap spat. We listened intently as we heard screaming and rumbling coming through the receiver. "Daddy, help me please, Daddy. No please stop wait. Leave my Mommy alone. My Daddy is going to get you," Hakeem Jr spoke through his cracked voice. Tears fell from Zap's eyes. Then I ended the call. "See you on the other side. Oh yeah and tell my Pops I said what up. This one for him," I said as I stared into his eyes. Then I nodded at M, and he locked the door to the car and left Zap trapped inside.

He drenched the car with gasoline and lit a match before he flicked it. We rushed back to my ride watching the car go up in flames. I threw the duffel in the trunk, and I hopped in. "That was a close call my dude," said M. "Yeah, it was," I said as I pulled off. I glanced over at M then I refocused my eyes back on the road. I heard a loud banging noise, which startled me. BOOM! I swerved almost losing control. M you straight? I asked him not taking my eyes off the road. Then I felt something wet on the side of my face.

I glanced over at M and saw his brains splattered on the windshield, the dash, and the seat. Then I felt a block of steel, pressed up against the back of my head. "Drive bitch," the person yelled, angrily. "Where to?" When I asked that question it must have triggered him because I was immediately struck in the back of my head. I swerved. Silence. "As a matter of fact, drive to your crib and don't try anything stupid Ghost, I'm warning you." My phone rang but I ignored the call. "Yeah, and uh run me that phone to you won't be needing that anymore." I reached down in my pocket with my free hand and handed him Zap's phone in place of my own. He snatched the phone from my hand, and he tossed it out the window. I kept on driving, trying to think of a distraction.

Save Her: Michael

A team of doctors sprinted in shortly after the nurse called. "Sir we're going to have to ask you to step out of the room for a minute," said the nurse. "No, I can't leave her again. Tell me what's happening? Is she going to be alright?" Silence. "Sir please, I'm going to ask that you step out of the room. We don't have much time. I will join you in the waiting area as soon as we have some answers for you." I stood there in silence. "Sir please let us do our job," she said with a little more urgency than before. I forced myself to the door and I stopped in the doorway before exiting. "She's going to be okay, right? You have to save her." "Sir we will try our best." I left the room and stood in the hallway. I looked inside her patient room window until the nurse closed the curtains. Feeling loss, I paced the floor.

TWENTY-NINE

Long Ride: Isis

We rolled in silence the entire ride home. Mike had Chase drop us off. I was still a bit shaken considering the circumstances. Chance was trailing us in one car and Fly and his girl was in another. I felt safe, Chase didn't look like anybody you wanted to fuck with either. He was dark skinned with tattoos all over his body, including his face. I stared out the window as I reflected on the day's events. I prayed, as I thanked my heavenly father up above, for his mercy and grace. I couldn't wait to get home. All I wanted to do was jump in the tub and soak my troubles away.

Shayna looked a bit dazed, so I grabbed her by the hand. "I love you Shay-Shay. It's going to be okay, it's over, it's finally, over. We made it, we're safe." She looked me in my eyes and nodded her head. Then she squeezed my hand tightly, as the tears cascaded down her cheeks. We stared at each other for a couple of minutes and then we turned away. Arriving to our gate I felt a sense of relief. We jumped out quick. Chase parked my car near the gate, and he jumped in the car with Chance. Before they pulled off, he rolled down his window and all I could smell was the weed smoke.

"Y'all, good Ma?" "Yeah, Chase we straight, I guess. I think we can handle it from here. Thank you," I said. "We family man, this shit nothing," he said, and he pulled off. I hopped in the driver seat of my car, along with Shayna and we pulled to the gate. Then I punched in our code and drove up to our driveway. I rushed in the door, anxiously hoping my man would be home but he wasn't. Before we parted ways, Shayna hugged me tight, and I didn't let her go until she released her grip.

After our embrace, she went up to her room. I walked into the kitchen and poured myself a glass of wine. Then I headed straight to my room. I shut the door behind me, and walked to the bathroom, with my glass in hand. I lit the lavender candle and sat my glass down near the faucet. I ran myself some warm water and added some bubbles. I slid my dirty clothes to the floor. Then I scrubbed my body so hard that my skin turned red. I sat in the tub until the water was cold. I hopped out, dried myself off, and rushed in the bedroom to lotion up.

I sprayed ever crevice of my body with some smell goods, just like my baby likes it. I slipped on my satin, cut out lingerie and I grabbed my handcuffs from the dresser drawer, and I sat them on the nightstand. Then I brushed my lose strands of hair back in one place. I don't know what it was about today, but I was feeling extra horny. I can't wait until my man comes home so we can turn it up a notch.

W.T.F: Ghost

This shit crazy, I told Pac Man, earlier to be on point and he couldn't even do that. Now come to think of it, I haven't seen that nigga since the meet up. I pressed my foot on the breaks trying to get the pigs (polices) attention, but that shit didn't work. "Slow the fuck down before you catch a bullet to the head," he spat. Silence. I drove around like I was lost, which cost me another dash to the head. "Stop playing with me Ghost before I send my people in your crib to get at your wife." I straightened up quick. I tried to get a view of his face, but he kept his hat hanging too low.

At the Crib: Ghost

"Get out," the gunmen said. "Don't try anything slick either I'm warning you. We walked to the gate, and I punched in some random numbers. "Hurry the fuck up. I don't see what Isis sees in you anyway," he screamed. That right there gave me the extra strength that I needed. I elbowed him in the face, knocking him to the floor causing the gun to sound. Then it slid underneath the car. I ran to my car, moved M's body back and ransacked the glove box looking for my piece. "Looking for this," he asked holding up my Glock-40 in hand as he stood to his feet. "Shit." "Nigga, you hit like a bitch to. Now open this gate before I pop your ass."

I punched in the code, and I walked up the driveway with the gun pointed at my head. I noticed my girl car was parked so I bumped the car and sounded the alarm. I unlocked the door, walked in, and I slammed the door hard. We walked over to the couch. "Have a seat," he ordered. I did what I was told. "Aw what you thought you could just kill Zap and the guys and not suffer any consequences?" Silence. "So where is that pretty little wife of yours that everyone loves?" Silence. "Zap killed her. Zap killed her and my sister, man," I said as I lowered my head.

Down & Dirty: Isis

I heard the door slamming downstairs, so I rushed over to the door. I hit the button on my key fob when I heard my alarm going off. I strutted down the hall in my sexy heels until I reached the top of the staircase. I grabbed the banister for balance before I proceeded. When I was almost at the bottom of the stairs, I drew my gun because I wanted to pretend like Mike was under arrest and I was his sexy little officer. Once I got to the landing, I immediately turned to my left scanning to see where my baby was so I could sneak up on him.

It was dark in the living room, so I turned around and flicked on the lights. When the lights came on, I was startled when I noticed a mask man sitting next to my man aiming a weapon at his head. "Well, hello, Isis, so glad you could join us," the masked man said. Then he tossed what looked like a voice changer on the floor and removed his mask. "What are you doing here?" "Well, I just happened to be in the neighborhood, and I decided to stop in. Surprise! You don't mind, do you?" Silence filled the room.

"Are you crazy or something? What is wrong with you?" Silence. "You're what's wrong with me. You've always been a problem." Mike had the look of confusion written all over his face, but he didn't say a word. I stood there never taking my eyes off her and I lifted my gun. "Ice baby, shoot this crazy ass bitch." "I can't Michael, what if I miss? I couldn't live with myself without you." "Well baby don't miss. Shoot this bitch." "Bitch you shoot me, I'm gone shoot him, period." "I don't understand. Why are you doing this?"

She laughed, "You don't understand. You always thought you were better than me ever since we were kids. Isis this and Isis that. I'm pretty, but nobody ever noticed me. All the boys wanted you, you, you, you...you and I'm sick of it. I deserve some recognition to. Even when we were in that play, I wanted so badly to play Annie but no, you got the leading role. I'm sick of being in your shadow. I even tried getting attention by being the class clown, but you took that away from me to. You remember that day when we had that fight? I've been waiting to run into you since then and the day has finally come."

"Man, say less, Ice shoot this bitch." "Shut up Ghost, I'm warning you." She looked at him, then she looked back at me. "That's old. How did you even find me?" "Finding you was a piece of cake after I met Shayna. I saw the two of you on a picture in her phone. At first, I wasn't sure if it was you. For a year straight I had to listen to her glorifying you which made me sick to my stomach. I even let her borrow my man Zap, but she started catching feelings for him though. See, my cousin Kiki didn't love know how to love him properly, so I had to cuff him."

As she talked, she became angry, and spit formed in the corner of her mouth. She turned to face

Mike, "I'm pretty right Ghost?" Silence. "Answer me dammit! I said, I'm fucking pretty, right?" He hesitated before answering, "Yea, Ma you pretty." She smiled. "Yeah, you're pretty alright...pretty fucking crazy," I said as I rolled my eyes. "What was that you said, Isis? I'll show you crazy." She grabbed Mike's face and forced her tongue down his throat. "Kiss me back," she ordered him. I stood there in silence wanting to gag.

She kissed him with the gun still pointing at his head. While she was staring at Mike trying to get a reaction from me, I saw my chance, and I took it. BOOM! I aimed for her head. She ducked and I missed. "Bitch, bag the fuck up off my man." "Your man? Fuck you and your man." Silence. "I'm warning you, you delusional ass bitch, back up off of my man and we can forget this ever happened." Mike looked at me puzzled. Then Shayna appeared out of nowhere. She squinted her eyes adjusting to the light as she yarned.

"Ice what's all that noise?" "Nothing sis go back to bed. Everything's smooth," said Mike. Then Shayna turned in Mike's direction and she froze. "Oh my God, Tommie, what are you doing here? What the fuck is going on?" "Tommie, is this the bitch that you been calling your friend?" Silence. "Yeah, Ice, I told you all about her. I don't understand, what's happening right now? "Tominique leave my house or else. I'm warning you." "Or else what Isis? What yo prissy ass gone do?"

I smiled, "Keep playing around with me and you'll find out. The next time, I won't miss." Mike gave me an approving smile. "Would everybody just calm the fuck down and tell me what the fuck is going on," Shayna screamed. Then Mike nodded, and he closed his eyes. I cocked my gun and made sure the safety was off. "Ice don't shoot her sis, please let me finish this fake ass bitch," Shayna spat. "I got this," I said aiming at her head. "Isis you don't have the heart to shoot me. If you shoot me, I'm gone shoot him."

I smiled, "Oh yeah?" "Yeah! Bitch I said what I said. I'm gone kill all y'all." My adrenaline was pumping. I took a deep breath, and I squeezed the trigger shooting her in her shoulder causing her to jerk back. Mike ducked. "Isis, you bitch," she shouted as she let off a few rounds. Me and sis ducked. Then Mike leaped over, and they started tussling for her gun, knocking the gun from her hands and it fell to the floor. He elbowed her in the face. She dropped to floor and reached around for her gun. I lifted my gun again and Mike jumped back. She grabbed her gun quick and pointed it in my direction.

She pulled the trigger, but her gun jammed so I squeezed the trigger and I struck her in the stomach. Then she fell to the floor. Mike opened his eyes slowly, he looked around and he joked, "Am I dead yet?" We laughed. "No, but you will be if you keep cracking these stale ass jokes," I said. I placed the gun on the table, and I ran over and jumped in his arms. "Ice where you learn that from? Who you think you is oh girl from Columbiana?" I smiled. Relieved it was all over, I kissed him passionately. I peeped him admiring my outfit, so I whispered seductively in his ear, "Baby take me upstairs and make love to me." He smiled.

"Yuck, I heard that get a room," Shayna said pretending like she was gagging. Then Mike held up his middle finger, and we laughed. "Hold that thought Ma, I gotta make a couple calls." I pouted before punching him playfully in the shoulder. "So, let me get this straight baby. You about to make some calls while I'm dressed like this?" I spun around and started popping to put emphasis on what I said. "Ugh, y'all so nasty," Shayna teased.

"Shut up, hater," I said to Shayna playfully as I looked at her then I turned back around to face Mike. Before I could get another word out, I heard a loud scream. "Ah, die bitch... die," Tommie shouted. I looked around for my gun, but it was gone. Then I heard shots being fired. When I turned back around Tommie was sprawled across the floor, oozing from the mouth. I looked back at Shay who was holding the gun in her hand, shaking. No words were exchanged. Then Mike made a call to someone sounding like he was putting in a cleaning order.

I walked over to Shayna, and I grabbed the gun from her hands and Mike snatched the gun from me to. "Shayna you and G.I. Jane, gone upstairs, let me handle this business." We all laughed. Then I punched him on the shoulder playfully. "I'll be up to join you in a minute Ice," he said as he winked his eye. "Okay baby. Hurry up," I whined while I was kicking my shoes off. When I got upstairs, I went to our room, and I fell asleep. Hours later I heard the bedroom door open, which woke me up. When I lifted my head Mike was standing in the nude, smiling. "Baby, what are you smiling for?"

Silence. "You, Ice I can't believe you shot somebody today." "I'm full of surprises baby." Mike walked towards me with his manhood swinging so I scooted to the foot of the bed. I grabbed his member and I placed it inside my mouth. I licked and sucked his controller until I heard him yell. Then I turned on all fours. He bit down on one of my booty cheeks and it gave me goose bumps. Then he reached in between my thighs and started playing with my cookies. Right before I creamed, he entered my right to passage. I positioned my body to match his thrust.

We were like a positive and negative charging ion. His touch was electrifying. Breathing heavily, I glided my ass on his tool. He played in my puddle while I felt him inside of me. As I felt his lava entering my passageway I shook uncontrollably. "Oh Shit Ice. Oh shit. Dam I love you Ice," he screamed. Then he kissed me on my neck. He rested on my backside while he was struggling to catch his breath. Seconds later we climbed to the top the of the bed and I fell asleep in his arms, the place that felt the safest.

THIRTY

Toast Up: Ghost

I don't know what it was about last night, but our sex was steamier than usual. I watched her sleep while laying next to her in the bed. I glanced down at my watch, and I jumped up when I realized I was late for the meeting. I tipped toed around the room, trying my best not to wake her. "Baby, where are you going? Stay home with him," she whined. "Ma don't be mad, but I have to make a run and holler at the guys." "Baby, don't go."

I ran to the bathroom and brushed my teeth and washed my face. Then I sat on the side of the bed, and I slipped on my shoes. "You, know I love you right Ice?" "Yes Michael, you better," she said half-jokingly. "And you love me, too, right?" She smiled. "Of course, I do. Baby, I love you so bad," she whispered. "Then let me go handle my business and we gone be straight. Just stay down and I got you. You trust me, right?" Silence. "Yes, baby I trust you with my whole heart." "Okay then say less. I'll be back in a minute, and we can finish where we left off." I leaned forward and we kissed. "Ice baby, meet me at the hospital at noon," I hollered back at her as I walked out the door and left. I stopped at the store and grabbed a couple blunts and soon as I started moving around.

I was in a good mood today, Ma is getting well, sis is back home safe, and those clowns that were playing with us are no longer walking these streets. All I needed to do now was to break bread with the guys, start back hooping, get out of this game, and get my girl pregnant. On my way to the spot, I started thinking about my love for basketball. I found myself drifting off wondering what my life would be like if I would've gone straight pro, instead of getting wrapped up in these streets. When I pulled up, I shut down my engine and hopped out. I popped my trunk and grabbed the duffel.

As soon as I walked in, I handed everyone back the money they loaned me plus an incentive. Seven's wife had been hounding him, so he left early to catch his flight. My phone was steady jumping (ringing), but I figured it was the wife, so I didn't even bother checking the ID. LaLa and Fly was across the table, sucking on each other faces like leashes. "Get a room y'all, damn," said Chance and we laughed. I walked over to the bar area, and grabbed the Rose, bottle of, Don P.

I popped the cork to the champagne careful not to spill any. Then I poured our drinks evenly, I raised my glass, and I made a toast. "Cheers to loyalty, good health, plenty of head, and plenty of wealth...Cheers," I shouted before downing my glass. In unison everybody hollered, "Cheers." "It's all love, Papi," LaLa said as she raised her glass. We emptied the bottle, then I threw the rest of smoke to Chance so he could roll up. It's been a long ass couple of weeks, I needed to smoke, bad.

Feeling Beat: Isis

I know Mike told me to meet him at the hospital at 12, but something seemed off. I been calling him since earlier and he still hasn't returned any of my calls. I forced myself out of bed, jumped in the shower, and got dressed earlier than I anticipated. I was anxious to see Mama. I hopped in my ride and sped off. I looked down at my phone and noticed I had a missed call, but I didn't think nothing of it. I swerved almost hitting a pothole, when my phone rang again but I missed that call to. When I got to the hospital I parked in the closest spot, and I jumped out. I stopped in the gift shop and grabbed Mama some fresh flowers before heading to her room.

Entering her room, I was startled when I saw an older gentleman sitting on the side of her bed. When he looked up at me, I clutched my chest as my heart started racing. The man sitting before me was a splitting image of my man. I spoke nervously, "Hello, sir. I'm Isis. I'm Michael's..." He stopped me and interrupted before I was able to finish my sentence. With tears in his eyes, he looked at me and said, "Let me guess, his girlfriend." Silence. "Close, no sir, actually I'm his fiancé," I said proudly then I flashed my ring.

"How is Mama doing?" Silence. He paused before he continued, "She's... oh my God... she's gone to a better place, my dear child." It was at that moment that the flowers slipped from my hand, and I stood there unable to move. "No, there must be some sort of mistake surely she's just resting." I rushed over to her bedside. "What do you know, you're no doctor. Where is the nurse?" Tears raced down my cheeks. When I laid eyes on her, my biggest fear had come to life. A sharp pain shot through my body, and I sobbed uncontrollably. I screamed, "Oh my God she can't be gone. No...No...No...Mama please No! Nurse please hurry, Nurse!"

Solace: Ghost

We sat around chopping it up for a minute as we inhaled the relaxing potency of the Za. "Pass that shit," I said to Chase. "You fuck up the rotation, it's puff, puff, give," said Chance in the best Chris Tucker voice he could muster. We fell into laughter. He sounded just like his ass to. I popped another bottle and I poured us up. Then I summoned for everyones attention, and they all raised their glasses before I spoke, "Here's to success, victory, survival and the good life...." While I was making my toast my phone rang and interrupted me.

I glanced at my caller ID, and I noticed it was Ice. She had been blowing me up more than usual, so I sent her to the voicemail. "Now, where was I? May we stack, and never starve and we always eat...Cheers!" "Cheers, gang," said Fly. "Cheers," they said simultaneously. We held up our glasses and clicked them together. While I was hitting the blunt my phone rang, and it was Ice's bug ass calling again. "Don't front your move man we all know you whipped, gone answer it," Chance joked. "Fuck you, bro," I said as I held up my middle finger. Then she called again, irritated I answered the phone. "Yeah, what up man.... She what, wait a minute Ice...slow down. What? Oh fuck! I'm on my way." My heart started pounding as I disconnected the call. "Shit, I got to go, cuz lock up," I shouted while I was rushing to the door. Before I made it the door, Fly asked, "You good dirty?" I didn't even bother to reply.

The Ultimate Betrayal: Ghost

I twisted the knob and as soon as the door flew open, I damn near had a heart attack. "Aw shit," I screamed.

"Freeze!" Guns were drawn. I eased outside and I closed the door behind me. "Michael "Ghost" Johnson Jr. you are under arrest." "For what?" Silence. They read me my Miranda rights and cuffed me. I didn't even resist. I saw Pac Man, and I could tell he was trying to avoid eye contact with me, so I already knew he had backdoored me. I couldn't believe he signed an affidavit. I looked at him callously before speaking, "Are you serious man? Pac Man you a fucking bitch man."

Silence. "They made me do it you know what I'm saying? I swear on my OG's grave I'm not lying Ghost. You know I'm not no rat." "What you mean you ain't no rat nigga? What the fuck you think you doing now? You a bitch." "Ghost man they were talking about giving my little brother life if I didn't give you up. On my kids I didn't have a choice. They promised me they would go easy on you though." I just shook my head. "There's always choice. You should've come to me first, man." While me and Pac Man were going back and forth, I saw the rest of the crew being hauled off in cuffs. LaLa saw Pac Man and tried to run towards him, but she couldn't.

"You fucking Punta," she spat. Fly was in the corner, getting ruffed up the other officers, forcing him on the floor face down. She cried. Chance was fighting off the officers to; nobody was being cooperative. Just when I thought matters couldn't get any worse, the look of hate appeared in my eyes. Then the news media started flashing cameras from every angle. I looked up and got a chill when I laid eyes on the devil himself. It was my right-hand man, the one I would go to hell and back for. My blood started boiling. That's when Officer Douglas bitch ass spoke up, "What's wrong Ghost? You look like you saw a… ghost," he laughed. "Naw, just another fuck boy like you, you pig!"

As soon as I made my last statement one of the officers hit me in the face, drawing blood. I shook my head in disgust as a single tear rolled down my cheek. "Nigga, I thought you was dead. How could you be this grimy?" I hulked up some spit and it flew in his face. He wiped his face with his sleeve, and he stared into my cold eyes. "This is business, my dude this shit not personal my boy." Meanwhile, Officer Douglas and his partner seemed to be enjoying this take down. The rest of the team was already in squad cars.

"I told you we were coming for you," one of the officers spat. I laughed. I kept laughing though because I refuse to let them see me sweat. I felt betrayed. "Mama always told me to watch out for them snakes in the grass, I wish I would've listened more," I said to him. "Trust a get you killed son. Nothing is ever what it appears to be," Money stated firmly. I looked at him with a look of uncertainty, "Damn Money, I guess you never really removed your mask." He looked at me and grinned.

"Detective Jones what do you want me to do with this one?" "Give me a minute," Money said while he held up his finger. "Man, so this how you coming?" He paused, "You already know how the game goes." "Damn man you were like my family, on bro." "Ghost, see that's your problem you are so predictable. You take everything personal knowing this game is cold." I stood in silence. "Then he turned to face one of the officers. "That's enough, get his ass out of here." Next thing I know I was being thrown in the back of a squad car. I felt like I was drowning and all I could think about was my girl.

Made in the USA
Monee, IL
03 June 2023

34947010R00148